THE LAMPLIGHTER

By

Pamela Hanson Ryder

To my parents, Alfred and Lois. One nurtured the stories while the other encouraged me to write them.
My husband, who leads the rest of the way - always believing, curiously questioning.
Cameron and Caitlin, when looking from the shore may you always find the warmth of the sunshine and true felicity.
Also, summer rosé. Without you, the glasses would be colourless.

A very special thank you to the Northern Lighthouse Board, Edinburgh, particularly Fiona Holmes for all of your incredible help, Michael Bullock and David Albutt.

Rod Hunt at the Scottish Poetry Library

Jamie Keller USMC (retired), weapons expertise

Mary Turner Thomson

Patrycja Zajak at Mr B Photobooth & Atelier

Jamie Stewart and Wendy Helliwell

Foreword

By Andy Ryder

We have all experienced Lamplighters in our lives. Perhaps an inspiring teacher, parent or good friend has helped change the course of your own life's events. Likewise, major changes in history may have taken a turn due to a simple, chance meeting or the sharing of views between strangers.

Lamplighters are everywhere for those who dare to hope.

PROLOGUE

The swelling stu'n sails now their wings extend,
Then stay-sails sidelong to the breeze ascend:
While all to court the wandering breeze are plac'd;
With yards now thwarting, now obliquely brac'd.

Again she plunges! Hark! A second shock
Tears her strong bottom on the marble rock!
Down on the vale of death, with dismal cries,
The fated victims shuddering roll their eyes,
In wild despair; while yet another stroke,
With deep convulsion, rends the solid oak.

William Falconer
The Shipwreck

The stillness of the ocean rested in a menacing mood, temporarily beautiful in its serene ambience. But for a sailor who was dependent on wind power alone, the calm was a useless, frustrating leisure. A day of doldrums would be spent repairing sails, cleaning decks and even less likely, bathing. However, taking time out for one's appearance among the men was viewed as an act of vanity, so bathing would be an unusual event. Nonetheless, a bath from a bucket would always be a very cold one.

Still, it was invariably a lengthy waste of time without the thrust of the constant wind by which to travel. Any seasoned captain knew well how to read the signs of the weather and the significance of the formation of clouds. Those that resembled the wavy lines on the sides of a mackerel were characteristic of strong winds high above. This display was also a warning, suggesting trouble was about to appear, as high seas often accompanied summer gales.

Such skyscapes were not an unfamiliar sight to highly experienced sailors, one of whom was Captain Bedford of the Lady Albatross. With the wisdom that such terrible hindsight brings a man, they knew only too well never to underestimate such romantic summer skies over the North Atlantic Ocean. With the years of experience they had and the calculations made in the developing weather, Bedford and his crew decided to continue sailing under the increasingly dangerous circumstances for the sake of saving time. They were the fatal victims in a violent shipwreck in the storm of July, 1869.

It was common knowledge that the south westerly early winds in June could suddenly sweep in to transform a quiet of an open sea into a scene of wild carnage. This was a symptom of the changing of seasons from winter into summer that could create disagreeable agitation.

On this particular day, the winds became very hostile, stirring and becoming darker as they gathered high above the North Atlantic Ocean. Clouds were aroused by both the warm and cold variations of air as they clashed for their place of dominance. Eventually, the canvas was complete and a heavy shroud covered the earth like a marquee, reaching to the corners of each horizon as far as the eye could see.

How easy it was to forget that just above the murky, dreich ceiling was a sublime contradiction. Rising beyond the clouds and resting much further into the clear blue empyrean was an effusive, glowing sun. In its usual peaceful, melodramatic continuance, it radiated its golden glow as it does every day without ceasing as the stand-alone beacon to an entire planetary arrangement. It serves as a light of hope, an instrument to life and the giver of warmth, life and growth for all living things. Throughout the ages, this has not excluded the vast number of people, as each one of them existing under it has tended to their daily tasks, indisposition and emotions, a nightly slumber or regretful insomnolence.

Descending back down into the chaos of the North Atlantic, together the wind and sea in their duplicitous liaison, often orchestrate sudden and treacherous fortitudes of nature. When a ship - a mere introspective invention of man, inconsequential in comparison - attempts to cross through these gales, there is no pardon.

The storm is unaffected by the slicing through of even the largest of vessels. A craft is not an offence or discourtesy, inconvenience or distraction. It is simply a complete nullity, for it changes nothing of the ocean's splendid purpose and grandeur. Any daring person with a sense of self-importance, disillusion or adventure to cross a gale is ignored in their idiocy by the intolerant, mountainous seas.

It happened in this way on that July morning. The winds battled without mercy against the taut sails of the Lady Albatross. As her bow fell into each steep trough, walls of spray deluged over her, washing her in the salty quaff. The crew were swept with bated breath every time the next surge lifted her bowsprit high into the air and they anticipated the pounding blow of the fall, not certain if the wooden hull would survive another bashing. Should one plank be pulled from its cleave of the frame or its balancing keel be split, the ship would be consumed in seconds.

With great speed, the water swept over the decks with unnegotiable force, pulling along anything it could come upon as the cold foam rushed down the gunwales, past the quarter deck, the captain's cabin, finally rushing its cold salt over the stern before returning to its chilly, dank inferno.

Captain Bedford ignored the eerie, piercing whistle which tore through the mizzen sails whilst side-sweeping lashings of rain blinded the crew into confusion. The men feverishly busied themselves with work, climbing up the windward shrouds next to the masts to stow the sails, holding on with every muscle in their fatigued, warped bodies.

As his wet, white knuckles clenched tightly to the wheel, Captain Bedford ceased to shout orders to the crew as he knew no one could hear him against the bewailing. He was blinded by the stormy rain beyond the door of the cabin and his legs straddled across the deck. In the enclosure of the helm, Captain Bedford steered the creaking, timbered ship with all his physical strength, hoping that he was sailing north to pass the Scottish west coast. But he could no longer see beyond the bow of his ship nor could he read the compass through the rain.

.oOo.

Somewhere not far from him in the same gale lay the beginnings of the Dubh Artach lighthouse. It was perched atop a small oval bed of sea rock on a long, skerry formed of black, rigid sheets, stretching under the water's surface for ten miles. Dubh Artach stood isolated fifteen miles southwest from Scotland's Isle of Mull. Also built on the rock just a few yards from the tower base, a barracks rose high upon steel stilts which were forced arduously into place by chiselling deep into the skerry by resilient craftsmen and their hand tools. The barracks itself was shaped like a large barrel, resting prostrate above. The work was often limited by short, low tides whilst they worked just a stone's throw from the barracks on the large, round lighthouse foundation. At this stage of the work, only a few layers of shaped stone, cut from the nearby quarry in Erraid, had been laid after careful planning for what would become a vital warning beacon for ships after decades of recorded shipwrecks.

Although the skerry remained unchanged and untraumatised by yet another storm, that fateful day the stony lighthouse base was subject to a devastation of its own.

As the storm brewed into force, the lighthouse workers were taken by surprise and they quickly gathered up what tools they could carry. The anvils were too heavy to lift, so they were left behind and only the lighter tools were taken. The men rushed for cover towards the barracks. The wind and rain increased so much that the skerry became slathered in foam and with one surge, the men who were waiting in the queue to climb up into the metal cylinder, found that their legs were submersed in water and with the rush of the waves, the rock was impossible to stand upon without slipping or being thrown off balance. After every final attempt, the twelve craftsmen and their supervisor, Alan Brebner made it into the safety of the barracks and the last man who scaled up through the bottom hatch closed and fastened the door behind him. When safely inside, the men looked around at each other, breathless. With their clothes dripping and their faces sprayed with the cold, salty water, they felt lucky to be alive and yet fearfully prognosticated how the storm would progress and how or if the barracks would even hold up to it.

.oOo.

Aboard the Lady Albatross, the waves continued to engulf the creaking vessel and pull her down under the water, rolling it with every swell and the bow dived into each dip, giving in to the hard blows as if she knew she was losing. The crew slid down the slippery decks, and in one final blast against a wave, the bow crashed into the unseen rock below. The timbers of the hull split open and scattered like a box of toppling matchsticks. Their screams were futile to the distant Inner Hebridean Islands as the men were hurled into the raw, dark waters, forced to their demise as they drew the fishy, salty liquid deep into their lungs. The Lady Albatross disappeared from sight and sound of the sea, as it returned to the writhing mass of power, devoid of any human voices or screams.

.oOo.

Inside the barracks at Dubh Artach and unaware of the sinking of the Lady Albatross, the men spooned down rations of porridge, followed by metal cups of beer. Alan sat alongside the eldest of the workmen, Kumbi, an African born into a slave family who had worked for the Stevenson family for many years. Together, they kept watch over the barrel and cauldron to fairly distribute the portions.

The chat amongst the men was not enough to drown out the pounding of waves and wind against the wooden capsule in which they waited. When the lantern finally exhausted its oil, to be locked inside meant day was just as dark as the night. In the black of the evening, they found it too challenging to sleep against the wild gale outside. It rattled not only the floor hatch and roof, but the very steel structure below. Some lay with their eyes open, unable to relax sufficiently to nod off, whilst others leaned on their comrade for a bit of comfort and warmth in their fatigue.

In the morning, the rain and howl of the wind seeped between the metal sheets as the men sat around terrified, sipping their rations. Should the rivets have begun to weaken and give way, they would have had no protection from imminent death.

Master Builder, Mr Goodwillie played his violin, while a jug on the floor collected the drips of water which fell in from the leaky ceiling. Tensions aroused in the cramped conditions as the men were aware it would be impossible for their ship to rescue them or bring food supplies. Frustrated with hunger coupled with the lack of space, an argument ensued between two of the younger men.

"Gie me space, ye scabby eejit; a'm nae yer milk nurse!"

The offended man backed off and took a stance. "What did ye call me?"

"Eejit. Yer as useful in constructing as a glass hammer. But, if ye dinnae like it, maybe ye prefer *reekie heid* instead, cause aye, ye reek as weil!"

"Well, if ah dae, it's only cause o' sitting next tae ye!" He shoved the young accuser, who fell to the floor.

Alan rushed to the men. "Order! Men! We'll have no tolerance of that in here, absolutely none. Men!"

The angry young man shoved him back and laughed, looking around to the other men for their approval. As his face was turned away from the man on the floor, he was kicked in the knees which made his legs buckle and sent him backwards. As a result, a full fight broke out. Shouting and pillage filled the small space. But before Alan and Kumbi were able to move in to hold the men back, a sudden and terrifying swell lifted the floor hatch open, magnificently flooding the barracks.

The men clambered together in the small, diametric room, finding elevation atop a table and bunks. The fear rendered them silent as they watched like helpless spectators, the floor shifting beneath them. The waves symphonically sploshed and lapped at their feet. Then it slowed and swirled around the table legs and bunks as a snake slithers around the floor, stalking with a divided tongue. The water played and clashed about the cups, bowls and cauldron in percussion, sogged the last of the bread and tipped over the crates of porridge before it rescinded, pulling all the food rations through the hatch and out to sea like a thief, leaving the upturned crates empty as the water waned. The men froze in bewilderment. Kumbi ran to the hatch, shut it closed and stood upon it.

Alan's anger grew within, believing the incident to be God's wrath. In a backlash he scolded the men. "Your sins have their consequences! Those of you who cannot practice self discipline by merely holding your tongue have inflicted us all with God's condemnation! You were all instructed on the very first day and you agreed to leave your differences ashore!"

Braving his chances, one of the workmen spoke up. "What now, Mr Brebner, sir?"

"We have no choice but to wait it all out. God help us not to succumb to death with the pains of hunger."

That evening marked the end of the fourth day of enclosure in the steel barracks. The mood was dismal, as there was nothing to fill their stomachs. There remained only the calm of resignation within. The men were in their bunks whilst in the darkness Mr Goodwillie played violin to pass the time and attempt to lighten the mood.

"Shut it up!" someone shouted, and the music lopped away.

.oOo.

The early morning of the fifth day was as quiet as the

dead. Kumbi was hungry and the rumbling of his stomach did not let him sleep. It was, in fact, louder than the sound of the drizzle from the ceiling. But the rhythm of the drips slowed to a long, delayed tap. He lay there, listening to the water releasing its final drops into the filled jug. The silence of it grabbed his attention and he jumped out of his bunk. He lept to the wall and pressed his ear into it to check on the rain outside. For once, the call of the gulls was glorious music to his ears.

"It's stopped!" he shouted. "Awake! Awake! Mr Brebner, come!"

Alarmed, Alan jumped out of his bunk and ran over to Kumbi.

"The rain and wind, Mr Brebner – they have stopped." Alan stepped close to the door and opened it cautiously, unsure as to what he would face outside. In place of the black sky above and waves which had grabbed at the steel legs below like encroaching, predatory arms, he found the sea had transmuted itself into a sparkly, serene deep blue. The glorious summer sky was raised high and infinite, flushed with the nearly forgotten sun's glare and warmth. There were sighs of relief among the workmen and great commotion as the men pushed each other along to step outside. With Alan's permission they climbed down onto the skerry.

The men walked around the perimeter of the barracks, inspected the steel legs and assessed the eleven metre wide lighthouse base for any damage. Eleven two-ton stones had not only dislodged from the course of the lighthouse work, but had disappeared altogether from the base of the tower, having been engulfed by the sea.

CHAPTER 1

Breathes there the man, with soul so dead,
Who never to himself hath said,
This is my own, my native land!
Whose heart hath ne're within him burn'd,
As home his footsteps he hath turn'd,
From wandering on a foreign strand!
If such there breathe, go, mark him well;
For him no Minstrel raptures swell;
High though his titles, proud his name,
Boundless his wealth as wish can claim;
Despite those titles, power, and pelf,
The wretch, concentred all in self,
Living, shall forfeit fair renown,
And, doubly dying, shall go down
To the vile dust, from whence he sprung,
Unwept, unhonour'd, and unsung.

Sir Walter Scott
Breathes There the Man

At Greenock, on board Aemelius, Alfred Henderson stood behind Captain Alexander MacIntosh whilst he studied the sea charts, contemplating their next sail.

A cold breeze blew outside, which made a sharp hissing at the windows. They had refuge inside the captain's cabin to save the charts from deterioration caused by the weather. Captain MacIntosh kept quiet, as he seemed to be uncertain of their plan. Trying to understand his hesitation, Alfred leaned over his shoulder to take a closer look. He slid his rugged finger across the paper, eager to come up with an idea which Alexander, or 'Tosh', as he was more often known as, would approve of.

"Following the route further west around Islay, we could possibly avoid the skerry to the east," Alfred drew the line he was suggesting across the worn chart.

"*Possibly* isn't good enough for a passenger ship. We clearly do not have enough information about the coast. It's wild, and the craggy coast has yet to be recorded in the charts." Tosh shook his head. "I won't take the risk," he retorted. His voice was commanding and his brow furled as he waved away the suggestion.

"But sailing south and around the coast of Ireland will increase the voyage by at least five days, even with both sails and steam at full power. The provisions for passengers and coal are limited," Alfred replied, raising his voice in order to sound adept and not too appeasing to Tosh's inclinations, however reasonable they were.

Tosh was quick to rebuke Alfred's plan. "Then we won't sail the Scottish coast until the light is built. I know you're keen to take the opportunities of emigration, but you must be patient. Alternatively, we could make a fair business of sailing the route from Greenock to Liverpool to transport passengers. Larger ships are bound for the Americas and New Zealand. We can continue this route until we are able to sail safely through to Nova Scotia when the construction of the lighthouse is complete. That's what I propose."

Alfred thought for a few moments before conceding, then withdrew his raised tone. "It's a smaller profit but ... "

"She's your last ship, Alfred. We must play it safe for a while, if you want any future in trading. And, as your captain, you must trust me inexplicably."

Alfred was unable to contradict Tosh's view on the matter and looked down from his captain to the charts. He sighed with resolution and nodded, "Again, you are correct."

"Indeed. Alright, that's that," added Tosh. In truth Tosh's opinion wasn't at all what Alfred wanted to hear. The added 'Indeed' heated some internal spite in which was fueled by a deeply embedded memory from his youth. When faced with the chance of a new opportunity, Alfred had a tendency to be stubborn and strong headed, not to mention impatient. But those traits didn't often serve him well, as they also had the capacity to disable him from making sound decisions. His ability to tell Tosh that he was correct or admitting that his opinion was the better of the two had taken years of practice, all the while biting his hardened tongue.

There was a lifetime of history between the two men; Alfred knew Tosh well. Twelve years his elder, Tosh was a man who had an even temper and was a highly knowledgeable seafarer with decades of insight and authority. As young men, Alfred was hindered by an injury to his leg in a steam packet incident, making him unfit to take to the helm as a profession. Tosh, on the other hand, carried on learning to skipper ships. And by the ripened age of fifty, the wind and salt had become permanently embedded into the thick, deeply lined skin of Alfred's face. He trusted Tosh more than anyone else in matters concerning his ships, though less so in his personal life.

Tosh was satisfied with himself at the conclusion of the conversation. He rolled up the charts as Alfred limped across the room with an uneven gait to the take the coats off the hooks, his stick giving him support and balance.

"Come now, let's go to my house and celebrate Lois's sixteenth birthday," Tosh said.

"Aye," said Alfred, "She's a woman at last." He passed Tosh his coat.

"Easy, son," replied Tosh. "This is my daughter whom you are taking delight in."

Alfred looked at him, pretending to be clueless. "I'm not taking any delight with Lois – or anyone." He knew he was lying and tried to dismiss his guilt, but nonetheless was embarrassed at his comment as he dug himself into a hole and felt miserable for doing so. "Not that she's not – well, delightable." He blushed.

They looked at each other. Alfred was momentarily apprehensive about Tosh's mute response but when he laughed, Alfred laughed back with him - and swore to himself that he would not talk about Lois like that ever again. Together they left the cabin, closing the door behind them.

.oOo.

Although Alfred grew up the son of a successful

ship merchant, his childhood was not without its faults or deception. The things he witnessed as a boy moulded him into the often opposing and emotionally distanced man he was as an adult. He was born a local lad of Greenock on 29 September 1842, the only surviving child of three. His father, David Allen Henderson, was a ship merchant whose main business was sailing Lady Albatross, one of his two finely built ships between Greenock in Renfrewshire, Scotland and the West Indies.

Measuring one hundred twelve feet long and sixteen feet three inches hull to hull, Lady Albatross was built on the Clyde River several miles to the west of Glasgow in the year 1832. This graceful and sleek ship was built for purpose. Not knowing that slavery would be abolished a few years later, she was already built fitted with plank for sleeping below two decks inside a hold for the merciless transportation of slaves to the United Kingdom. Below this deck, in the bottom of the hull, large barrels of rum, sugar and dried tobacco were packed to full capacity. This added weight kept the ship steady at the keel. There was little reserved space for other things, such as sleeping bunks for the sailors and food rations, which were proportioned mostly to feed the sailors and the very minimum with which to feed those on board in captivity.

En route from Jamaica to Greenock and bound by their ankles in chains, David gave each slave a number. Under sail, he would bring them up from the smelly, hot bowels of the ship where they spent their days without sunlight in their faces or inadequate food. In the mornings, he had small groups of s i x slaves work alongside the more experienced sailors for their morning exercise. Training up slaves during sail wasn't necessarily an easy task, as their ankles were tied together and each man had a gap of than two feet away from the other. David called these slave lines, and their main responsibility was heaving in the sails and anchor ropes, usually weighed down heavily after having been soaked in sea water.

On return to the West Indies, David transported British folks who were keen on securing land in Jamaica to profit from the few white entrepreneurs who were already living there. Each British farmer and potential shop keeper who wanted to take the chance of prosperity in the better climate were charged the hefty fee of forty pounds for the one-way journey.

After slavery was abolished, the black apprentice trade was established. Although slavery was formally banned in 1833, the British did not immediately adjust to free labour. Slaves had to continue to work for their former masters for a duration of up to to six years in exchange for board and food. This apprenticeship was eventually stopped in each of the colonies by the year 1838.

David saw an opportunity in those black people who wished to seek out available work in Britain during the greatly flourishing Industrial Revolution. He enticed them with the offer of work on his ship, only for them to discover shortly after leaving Jamaica that food rations were an absolute minimum and offered no pay, which they would have needed once landing in Britain. If they were fortunate enough to have survived the calamitous voyage, a good number of them would arrive ill as well as penniless.

David and his wife Kathleen had struggled to have children for more than three years, so in 1839 when she conceived, he was thrilled. Infant death wasn't uncommon, as one third of babies died in infancy. Against the doctor's advice, with an adolescent and vociferant nature, David was unable to contain his delight. He indulgently boasted to his fellow churchmen and everyone he knew about the impending birth. However, as fate would have it, the baby was born significantly underweight and unable to latch on to Kathleen's breast. He was struck down with dysentery and dehydration at six weeks old and died.

With his ego now badly damaged, he was both embarrassed and devastated by the loss and was left to wade heavy, awkward feet for his months of bravado. Swamped by this emotion, he arranged to embark on another voyage to the West Indies, a trade deal which he told Kathleen would expect to last several months, taking him from island to island. He was eager to leave the tragedy behind him. Whilst absent, Kathleen, now pregnant out of her husband's duty, suffered terrible depression from his alienation. Although she had the support of her mother and two sisters close at hand, she was without the company of her once affectionate husband, who seemed to have disappeared as if lost at sea. He spent most of his days away filling his apathy as he dangerously bonded with the vacant ocean, growing increasingly detached and caring less about the consequences of mingling with all sorts of shifty merchants. When David returned home after twenty-two months away, he had changed into someone whom Kathleen no longer recognised.

David went into a deep, downward spiral, one into which his suffering distanced him further and further from his wife and now second child, Alfred.

The growing number of large steam ships sailing in and out of the Clyde were on the increase and difficult to ignore – and more difficult to compete with. They were a threat to David's trade. In the challenge with the other merchants, he was called away from Greenock more often.

As a result, Alfred grew up not knowing David well, and his mother fed him exaggerated, inflated stories about the wonderful, yet absent man whom he was to call his father.

Several years after slavery had ended, David still continued to trade in secret. His corrupt methods carried on for three more years and it was a sneaky way to try to get away without the so called 'free labour'. Surprisingly, there were still buyers on the receiving end who traded inconspicuously. As long as the interest continued on British soil, David was keen to oblige in the opportunity. He offloaded small groups of slaves onto the Greenock docks in the darkness of the evening. In summer, the sun refused to taper off until ten o'clock in the evening and it was very difficult to hide the innocent captives from potential onlookers.

David's illicit dealings were kept quiet by the dockworkers, because there were other unsavoury traders who participated in activities of the like. But a single leak within the maritime community sparked a rumour as fast as a fire in a fuelled furnace and tainted his reputation as a ship merchant beyond repair.

The story goes that on one particular voyage from Jamaica, a slave line of six men were brought up from below deck in strong winds. With their ankles still tied together, they fought to pull the ropes in to secure the sails in the swell of the seas. The wind was furious and filled the sails to taut that they didn't allow for any yield. Because the front man had lost the use of his ulcerated and bleeding hands, he wrapped the rope around his arm for added strength. But he lost control of the rope as it all at once tightened, constricting it like a clamp. Losing his balance, he fell to the deck. The wet rope dug into his arm, dredging deeply like soldier's trenches, ripping off the skin and nearly severing his arm. All six men who were linked to him lost their footing one by one and the ill-omened lot of them fell into the sea screaming to be saved. But their pleas were cast in vain. They disappeared below the water's surface within seconds as the current pulled one in, then the other, till there were none left. The innocent men, known only as a number, were never to be heard of again.

David was on board on that fateful day and between the men who observed it, they said that David could have helped the situation if only he had given orders to soften the sails by marginally changing direction, but he didn't give the command. In fact, there was a very audible argument between him and the captain. David insisted that the captain obey him or face getting the sack.

.oOo.

This gossip, although a terrible thing to have believed, was overshadowed by what happened to eight-year-old Alfred one evening. He had heard the whole story about his father earlier that day from a group of boys at school who had cornered him. Although he was a shy lad, his sense of pride made him stand up for his father. He called back to them demanding they retract their untrue story, but the boys vexed, pushed and spat at Alfred, making him run from the gang and he cried as he rushed home to his mother.

One evening later in the week, a messenger boy came to his door to tell his mother that his father's ship had returned to the docks. Alfred overheard the conversation and decided to meet his crudely treated and unfairly cited father in secret. He wanted to walk home with him and hear words that would reassure him that the giant of a man was, and had always been, an honourable one.

Alfred grabbed his coat and slipped out of the house when he ought to have been in bed and ran down the lane to the docks whilst the sky was still dusk. He stood at the bow of the Lady Albatross and gazed at her grandeur as he imagined the lands she had seen and the vast waters she had crossed - all at his incredible father's hand. The ship was tidy and her decks had been mopped, so Alfred could not piece together in his young mind why his father had not yet returned home.

Unsure of what to do next, Alfred sat his tired body next to the ship atop a bollard which was bound up with fat ropes tied with several Lighterman's hitch knots. He studied them and ran his fingers over the detail, impressed with the smooth art. As the night closed in on him, he yawned wide and long and watched in amazement as the sky turned from blue to pink, then dark orange and grey over the southwestern-most silhouettes of Scotland - the Isle of Bute, Mull of Kintyre and Islay. Then, the sun finally sunk over the sea, pulling the bejewelled banner down with it.

The elaborate spectacle reminded Alfred of the travelling circus his mother once took him to see in the outskirts of Glasgow. Some of the fairground entertainers rode out with horses and wagons to the smaller towns outside the big city, offering them a taster for the bigger show. Children and adults alike were mesmerised by the dynamic acts displayed in front of them: trick riding on horses, acrobatics, jugglers and battle displays using fake ammunition.

Like all of the other children, Alfred was thoroughly amused at the spectacle and stayed as long as his mother allowed which, luckily for him, was all the way until the very end. A contortionist appeared in front of them. Whilst others gawked, clapped and gazed, Kathleen winced at the awful sight and covered her eyes. The show then ended with the ring master asking for donations as the entertainers harnessed up the horses and loaded up the wagons. He took off his top hat and passed it around like an offering plate to his congregation. As Greenock was not a very wealthy town, only a few coins clanged as they tumbled into the hat and he walked around the towns people calling at them for support of the show before he jumped onto an open wagon. The crowd gradually turned their backs on him and trickled away. As the circus parted down the high street, it rolled off with an exciting noisy racket of horns, a shrill tintinnabulation of symbols and its colourfully painted advertisement sign which read "Circus Beebe" closing behind them.

That happy memory vanished into the dark sky in a snap as Alfred heard a sudden, harsh commotion from within the ship, directly next to where he was sitting. Scornful jeering and crying became more audible. He stood up in fear, not having any idea what was happening beyond the planks of the hull. As no one was around on the evening working docks, he was compelled to listen to the noises of people busying in the ship, some walking, other sounds of shuffling feet across the wood floor and the sound of a man shouting orders in a voice which was oddly familiar to him: his father.

Alarmed, Alfred jumped off the bollard. His eyes widened. Feeling very uneasy, he crossed his arms tightly across his chest.

A rather tall horse-drawn carriage then pulled up on the lower road at the dock. A man, dressed in a suit and a hat which shadowed his face, casually stepped out of the carriage. Leaning against it, he casually crossed his legs at the ankles and watched the ship, waiting. In a few minutes, several black men, as if marching, emerged above him on the deck forming two slave lines. Alfred's father walked up from behind them and ordered them to stay quiet, whilst two other sailors stood beside them holding sticks and measures of cut, linked chains.

Afraid of being seen, Alfred hid behind a wall of empty crates, stacked on top of each other by the bow of the ship. The young lad froze in outright fear as he watched as his father took the chain attached to a metal collar around the neck of the slave at the front on the line. David yanked on the chain, pulling the man forward - followed by the rest, as if he were walking out a team of shire horses.

David then led the men down the gangway, each only able to take short steps in sync with one another. He marched them down to the man who was waiting at the carriage. The stranger walked around the slave line, inspecting each one, feeling their arms and legs and slapping their hind quarters as if it was a sale of a herd of cattle. There was an exchange between the hands of the two men, the blacks for a small sack of what Alfred assumed to be money.

Alfred knew that slavery was no longer allowed and he was horrified to be witness to his father's disgraceful behaviour. The cruel, aggressive behaviour to those men by his father left him disturbed, for he could not correlate what he had seen with the man he thought he knew.

This scene was an overwhelming one to the eight-year-old Alfred, who from that moment, placed his father in a new, very dim light. It diminished his father's redemptive value for the rest of Alfred's life. He ran home on his own that evening without the comforting accompaniment of his father. Slipping quietly back into bed, he shivered with nervous discontent under his blanket. When he heard his father enter the house soon after, Alfred felt both angry and afraid of him.

His mother did not understand the change in young Alfred after that. He kept to himself and out of embarrassment he became silent to the boys at school who had teased him that day.

Regardless of his record of wrongdoings, David found financial success. This meant that he coud now expand the company, and so in the year of 1842 he commissioned the building of a second ship. she was a new type of vessel which, although retained the traditional sailing aspect of three masts – the forward mast, main mast and a mizzen mast. She now had the added benefit of steam power run by coal fuel. During its construction, a smoke pipe was built in the centre of the ship between the forward and main masts and stood tall enough so that the men could see where the ship was headed without the interference of gagging in heavy soot and being blinded by the impenetrable, black smoke. She was a smaller ship and though heartier, she lacked the elegance of Lady Albatross, with just eighty-eight feet in length and fourteen feet six inches from hull to hull. With no time to waste, she was purchased, christened Aemelius and launched immediately, taking her maiden voyage to Jamaica.

David had grand visions. If not for the first son, then for his second, Alfred. But he was reluctant to put his faith in Alfred because he was a disinterested and distant adolescent, whom he thought lacked discipline due to David's absent years. There was no solid promise that the shipping business which he worked so hard to establish would be continued one day by his son. So, he looked onto the third child, Alfred's younger brother, for this. But it was never meant to be as the child was struck down with pneumonia and didn't live beyond the age of nine. This left David depending on Alfred, but he knew that the lad would require the extra time to be instructed, given the right discipline and to acquire enough knowledge of the anatomy of the two ships and how they both functioned. It would take years to teach him this and David knew he would have to be the man to take on the task.

During the early days of Aemelius, there was quite a demand on ships to carry people to new lands of opportunity, in particular New Zealand and Australia. David found a very good business of emigration from Scotland to Nova Scotia as the economy in the Highlands collapsed.

Joining his new Lady Albatross crew, David hired Tosh, a sharp young man at the time, to work as 2nd Mate to Jamaica. Tosh was everything he wished Alfred would become in time: responsible, bright and willing and David rewarded him with respect.

In turn, David began to see that if he wanted his business to survive in the West Indies, he had to do things very differently. And the once good name of the Lady Albatross was attached to his diminished reputation. So, in a bid to rectify his past and create a fresh start, he switched the purposes of his ships. He chose to sail Aemelius to Jamaica, importing higher volumes of sugar, rum and dried tobacco. They filled the airy spaces below the main deck, mainly concentrated in the bow and stern, well away from the heat of the steam engine. Lady Albatross became reserved only for the voyages to Nova Scotia.

The new steam engine required several tons of coal to be kept close at hand in the lower deck, two men in a shift at one time to feed the fire and two other men who would change over the labour every four hours, rotating all day and all night. The part sail, part steam ship was also fitted with a new invention to make them travel even faster - an underwater propeller.

As large ocean crossing ships go, his two ships were still considered modest in size in comparison to some of the other merchant and passenger ships who were now busily crossing the great oceans of the world. Yet, Aemelius and Lady Albatross were still large enough to withstand the brash Atlantic Ocean currents and storms to keep his business afloat.

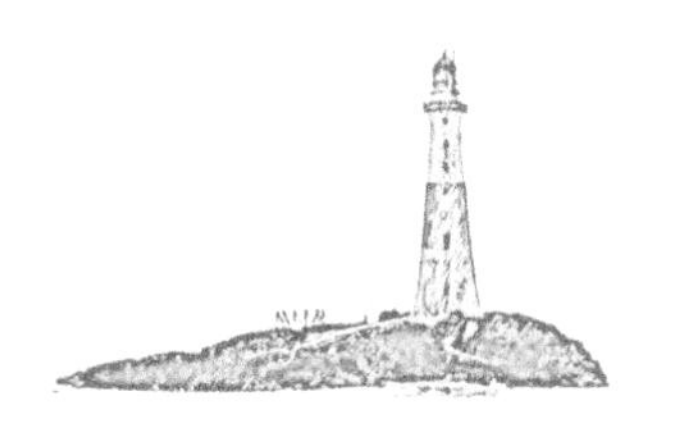

CHAPTER 2

I hae seen the smiling o'fortune beguiling;
I hae felt all its favours, and found its decay:
Sweet was its blessing, kind its caressing:
But not 'tis fled – fled far, far away.

I hae seen the forest, adorned the foremost,
With flowers of the fairest, most pleasant and gay,
Sae bonnie was their blooming; their scent the air perfuming;
But not they are wither'd and a'wede away.

I hae seen the morning with gold the hills adorning,
And loud tempest storming before the mid-day.
I hae seen Tweed's siller streams, glittering in the sunny beams,
Grow drumly and dark as they row'd on their way.

O fickle fortune! Why this cruel sporting?
Oh why still torment us, poor sons of a day!
Nae mair your smiles can cheer me, nae mair your frowns can fear me;
For the Flowers of the Forest are a'wede away.

Mrs Alison Cockburn
The Flowers of the Forest

After a fair number of Atlantic crossings, Tosh soon became David's closest comrade. He was barely Alfred's senior, yet already an austere, experienced captain. Married to Marion, together they had a growing family. He was also a kind and forgiving man who had the inner strength to overlook David's bad temper and harsh attitudes towards the black people when they were spending time in Port Royal and Kingston. Knowing the sailors faced every possibility of disease, Tosh was empathic. So, in the early days of his apprenticeship and at his own expense he often slipped a small, concealed crate of June plums, mangoes and papaya onto the ship to prevent the men from getting scurvy.

Alfred's mother, Kathleen Gordon was born in Glasgow, where she met David through an introduction by each other's families. They were married and moved to Greenock to start a family and to support David's nautical pursuits. At such a young age she was unaware of his racial intolerance and that his malicious treatment of others would eventually spin out of control. And even when it did, she chose to turn a blind eye.

When Alfred was fourteen David began to spend time with him at the dockyard teaching him the ins and outs of ship responsibilities. Alfred gradually grew an interest in ships and trading.

Becoming a ship merchant was expected of him and although David was hard-nosed and demanding, despite their past, Alfred had an innate need to prove himself as a competent, capable adult to his father regardless of David's shortcomings. Having lost both of his siblings, watching his father import slaves and then losing his adored mother to consumption when he was aged fifteen, his mind was often wandering in his solitude and his home was quiet and vacant even when he was there. He kept to himself, becoming more introverted and his awkward approach to women made him feel uneasy, as growing up in a shipyard didn't give him experience to communicate with them. Hence, he lacked charm, and as an older teen his approach to any woman was unattractively far too direct – often considered coarse, however unintentional it was.

Alfred grew up in the church and was well rehearsed in scripture and as his mindset was quite a disciplined one, he followed the Bible with reverence, with a serious frame of mind and regarded it with great importance to everyday life.

There were many maritime superstitions during the 19th centuries which were born of happenstance and had taken on life during the centuries before. Alfred chose to put much of that aside and rely on his faith as his guide. It was the general belief among sailors that if someone was swept overboard, it was God's intention for that to happen, and no one was to interfere with this by means of an attempted rescue. Alfred, though, had other thoughts which were more compassionate and heartfelt towards humanity. In contrast, he often envisioned a rescue should he be out at sea and the need occur. Because of this, he was considered guileless, and fair hearted by some of the other ship merchants.

As any young man might do, Alfred ran his first yawl aground during a practice sail, to which incident he was bound to quite a punishment by David. According to the story that Alfred told his father, the degenerate sailor who took him out had been on a three day bender before showing up on the docks and convincing Alfred it would be a good idea to turn loose the ropes from its bollards. He should've been forewarned when the man showed up on the day unshaven, stumbling and reeking heavily of whisky. Yet young Alfred was not wise or sensible enough to tell him he was uneasy with the idea.

In a matter of a couple of hours and some pretty gusty southern winds, the boat shot across the inner seas and onto a sandbank between Bute and Argyll along Kames Bay. There, she laid sideways and the hull exposed her split timbers like a prostitute had been stripped of her dignity by the crude drunkard. And in that position, they sludged their way to shore. The abandoned, reclined ship lay in the cusp of her crypt, awaiting a dignified burial of the tides on the sandy shoals of the bay.

The realisation of the unfortunate result came to the sailor only too late to retract his err. He sobered up just in time to realise what he had done as the fear came over him knowing he would face not only an immediate sacking as a result, but a rebuking of gross proportions from the now respectable ship merchant who was Mr Henderson.

Although evidently not surpassingly mature, Alfred was able enough to negotiate places for them on a fishing boat to Largs Pier and walked the fourteen miles home with his less than savoury companion. It was a learning curve for him, as he had taken the ship out against his father's wishes, and unquestionably with the wrong instructor.

Eventually, David believed that Alfred would have paid his dues after giving him a month of punishment with daily jobs of polishing brass and repairing ropes, rigging and mending sails on Lady Albatross. The chores were long and arduous hours on end. As if polishing the Muntz metal wasn't itself taxing enough on the hands, it was a tediously boring task of rubbing a cloth against the yellow metal for hours. Alfred became resentful at his overly harsh father for giving him this duty.

The previous brass finisher, Mr Williams, died of pneumonia at the age of just 34. It was becoming well established at that time that the common cause of death among brass finishers was coronary and lung diseases. Thus, not many wanted to take on that job, seeing the horrendous pain Mr Williams lived with for four years before his life had finally succumbed to the illness. The job was passed onto Alfred in order that he would learn his lesson. Without success, he tried to convince his father that the mere thought of polishing was in itself a severe lesson.

The mending of the sails was a more sombre test and for this Alfred was given a ditty bag. This bag contained all the tools required by a sailor for repairing sails and ropes: a palm, a cake of wax, strand line and sewing needles. Once a sail was lowered off the beam and untied from the rigging which was attached vertically to the mast, a repair would then be made by way of stitching the tear and reinforcing each end, ensuring that the strands and scrim of the weave would be sewn in with the new stitches. This was to prevent premature unravelling or ripping as the winds pulled at it whilst under sail.

Then, a larger sized patch of cotton was cut and sewn over top the mend. The difficult push of the fat needle with each stitch would have ripped through his hands had he not been given a metal palm, a special thimble designed for sailcloth repair. It was individually made to fit over one's hand with a protective and secure thick leather strap.

The ship's ropes were heavy and long. So, from the dark and musty rope lockers the sailors heaved up only the tattered portions to the deck, where the frayed areas could be better seen and easier to work on.

He quite enjoyed the mending of ropes, as it was organised, methodical and in line with the way in which his brain worked. The delicate splicing of the strands, connecting new ones and grafting them together was in a sense quite like a surgeon's work. It required problem solving skills which seemed to pluck at Alfred's satisfaction and gently appease his rational thinking.

He also learned that alternating the tasks eased the boredom and sore muscles. A little bit of rope mending, some polishing brass, then more rope mending followed by sail repair. His father overlooked his style of work and although David believed Alfred's thoughts were somewhat scattered, he was content to see that the chores were all being done.

The punishment kept Alfred busy and out of any potential mischief. Although he was not the sort to seek out trouble, his father still felt it best to keep him away from the other young men his age who were not so accomplished, and to acquire a new set of career prowess, which he did.

When the opportunity arrived, youth had shed its doubtful, defiant, skin and he had gained a higher level of responsibility. Now that Alfred knew all the ins and outs of a sailboat and how everything worked, his father bought his learned young man the Consolation so that he would be able to start his own small trade of goods to the Outer

Hebrides. Quite the fitting name of a boat, considering the outcome of the circumstances for which it was given; one final job remained, which was learning to sail with confidence.

She was a small, two masted vessel which required two men to sail her. When Tosh returned from sea, he spent every morning apart from Sundays teaching Alfred how to sail his new boat to a good standard. After two weeks, Alfred was put to the test and sent out into the Clyde without Tosh's help, apart from one sailor who helped manpower the hoisting of sails. He did fairly well, and after Tosh gave David the nod of Alfred's competence, it was assumed he would commit to his father's business ventures.

His skills did sharpen over time, and yet after only five months developing his sailing on Consolation, he was offered a job working on a steam packet ship for the Royal Mail, sailing between Douglas on the Isle of Man and Liverpool. The opportunity was one which he could not disregard. He had the important task as a Third Officer transporting parcels and domestic mail as well as people back and forth. But the real pleasure in working on the steam packet was that he could leave his father and hone in on his sailing skills without having David stand over him, constantly correcting him and shouting orders. After all, Alfred was now in his twenties and felt as if he was too old to receive his father's direction.

Alfred was unconcerned about Consolation as she was kept tied up back in Greenock while he worked on the company's own small fleet of part steam part sailing ships which were based on the Isle of Man where he now lived in a small room above a tavern.

He was issued a uniform which included a brown, wide legged trouser and over it he wore a heavy green mid length coat. The coat was furnished with brass buttons and cuffed with the same. The buttons were embossed with the triskelion, or three-legged figure, the symbol of the Isle of Man. This ensemble made him look particularly smart, fitting for a new captain.

Just eight months into his career, there was a terrible accident deep within the ship as he was making the trip back to Douglas. A fire broke out in the engine next to the coal store. The Bosun came running down the deck and into the captain's quarters shouting "Fire!" Alfred ran past him and scrambled down below deck to extinguish the flame with the help of the Engineers when the fire spat out at him, igniting his left leg. The engineer grabbed some rags and vigorously patted the fire out, saving Alfred's life. After months of care in recovery and strict doctor's advice, he finally regained the ability to walk on the leg, but with limited use and the help of a walking stick. This ended his career on the steam packet, and Alfred went home to Greenock.

Friendly neighbours started pushing the idea of having their daughter Fiona talk to Alfred. Each was just as nervous as the other. Although they had known each other from church since they were children, it was assumed between the families that finally, at the ripened age of sixteen their daughter ought to marry. David thought that marriage would indeed teach Alfred to be more respective of his future businesses and lock him down to Greenock.

As the weeks and months passed, Fiona and Alfred grew fonder of each other. She, patient in nature, accepted his lack of engaging conversation. She would smile at him in passing and not be tempted to nag or fight him for attention. This behaviour attracted him and drew to her physically. So, their desire for romance was slow growing but eventually they became entwined with each other. There was a neediness for consistency and certainty with one another that neither had felt before. However, just like his own parents, there was not any sign of an occupied nursery at the end of the hallway for three years.

After three and a half years of marriage, Fiona finally fell pregnant with a son. During a premature labour, she bled heavily until she died in childbirth. The child was stillborn. His reserved demeanour did not lend his grief any favour. Heartbroken and withdrawn, Alfred struggled to come to terms with the tragedy. Not the most emotionally resilient man, it proved to be two too many losses for him and as he was unable to communicate his grief to anyone. Much like his father, he turned exceedingly inward. He only grieved alone when his vulnerability took him suddenly in the quiet hollow of the whisky glass.

The evening of September 1863 his father David died of heart failure in the family home. He had bequeathed his merchant ships to Alfred, and only then embraced the responsibility of running the business with Tosh by his side. Tosh possessed the good intellect of chart reading and the cleverness to manoeuvre ships through all changes of weather. He was less in favour of dead reckoning, or impromptu decisions, without the aid of celestial navigation and he opted for the use of the latest transit circle, the sextant, with which he was an expert in measuring the horizon.

Alfred grew into an ever-closer relationship with his comrade and neighbour Tosh and his family, almost as if he was adopted. After a day's work at the shipyard of planning and updating charts, the extended friendship continued with Alfred dining with them in the evenings instead of dining alone. More often than not, Tosh's wife Marion would expect them to walk through the door together. When he did, he was often received with cheerful greetings from their daughter, Lois. But when Tosh was away at sea, Alfred had his meals at his home which was managed by his housemaid, Ede.

The MacIntosh home was a modest Victorian terraced house built of stone on busy Inverkip Road consisting of a small garden laid to lawn. In the very front grew a silver birch and every spring a patch of colourful Dutch tulips encircled it. The house sat unobtrusively within a newly built scheme behind the south hill of Greenock's town centre, not a far walk from the docks which lay west, close to Port Glasgow.

Apart from Sunday service, Marion inadvertently kept to herself and their only surviving daughter. She was left alone when Tosh was on a voyage and deliberately busied herself with methodical patterns of the daily chores, in case he was to return home unexpectedly. The scrupulous washing of the bed linen and clothing and scrubbing of floors became the measure of her value. It was obsessive, but the upkeeping of the house and tending to Lois kept her mind off her loneliness and as if a cure of purging her negative energy and then - just like that - she would be the epitome of merriment when she needed to be.

Marion was just as deeply grateful as she was resentful of Tosh's work. She never outwardly complained for fear of living an existence in violation of God's word. She was well aware that it was written in the Bible in Philippians 2:14-15, to *"do all things without complaining and disputing, that you may become blameless and harmless children of God."* This knowledge took a toll on Marion's youthful looks as her once glowing now fully ripened face reflected her internal, secret sin of not trusting God as she ought to. She continued to wander in her own private desert, waiting for God's deliverance and watching, hoping for Tosh to return from the sea and relieve her agony with his presence and comfort.

CHAPTER 3

Venturing the dark for a stroll slow in stride,
A nicht o' an itch fae bonnie my bride;
Babie lambs dot the braes in plenty and quicken fancy,
As do stars out of reach upon wishes are many.

Alas, succee'd my sore and wither'd request,
Appealed to the Higher have I in my test;
May be heard her sweet sound, nae by the wind blown,
Afore I depart this falter'ed life that I've known.

Anonymous

Tosh and Alfred came through the front door, hung up their coats and walked in through the hallway welcomed by the delightful aroma of lamb and potato stew wafting through the air. Marion eagerly appeared from the kitchen, Lois rushing behind, restless and curious to know if her father had remembered her special day.

"Papa!" she cried. "You're home!"
Marion looked at Alfred and commented sarcastically, "Alf, you're here! What a nice surprise!"

They cracked sneers at each other.

"Papa, did you remember what special day this is?"

Tosh kissed Marion respectfully on the cheek, then turned to Lois to give her a birthday peck on the forehead. "And this is for my lovely daughter who today is sixteen years old," Tosh beamed as he handed her a small sack made of a remnant of sail cloth. The cloth had faded stains of dirt rubbed into it and a piece of red string at the top which clenched it all together in clove knot. "Happy birthday, Lois."

Taking the sack, she pulled the string until it let loose the four edges, exposing a large tulip bulb inside.

"Oh, Papa, you did remember!" Lois replied in delight.

"This one will be yellow."

"I'll plant this with the others. Thank you, Papa." She leaned over and kissed his cheek.

Alfred waited for his turn to greet her. When Tosh stepped aside and the space allowed, Lois looked up to Alfred and grinned at him with a twinkle in her eyes.

Alfred caught sight of this and it made him look down at the floor shyly as he stepped forward to give her a birthday handshake. A smile twitched on his face. "Happy birthday, Lois."

"Thank you, Alf." She giggled at being the cause of his awkwardness.

Alfred sat down at the table as he watched Lois help her mother put plates of food in front of them. "Lois is now of the age to find a suitor, don't you agree, Marion?" Alfred had rehearsed the conversation to himself several times earlier that evening, hoping he might be considered.

"That is up to Tosh, of course. Do you have someone in mind?"

"Well -," began Alfred.

Tosh interrupted. "I am not sure I'm ready to let her go just yet. She is becoming quite the young lady, all credit to her beautiful mother, of course. Isn't that right, my dear?"

Marion smiled at her husband as if she had heard it before.

When she sat by Tosh in the dim light he could see signs of age in her face and her working hands. Through the shadows he noticed the new lines which had formed around her mouth and forehead which he had not noticed before he left on his last journey. He smiled at her with the glint of complete devotion.

Marion smiled back, the sides of her mouth creasing a little. "I wouldn't argue with you there," she replied.

Marion sat down next to Tosh. He put his hand over hers, rubbing it gently and they smiled at each other, then Marion lowered her voice to Tosh, changing to a dourer tone.

"If she is married off, I will most certainly be alone and without help," she said, meaning for it to only be heard between the two of them. "Not that I'm complaining."

Tosh was surprised at her concern and raised his voice as if to scold her self-interest. "You can't keep her locked up here, utterly destitute for love, Marion."

Marion felt ashamed of her comment and she looked around at the others, quick to defend her reasoning by turning the blame back on Tosh. "I realise this. So, just as long as you keep coming home alive, I will be fine."

"Don't worry yourself, my dear, not on Lois's day." Tosh looked up and saw that Alfred and Lois were watching the conversation. He decided to not make a big issue out of it and changed the direction of the conversation.

"She would be a fine match with the Douglas boy. He has shown quite a lot of interest recently. Eh, Lois?" Tosh gestured with a wink.

Lois looked at her father and hesitated. Her face turned red, embarrassed of exposing matters of the heart, but she smiled at him. "Yes, Papa, I suppose he has."

Lois was not altogether comfortable at where this was going and looked at Alfred for some support.

Clearly disappointed was he that Alfred inadvertently pushed his napkin so far into his collar that only an inch and the hem of it was left to catch any drips of the meal. Tosh looked to Alfred for a response and as if to obey the captain's command he replied, "I am sure you are right."

"Settled. Marion, we will invite Douglas and his family to visit next week. Now, let's say Grace," Tosh instructed.

Each of them clasped their hands and lowered their heads. Lois didn't look keen on her father's insistence of the impending plan. But she would obey because she respected him, nonetheless.

After supper, Alfred and Tosh sipped whisky together in the sitting room. They were well mellowed when Alfred was drawn to the window at the sound of delightful humming outside. He walked over to the curtains which were pulled open at the side and fixed with a metal tie back. Together they flowed high from the top of the window frame from under a pelmet of matching brocade and like a waterfall, poured down to the floor, creating the rounded shape of a woman's hips, much like the decanter of whisky from which they poured.

Alfred pulled one draped curtain further over to the side to see out into the garden. The radiant summer sun hovered at the edge of the treetops in the long, drawn-out

Inverclyde sunset, and Lois was at the washing line taking down white sheets which fluttered about like crisp, white sails in the wind on the luff of a mainsail. He noticed how grown up she had suddenly become, and her young body had developed breasts which pushed through her blouse, tightening her dress at the top. He was also quite impressed at the speed in which she took in the linen against the accelerating wind and in haste pulled them in, furling them in the same way as a well experienced sailor would work sails.

With the curtain pulled back, Tosh saw Alfred staring at his daughter. Now aware of the attraction to Lois, he tried to break Alfred's stare by clearing his throat. "Tomorrow we will inform the crew of the change of our route to Liverpool."

Unable to take his eyes off Lois, Alfred replied, "Before we take to the sea, I will very much like to sail Consolation to Erraid to see why the lighthouse has been delayed so long."

"Very well," he replied. Tosh rose from his chair and walked over to Alfred. He stood close next to him and shared the view into the garden to confirm to himself what Alfred was looking at.

"Something caught your eye, eh?" he asked.

Alfred looked up at the tops of the mix of tall silver birches and pines. "Listening to the trees in the wind. It's the one envy that is never satisfied. You don't get this out at sea."

"No, but it appears rustling trees aren't your only envy. You should get home to your slumber; we have much to do over the next fortnight."

There was a pause from Alfred as he turned away to hide his blushing face and emptied his glass, wiping the corner of his mouth with the back of his hand.

"Go on then," pushed Tosh.

"Just so," replied Alfred. "We have much to do".

He was about to leave when Tosh stopped him by taking his arm.

"One day, son, you'll find you are no longer a lone man. But that's not today. After so long you still haven't grieved for your loss. Make your peace with it, then will you move forward."

Alfred nodded with a dismissive absolution. "I'll see you in the morning."

That evening, Alfred was alone in the house apart from his housekeeper Ede, who had many years before began work with the Henderson family when his mother became ill. Visiting Kathleen in the house every day, Ede nursed the suffering woman until her death and stayed on to work in the house. She was given a small bedroom at the end of the hallway in which she lived.

Alfred sat back in his chair. He rolled a whisky round in its glass, watching it as the honey-coloured fluid smeared the insides of the clear glass. He took the final gulp without a flinch and set it down with a clang. Noticing the photograph of Fiona in its case on the table next to him, he reached out and took the picture into his hand and studied it, just as the alcohol warmed his sentiments. Setting it down gently, he rubbed his tired eyes as he thought of her fondly. Despondency and loneliness overcame him and he longed to hold her again.

In passing Alfred outside of the drawing room from the kitchen, Ede stopped to speak with him momentarily in the doorway. "Good night, Mr Henderson," she said. "We're all locked up and your clothes are ready for the morning."

Alfred paused then looked up at Ede with his drink fuelled glossy eyes. "Good evening, Ede." He smiled out of politeness but only from the half honest edge of his mouth. Then he took his glass into his grip again and sipped on it before realising it was empty.

Ede walked down the hall, her bedroom door closing behind her. Whilst she sat at her vanity table, she removed the pins from her hair. Her long, greying hair fell below her shoulders when she heard Alfred crying, sobbing like a child. But instead of reaching out to him, she got up and locked her door to keep herself from having to console him through the night. She knew she would have to let him sleep this off as he had done so many times before.

.oOo.

Alfred left Greenock at sunrise while the seas were calm to the south of Arran. He sailed round the south tip of Mull of Kintyre in the North Channel, through the Sound of Islay, to the east of Colonsay then westward in search of the black rocks where the new beacon was said to be built. He was chaperoned by a crew of two, Captain Andrew and Duncan.

Far off the coast of Mull, they tacked close to the area where his ship was believed to have been wrecked. There was a lump of solitary rock which hid miles of black rock that promiscuously waited below the surface of the sea. Upon the protruding rock was a partially built stone structure, slowly taking a gently rounded shape from its base. Above it hovered a steel horizontal contraption on supports, and just a few metres away stood a strange looking cone-shaped steel tower.

As they sailed past on a slow breeze, they could hear the workmen calling out orders to one another in the distance. The ship skimmed past the skerry gingerly at a safe distance, several fathoms in length. As the crew of three watched in wonderment and fascination, each man stared in silence. The ship came about and the boom swung out to the starboard side, turning the vessel northeast toward the southwest coast of the Isle of Mull, the white coved and rocky cliffed little island of Erraid at its tip, now in sight.

Once moored up against the pier, Andrew and Duncan watched as the independently minded Alfred stepped off the ship with his stick alone, giving a bit of a wobble. Alan Brebner, the site superintendent, came running down to greet him. He ushered Alfred up the path and towards the row of cottages that lay quietly at the end of the track of a railway. Nearby, at the side of a hill that was used to quarry stone, two dozen skilled workers chiselled away at the rock, squaring the edges into shape. Some assembled the stones together while other men hoisted the finished slabs up and onto a platform on wheels, which sat atop the tracks. The platform was then pulled along the tracks down to the mooring and transferred on the awaiting barge by using pullies to lift and lower them. They were then bound for the lighthouse.

Alfred was fascinated by the buzz of industry taking place on the tiny, isolated island and how it was purposefully furnished for the sake of constructing a lighthouse.

"All that you see here – the cottages, church – we built for the families of the workmen. Having them stay here keeps morale high and gives a sense of normal life," explained Alan.

"And the rail line? There are no trains in Mull, or even at all on this part of the west coast," queried Alfred as he looked around.

"That's right, there are no trains for further than one hundred miles. These tracks are short and used to transport the stone from the mason area to the ship, which then takes it to the skerry. You see, Mr Henderson, all of the stones are shaped and fitted on Erraid like a puzzle, piece by piece, each one fitting into the other with precision. We have learned over the years to assemble it this way for the best result. After this is completed, the stones are dismantled, taken away and rebuilt like for like on the skerry."

Alfred was bewildered at the setup which surrounded him and he looked across the yard as Alan explained each man's task, introducing him to a new world of maritime engineering that he had never heard of before that moment. "I am very much impressed, Mr Brebner. Very much impressed indeed. I am curious to know of your background and your dialect – are you from the lowlands?" Alfred listened to the compelling man speak expeditiously before him about his long-standing career.

"Many years ago, I was appointed by Robert Stevenson, the civil engineer for the Northern Lighthouse Board."

"I know of his work", Alfred declared.

"Aye, but it didn't come easy for this headstrong lad from Leith. I had to set out to prove myself – that I was a man of faith and gain trust by having good standing of my word. This was important to Mr Stevenson, who was a man of great conviction."

"I understand this - the importance of his approach is to ensure everyone works in accord with one another."

Alan continued. "Aye, of course. I was a young apprentice builder under the guidance of my father, who was a stonemason. He worked directly under Mr Stevenson. But being a contrary sort, I didn't care to take the same path, so, I studied civil engineering and finally earned the responsibilities of superintendent."

"And here you are now, risking your life around Scotland's most difficult coastline", Alfred said, sharing his sense of pride.

Alan laughed. "Aye, that is true. We all sacrifice ourselves for a cause, don't we? I didn't get to where I am today without understanding the severity of loss."

The two men arrived at the row of cottages. Alan stopped in front of a door and knocked. There was a long pause. As they waited for someone to answer it, he glanced over at Alfred, who was looking down at his dust covered shoes and their new scratches made from the short walk up through the stonemason's rubble. He was annoyed that they required another shine and gave a huff. Alan ignored his self-absorption and he knocked harder, calling out, "Robert!"

Just then, a tall, slender young man the age of nineteen opened the door. He wore a grey, single-breasted coat which had a slightly squared lapel. It swung open with the breeze exposing a flapping, billowing shirt the colour of oyster and his loose beige trousers waved wildly like flags on poles. He lifted his head to the men, stood jauntily in the doorway and gave a relaxed, youthful grin as he looked at the stranger and then to Alan.

"Mr Brebner, I apologise for the delay. I didn't realise who you were calling out to", said the young man. He rested his long arm within the doorframe. The left sleeve of his coat was stained black, smeared with ink from his forearm, across the cuff and up the side of his little finger. He continued, speaking coolly. "Anyway, I am sure I have told you several times before to call me Louis, my name is no longer..."

"Mr Stevenson, I'd like you to welcome Mr Alfred Henderson, a ship merchant from Greenock," interrupted Alan.

"How do you do?" Louis stretched out his hand as he stared at Alfred's pleasant taste in clothing, admiring his dark green coat in particular.

"Very well, thank you," replied Alfred, shaking Louis's hand.

"May we?" Alan held out his hand between Louis and the doorframe.

"Oh, quite right! Do come in," said Louis.

The men lifted off their caps and entered the cottage. The young gentleman returned to his desk and stood in front of the many scattered papers with drawings, notes and poems written on them. He attempted to block the mess with his thin frame and his arms stretched across to both corners of the desk like a long barrier of draped rope as if to hide from Alan the hills of paper litter and lack of actual work that awaited his completion.

"Mr Henderson, Mr Stevenson will be here for three weeks on Erraid, completing his dissertation for an Engineering degree at Edinburgh University." Alan turned to Louis. "Mr Henderson's ship was the Lady Albatross, the unfortunate vessel which was wrecked in the big gale."

"How unfortunate it was. We were all very sorry to have known of the accident. So, tell me Mr Henderson, what brings a ship merchant all the way to Erraid?" questioned Louis.

"He is here to quench his curiosity about the building of the lighthouse," Alan replied.

"Just so," said Alfred. "I do have questions, such as where you are in the progress of the construction of the light."

Alan faced Louis and dismissed himself, passing off the interrogation. "I thought you could take time for Mr Henderson and talk to him about Dubh Artach and where we are with regards to the building of it. He will stay here in this accommodation with you.

"I will help as much as I can. Mr Henderson. I was full of sorrow to hear of the loss of your men," confessed Louis, holding his hand to his chest solemnly.

Alfred nodded, then curiously he asked, "Stevenson, not per chance a relation of Robert Stevenson, are you? The great engineer?"

"Indeed, he was my grandfather. I was named after him."

"It is such a genuine honour to be meeting with you, his grandson! He was a legend in one's own lifetime; a pioneer in the art of engineering. It is fortuitous that such a skill continues to pass down the generations! What a privilege you have here, to follow in his footsteps. You do realise this, young man?" Alfred said with a rare thrill in his voice. Alan looked pleased and smiled in accord with him.

"I am aware of my family's fortunate history, thank you," said Louis, glancing between the two men. He tried to hide his irritation at Alfred's compliments, receiving them as if they had been given with some measure of criticism.

"It's not the fortunate history that is important, but the fortunate future that lies before you," said Alfred.

Wishing to ignore Louis's change of attitude, Alan closed the introduction. "I shall leave you both now. I have work to do which calls me. Son, you mustn't forget to enter your notes into today's journal. Gentlemen."

"I won't forget, Mr Brebner," quickened Louis.

"Mr Brebner," Alfred acknowledged him with a nod.

Alan left the cottage, closing the door behind him.

Louis sighed. "It is much to realise. My hope would be to please my grandfather if he could only look down from the heavens and see me in this capacity. However, I don't suppose any of that is truth."

"What do you question to be truth?" asked Alfred.

"My grandfather floating somewhere above in the sky. The evidence of religion, of an afterlife in which all good and faithful men, when they appear before the gates of heaven, are welcome and that they may receive their deserved favourable, eternal hospitality. And the likelihood of anyone passing through the eye of a needle! It all seems like foolishness to me."

"I don't think it foolish. I, too believe. The eye of the needle represents the difficulty each one must face in order to change themselves for the betterment of their soul to reach eternal life."

Louis nodded sharply. “Yes, yes, I understand that. The rest of it sounds like it is made of whimsy – complete poppycock!”

Remembering why he was visiting Erraid in the first place, Alfred decided not to get in a heated religious discussion with the young man. So, he recollected his thoughts. “I do not wish to challenge your faith, Mr Stevenson. I have arrived this day only to understand the delay in the building of the lighthouse.”

“Forgive me and my distractions, for I have many,” declared Louis as he looked around his desk seemingly lost in disorganisation and clutter.

Alfred explained. “You see, I must pass here from Greenock to Canada with a ship of emigrants at summer’s end. My captain, who although is most capable and experienced, cannot be certain of safely navigating the journey past the black rocks. They are not yet established on any of the charts. We need the beacon to be alight for us.” Alfred explained.

Louis looked at him with dubiety. “At summer’s end? But I fear that won’t be at all possible! There is much to do and a mere few weeks a year in which the men can work. At the beginning of the construction, they were delayed due to the most wretched two years of gales. The foundations which were set into place within the rock were lifted from its base and taken to the sea each time they tried. Working only a few months – or weeks each year means that they are limited to the constraints of time and tide. And what with the winds and rough sea, it has been a near impossible task to reach the rock.” Louis continued after catching his breath. “Finally, we now have a solid base established and are making haste.

As you have seen for yourself in passing, today we have a clear and calm sea. If this upholds, we can steady onward and upward to build the light for you and all sea men. But not by summer's end, Mr Henderson. That just isn't going to be."

"I am impatient and for this I apologise," Alfred sighed. "But with the increase in emigration, there is profit to be made. We were wanting to sail this September. If we don't sail, the people will leave by other means by way of Liverpool or Skye. As well, we cannot leave later in the season, or my ship and her 200 crew and passengers will face the impossible Atlantic storms and will be battered to fragments."

"Your emigrants will have to wait. Dubh Artach will not be finished this year and doubtfully the next." Louis turned away to look at his work laid out on the desk, scratched his head and coughed deeply. "I have some work here to finish before supper. But first I will show you the room in which you shall stay and I will come for you in time to eat." Louis motioned Alfred to follow him away from his desk and into another room.

That evening in Louis's cottage, the two men sat in small chairs with the seats woven crisscross in straw and covered with cushions. Their empty plates lay on the table in front of them and flames from the fire danced in the shine of the broth left on them. They drank beer and relaxed together as the fire crackled. In the pause of conversation, Louis sang a verse of a song:

"It's almost just a week the morn
Since I was weill and harvesting corn
As full of health, and strength and fun
As any man among the crowd."

Alfred giggled at Louis and the joviality in his tune. "So, you are a musician as well as an engineer."

"No, I would not claim to be a musician!" he laughed. "And yourself?"

"I couldnae carry a tune if it were strapped to mah back," Alfred said as he took another swallow and sent Louis laughing.

The men stared at the flames and a quiet pause filled the room as Louis worked up the courage to confess.

"And I'm not yet an engineer, nor even certain of it."

"How so?" questioned Alfred.

"Mr Henderson do let me trust this to you and you alone. I can trust you, isn't it so?"

"Of course. Have I thus far given you reason not to?" asked Alfred.

Louis replied with caution. "Seeing as we have only met today, I hardly know you at all. But my senses say that I can."

"And my senses tell me you have good intuition, lad, something not everyone has. You have no reason to not trust me, that is true, so why not put me to the test."

Louis opened up to him, "Well then. Yes, I am indeed practising to become an engineer. I am, just as my father has intended me to be. But, even stronger than that, I have other ideas which I fancy." Louis sat in closer and faced Alfred. "When I close my eyes, dreams appear to me."

"I don't understand," said Alfred. Feeling the effects of the beer rush through his veins and flow into his head with a sudden and delightful jolt, Louis let his inhibition loose. He tapped the top of his head. "It is here and as real as anything. Take music. Is what we hear not real just before it vanishes a moment later? Just like that?" he snapped his twig-like fingers. "Not like my father's outdated fables he calls religion."

Alfred gave Louis a look of disbelief. "I warn you, be careful as to not tempt the Lord God. The Almighty will not see pleasure in your mockery."

"No, let me explain. It – it's not mockery, try to understand. All sorts of stories of adventure come to me; they always have." Louis grew excited and bounced over to his desk, picked up random pieces of paper and continued to animate, his arms flying freely in the space around him. "*This* is what is real to me. Surely, it is in these that I am to believe!" He said, shuffling the papers.

Alfred bent down to tend to the fire, wondering to himself what sort of tapestry of a man had appeared before him within Louis and even with his supervision, he had allowed him to let loose by way of alcohol. Rotating the dissipating, glowing logs with the tongs, he looked over at the dried wood which was carefully stacked neatly next to him. He chose one to add to the fire, then returned it back to the pile, deciding not to continue the fire and prolong the charade. Instead, Alfred stood up to end the night.

Louis noticed he had lost Alfred's attention. "I'll have you know that I have published one book already."

Alfred looked at him, stumped. "Have you now?"

"Aye, well, a small book called *The Pentland Rising* - three years ago. My father funded its publishing. I have continued to write more poems and stories. Some are in verse and perhaps I will publish them one day. Everyone must record their thoughts, even you."

"Me?" Alfred questioned. He started to laugh.

"But why not? A man such as yourself with age and many life experiences would have much to pen. I have heard it say that it might unlock all the tension one carries. You ought to try it."

Alfred grew defensive. "I see no fault in your desire to write stories. However, Mr Stevenson, perhaps you ought to concern yourself less in matters of my tension and take more concern for your soul!"

"Oh, but I have no shame in being a sinner. The saints are the sinners who keep on trying." Louis took a moment to think about what he had just said and turned to his desk to find his pen. "Just a moment, let me write that." He dipped his pen into what was left of the small glass pot of ink on his desk and carefully tapped the excess back into it. He searched for a blank sheet of parchment and as he could not find one, he took a piece which had already been scribbled on, turned it over and wrote on the back of it quickly, so as to not forget his magnificent line. He repeated under his breath as he scribbled, "I have - no shame - the saints are the sinners - keep on trying."

Alfred sat down in his seat. "I have not this talent; the skill to define what it is that I feel or think."

Feeling sadness for Alfred's lack, Louis tried to explain. "The words are there; you just have to find them in here." He tapped on his chest. But he could see that Alfred was clouded. "Allow me to ask this of you: did it once happen as a child; you pulled the boat up into the sand and as you did this you began to sink into it?"

Alfred leaned forward inquisitively. "Why, yes."

"This is your problem today. The tide is well out and your legs are trapped. You stand there, waiting, unable to move. As that child you were not able to dig yourself free and you became frightened, requiring help.

As you grew older, you were able to free your legs with ease. This wasn't because you were any taller or wiser, but only that before you were stiffened with fear. With some practice, that fear no longer controlled you."

"How does this help me the now?" Alfred queried.

"Mr Henderson," Louis added, "you have always had the ability to free your feet."

Alfred rubbed his chin to a point. "This is a sensible explanation."

Louis was elated. "Very well then!"

"I shall take it to heart", conceded Alfred.

Louis then looked upward to remember what was previously on his mind. "Now, what was I saying before?" He thought for a moment. "I have so many ideas. I would like to write stories of the wild coast and pirates and men and new places. Who knows what else! They will come alive from the pages on which they were written. And, just like you, Mr Henderson, I have for myself read the Bible and it, too, is full of adventure. So, we are both lovers of fine stories. I was *sure* we would find common ground - the muse and the student! I find inspiration in you."

"Mr Stevenson, I am sure that your visions of mischief are exciting in themselves," said Alfred.

Louis interrupted madly, "Oh, but mischief it's not; I'm writing and I'm creating life!"

Ignoring Louis's last and ever confusing statement, Alfred grew ever more impatient and his voice louder and he spoke over him. "If only you had the possibility to tell me the whereabouts of my loot."

Louis stopped himself as he saw the annoyance in Alfred's eyes. He threw his lengthy, drunken arms into the air and they landed craftily upon his hips. Then he took a deep breath and exhaled audibly, adding, "How could I possibly do that?"

Alfred regathered his disposition. "When my ship was wrecked, she took with her a full cargo of sugar and rum en route to Norway. It was a great financial loss to me."

"It is hardly a conundrum, Mr Henderson. It would have been taken by the coastal wreckers had it not sunk to the sea floor," Louis answered.

"Coastal wreckers? What wreckers – where?" Alfred asked inquisitively.

"Chances are that it's sunk instead. But there is talk that some small communities still live along the south coast of Mull of Kintyre, Iona and even much further north," he tutted, "if you consider that living by anyone's standards." Louis raised his eyebrows in distaste.

"Is this one of your fictitious stories?"

"Not at all!" Louis stepped forward. "I implore you to believe me that what I tell you now is what has been said to me by reputable men."

Alfred paced around the room, contemplating. "I didn't know wreckers still worked the coasts."

"If they do, however, the law is on their side. Everyone lives by selling something, whatever be his right to it." Louis turned quickly and took another piece of paper. Adding more ink to his pen, he wrote what he'd just said, again repeating it under his breath. "Everyone – lives – by – selling - something."

Alfred was frustrated at watching this one-man band before him, who clanged his symbols whilst blowing tunes out of a one-holed flute. Alfred finished his ale and bashed the tankard down on the table. Then he took Louis's tankard and drank the rest of it, maintaining a sober posture. Louis looked at him in bemusement and puffed.

Alfred ignored him. "Well, once again, this justifies the exact reason why I, among many other ship merchants, have signed the petition to the Northern Lighthouse Board. I have one ship left; nothing else do I own. I cannot, shall not, lose her."

Alfred set Louis's empty tankard on the table with a soft thump and wiped his wet gob with the back of his arm sleeve.

Louis took his tankard and looked into it. "Have you just finished my ale?"

"It's clear you've had enough for tonight. Time to sleep."

Louis sighed.

"Trust me," Alfred said.

Louis grabbed Alfred's arm and looked intently into his eyes to reassure him. "We will not waste time, Mr Henderson. I, myself, will keep you informed of all our progress by letter and will do my best to see that you have your lighthouse." Stepping back, he placed his hand on his heart, bowed and spiritedly added, "I will be a proud man to have had some part in it and have helped to make a safe passage for your captain. This is my promise to you."

Alfred nodded satisfactorily. "Going forward, you must call me Alfred."

"Likewise," Louis agreed.

Alfred appealed. "Don't be absurd; I will not call you Alfred."

"Call me Louis."

"But did you not say that you are Robert, the name of your grandfather?"

"I did, yes, but I now prefer to be called Louis. I am my own man."

Alfred smiled just as equally in amusement as he did in respect for the young man, who was simply trying to find his own way in life outside his father's and grandfather's fame and make a name for himself just as Alfred had once done.

"Just so, Louis. Just so."

.oOo.

The following morning, Louis took Alfred on his ship to the skerry, and the Consolation followed closely and cautiously behind by less than a quarter of a nautical mile. Although the sea was again calm and the currents rested at a low tide, looking back towards Mull one could see the edge of the thick, grey haar slowly dragging across the sea. Young Captain Andrew did not trust his own limited knowledge of the waters enough to venture into the North Atlantic beyond the Outer Hebrides, so he tacked in tightly close to the other ship before him to keep the figure of the hull of Louis's vessel and the increasing swirling current of the eddies in plain view.

Mr Irvine, the landing manager at Dubh Artach, waited to greet them at the rock's edge. His job was to secure the ship's ropes to the steel mooring. This consisted of several rings attached to the base of the rock, forged by the blacksmith on hand. Mr Irvine noticed Alfred's walking stick, so he offered to help him off the ship with a long reach of his arm followed by impromptu pretzel lock at the elbows. It was obvious that Louis had young, reliable sea legs, as he confidently dismounted his ship by taking one, long legged stride across the gap between the ship and the black skerry.

Although the Consolation found a safe distance away from the skerry in which to anchor, the other ship stayed tied up whilst the men offloaded rations: barrels of beer, bags of bread and porridge. They rolled the barrels up the rock and carried the bags on their shoulders up the ladder which was fixed underneath the barracks. They then carried the supplies in through the bottom hatch. Once the delivery was made, the vessel was untied and pushed away from the skerry, sailing back to Erraid.

Sitting just a few metres from the lighthouse, the barracks was built to accommodate the workmen. Below this structure steel legs stuck deep within the black rock to support the top-heavy barracks which appeared like a barrel on stilts.

Before the barracks was built, their ship sat anchored some way off while the men worked. There, it waited for the rising tide or sundown, whichever came first. It had to maintain a safe distance from the rock to keep her from bashing against it just in case the sea was to take on a swell, which it had been too often known to do.

The sight of the men working quickly, yet in sheer cadence, impressed Alfred. He watched as the workmen guided the one and two ton, perfectly carved granite blocks via short tracks, the same method they used on Erraid. These tracks stretched from the mooring to the lighthouse base. Using thick ropes and small wheels, the stones were hoisted by way of a pulley system on a steel frame and crane, the same rig that Alfred and his men saw poised over the lighthouse base the day before as they sailed passed it.

By this time, the base extended several metres above the platform of the rock and next to it the lighthouse base looked as sound and solid as anyone could have imagined. The building was well on its way skyward.

Louis and Alfred gazed at the site. There was a deep sense of awe at the immense effort being made in the middle of the sea.

"If you think the building of this lighthouse stands precariously, Alfred, then surely you must have heard of Bell Rock?" asked Louis, testing Alfred's knowledge.

"I have heard of it, just as everyone, but have not yet seen it," Alfred replied.

"It was built by my grandfather and his sixty men in the year 1810", Louis informatively boasted. "In the same way, the engineering of Dubh Artach is not an easy task, due to the extreme danger of the tides, navigating the currents and enduring the weather."

"Aye, I imagine this is so", commented Alfred. Louis continued, "It was based on the same methods used at Bell Rock. Originally, that itself was modelled on the Eddystone Light, the John Smeaton design of the mighty oak tree. Because of the success of Bell Rock, we have learned much about lighthouse engineering and there have been many improvements in the sixty years since Bell Rock. Not alone the planning and constructing of it, but the lenses! How they have changed so."

Alfred was moved to profound respect as he grasped

the earful he was in receipt of. "This is commendable, Louis. It makes me feel..." There was a long pause and his face turned downward in his difficulty to find the words. He looked down, growling bitterly in his hesitation.

Louis noticed Alfred's uneasy shift of mood and thought he would help him by injecting his own choice of words. "Educated? Full of cheer? Delighted?"

Suddenly, Alfred looked up and snapped at Louis, which made the lanky lad jump. "Enlightened." Alfred took a deep breath in relief after undergoing the momentary agony.

Louis's eyes widened with excitement that he now felt a connection to Alfred with his unlikely, illustrious choice of words. He was thrilled that the despondent, unsettled man he had promised to keep in communication with just the night before now had, curiously, a willingness to explore the thoughts within himself. He smiled at Alfred. "Enlightened. Such a splendid word."

Alfred was awkward at this sudden revelation and closed himself off back to the dunes of doubt where he was most comfortable. "Well, I wouldn't go so far as that."

Kumbi, walking past the pair, held his head up looking filled with an unmistakable sense of purpose. He greeted Louis with a big grin.

"Mr Stevenson, young Sir, progress is being made on this sun filled day!"

"Indeed, it is, Kumbi!"

Alfred recalled the black sailors he had seen on his father's ship when he was just a young lad. His father had taken advantage of their capabilities and strength and the shift from slavery to freedom. He felt ashamed of the sins of his father when he compared it to the friendly banter between Kumbi and Louis. Much had changed since the 1830s and Alfred, too, wished to absolve his father's immorality which he felt hung displayed around his neck like an oxen's yoke. For this he was glad his father was dead.

Although Scotland once had its own number of slaves, most of the trade by Scots was in the West Indies. They had the reputation for being the most brutal of masters. However, for the many in Scotland who were against the slave trade, these people played an important part in its abolishment. It was because of this empathetic view that many former slaves from England made their way north into Scotland to find work and were welcome to begin anew.

But there was a more sinister side to slavery and Scots. The many Scottish men who supported and defended slavery in the Glasgow West India Association tried to convince the public that slavery was not only a good thing for Scotland both economically and socially, but beneficial for the slaves.

In sharp contrast to his father, when a young Alfred made his first week's pay of fifty pence as a basic seaman aboard the Lady Albatross, he made an example of the Association which his father supported by giving the two black sailors his pay in an effort to match what their white, fellow seamen earned. This gesture did not go unseen and after his father was informed of this, he was so infuriated his son had mocked him by making himself equal to a slave's pay that he flogged his boy's arms with the same leather that he used on the slaves.

This terrible punishment broke his mother's heart and she was bitter with David till her end. As much as she cared for his wounds, Alfred was left with long, thin scars on his forearms. The years passed and although the scars were somewhat faded, the trauma of his father's beating remained and the memory of this made him tenacious enough to deal with any acrimony among his own mixed-raced sailors.

.oOo.

The two men left their post and began to make their way back the short distance towards Alfred's awaiting ship.

"I am curious, what is his story?" asked Alfred.

"He was born into a slave family," Louis explained. "Just after slavery ended. In fact, Kumbi was the first of his family to be allowed to find a trade of his own liking."

Alfred nodded perceptively as Louis continued.

"My grandfather trained him in the lens workshop in Edinburgh when he was young. Here, in the lighthouse, he is preparing the interior space for the fitting of the new paraffin tanks. Later, when they're ready, the lantern pane will be installed at the top. Kumbi will oversee the assembling of the lens when it arrives here on the skerry."

"Is that so? I believe your grandfather was an admirable man to have given the lad a fair chance."

"Everyone has a story to tell," replied Louis. "Even you."

"Indeed, they do", mumbled Alfred.

When they reached the simple mooring, which was really little more than the edge of the rock, Mr Irvine joined them and remarked earnestly, "Would you believe the gales here could become so wild as to lift two-ton blocks of stone from this reef, wash them out to sea, never to be seen again?"

"Is that so?" asked Alfred, humbly.

"Aye, it is. You've had your great loss, Mr Henderson, yet on the very same night, this lighthouse base, in its entirety, was ripped apart and swallowed by the sea. The only luck we had was that nae lives were washed awa with it."

"To hear this - I am sorry; I wasn't to know," he retracted.

"God's hand protected all the men. Every one of their lives were spared," Mr Irvine said, clasping his hands in gratitude.

"I suppose this is all here to test our faith and endurance," piped in Louis.

Mr Irvine smiled at this and waved his arms to the men on Consolation to come forth.

"Perhaps we test God too much with our own man-made ideals," Alfred spoke with consideration.

"And not accepting enough of nature's own pace and its own idea of progress," Louis added.

The two men looked out to the open sea together and in reflection they remained silent as they waited for the Consolation to arrive.

Alfred recollected the evening and severity of the hellish storm. And while at the same time he was safe in his Greenock home by a warming fire and sipped his whisky, watching the rain through the window, the barrier between him and the blowing rain, how much more out of control the storm must have been out at sea. On the land it was tempered by hills and islands. At sea it would have been given the wicked and unsurpassed possibilities which not only wrecked his ship, men and cargo, but had also stripped clean the rock from which he was, at that very moment, standing.

Louis looked at Alfred. Not wanting to interrupt his thoughts, he looked out to Alfred's approaching ship and noticed the name painted on it as it came into focus. He closed his eyes and sighed and then whispered, "Consolation".

Alfred stepped away. "I will be away the now; my men must seize the day's good weather", he concluded.

Louis snapped out of his trance. "Oh, indeed, Mr He- I mean, Alfred."

Alfred grabbed his hand and as they shook, Louis surprised him with an embrace like the hug of an old friend. "I wish you well on your travels today, and much good fortune."

It was an uncomfortable moment for Alfred and without embracing him in return, Alfred opted instead to pat Louis's arms and left him standing there alone on the mound of black rock.

.oOo.

The Consolation sailed away from Erraid, homeward bound. Alfred emerged from down below the deck and looked around, admiring another day of fair weather to the west, and the wind was beginning to pick up.

"It's a fine day to have the wind in our sales, men!" Alfred shouted over the sweeping gust.

Andrew looked up at the sails bellowing with air in full measure of their worth. "Aye! We will beat the haar and be in Greenock in time for a late tea if the weather stays in our favour."

Looking at the skerry quickly disappearing behind them, the horizon ahead grew bleak and lonely, and the sea and the men on the ship altogether went quiet. The only sounds to be heard was the meditative slosh of the parting water below as the 'V' of the bow cut through it like a hot knife slicing through a brick of butter. The hissing of the wind passed between the tightened ropes and masts as they tacked south-easterly to pass around the isle of Colonsay.

The open sea was a grey, solitary wilderness not designed for the weary at heart. A character inclined to any degree of instability of the mind would undoubtedly go mad if having to endure prolonged lengths of such isolation. Neither the richest of men with all their ego, nor the strongest, clearest, most level of minds were any match for the unbridled power of the pewter tinted expanse. Days, weeks and months spent at sea was a test of the very fittest.

CHAPTER 4

The toils are pitched, and the stakes are set,
Ever sing merrily, merrily;
The bows they bend, and the knives they whet,
Hunters live so cheerily.

It was a stag, a stag of ten,
Bearing its branches sturdily;
He came silently down the glen,
Ever sing hardily, hardily.

It was there he met with a wounded doe,
She was bleeding deathfully;
She warned him of the toils below,
O so faithfully, faithfully!

He had an eye, and he could heed,
Ever sing so warily, warily;
He had a foot, and he could speed –
Hunters watch so narrowly.

Sir Walter Scott
Hunter's Song

The very idea of wreckers relishing in the discovery of his ship's haul at his expense played on Alfred's mind. He tried to dismiss the incessant nagging in his head, as Louis had said it was only a rumour by credible men of their continued existence and not necessarily a truth. At the same time, there was no rush to return to Greenock. Tosh would not be needing Alfred for another four days. A date would be fixed and a notice to emigrants bound for the Americas would be posted at the docks. They would then decide on the morning hour for the sail to Liverpool, depending on weather, wind direction and tides. Over the coming days, the sailors back on Aemelius would be busy preparing the ship by stocking provisions for themselves and inspecting the condition of the sails and each measured foot of the ropes for their tautness and durability.

With every passing minute, Alfred convinced himself that the right thing to do was to turn the boat around and sail north to Iona. Partly out of anger and partly out of seeking truth, he finally retorted and called out to Andrew. "Turnabout!"

"What was that Mr Henderson?"

"You heard me, turn about. We're sailing to Iona."

Andrew and Duncan looked at each other, confused. "Whatever for, Mr Henderson?" asked Duncan.

"I'm in search of wreckers. My instincts tell me if anyone has my loot, it's them."

"There's nae chance of that. I'd place my bets on it. If we go, we won't make it back to Greenock this night," said Duncan.

Andrew agreed and told Alfred, "Aye, he's nae wrong there."

"We'll stay the night along the shore, or a cove, if we must. We have rations for two days and aren't needed in Greenock today," replied Alfred.

Duncan looked to Andrew with uneasiness at Alfred's sudden desire to encroach on a strange wrecker community - if there even was one - but as their duty, they obliged.

Superstitious in nature, Andrew was mindful to not end the day on a negative note so he lowered his voice. "Aye, Mr Henderson. Duncan, prepare the sails to come about!"

"Aye, Aye!" shouted Duncan. He loosened the ropes of the sails. "Ready to come about!"

Andrew span the ship's wheel to the port side as fast as he could. The sails rustled and flapped loudly before the boom swung out and they filled again with a steady stream of wind. Duncan secured the sail rigging onto a deck cleat.

They glided swiftly and, in an hour or so, the isle came into view ahead. Her landscape appeared slate grey under a misty cloud whilst the mountains of the Highlands crowned the frame behind her in silhouettes. As the men neared, Iona's coast became clear and black rocks and white sands surrounded her, with a few gentle hills and humps rolling down her back.

Approaching the tiny Hebridean island, Alfred noticed a strange looking row of small cottages clustered within a cove. His eyes lit with interest and curiosity burst within him.

After a time of searching for a safe place to anchor, the men arrived in a small, quiet cove out of the wind on the north side of the island, where they were to stay out of sight from the wreckers, if they were actually there.

With the help of Duncan, Alfred stepped onto the shore, leaning heavily on his stick. He walked alone towards the cove of cottages, his shoes parting sand, strode over the dunes, then finally walked through the long grasses in the direction of the cottages which he had spotted earlier from sea.

After a short time afoot, the tops of the cottages came into view. He was shocked by what he saw; a community of which he had never before known. With the aid of his stick he pushed aside the tall, prickly nettle and sank his body down into a space in which to hide. He sat silently upon damp tufts of grass, clumped between the thorny gorse and delicate, pink starry wood anemones to observe the people below.

The rumour was true, and in full view before him. There, laid out on the western shore of Iona, were two small fishing boats and six shoddily built houses. These unique makeshift dwellings, made to look like cottages, were wholly out of sync with the fine edifices of modern housing in Greenock. Pieced together with parts of broken up and abandoned ships, doors were crudely assembled with odd fragments of wood. Ship-wrecked hulls, thatched with dried heather were placed upside down on rough stone walls and used as rooves. In spite of their messiness, there was a pleasant and surreal look in the way the gunwales curved elegantly upwards to form roof ridges, much like the peaks of a meringue.

At the top of the path, away from the row of houses, was a rudely made fence made of the remains of boat timbers and bits of washed-up wood all thrown together, fashioning a barrier to mark their territory.

Further up on a hill and well away from the houses, there was a stack of some old split wood and dried grasses, piled into a high mound.

The shouting of two children caught Alfred's attention and he looked over at them to watch them play with the shabby remainder of a ship's helm. It was fixed in the ground next to a ramshackle turned over hull.

An older boy shouted orders to the younger. "Secure th' sails! Git everyone below deck, 'ere comes another wave!" He swung to the left, mimicking being thrown about by the sea. "That was close. We mustn't lose oor ship!"

"Wha' noo, Captain?" the wee boy queried with a squeaky voice.

"'Ere comes anither wave, hold oan tight!" The captain ignored his sailor as if to prove his authority.

The wee boy crouched down into the marram grass and grabbed a handful. "A'm holding on 'n' everyone is safe below deck."

"Woah!" they both wailed.

The captain swung to the right and jumped out far as if he had been thrown off the ship. "Ahh, a've been thrown tae th' cold sea! Bye bye brother, bye mother!"

On the ground the captain clenched his elbow, moaning. "Och, ah hurt mah arm."

"Alright, Ewan, a'm tired o' this game. Let's play something else. We always play wha' ye want. Ah want tae play soldiers," griped the younger of the two.

Alfred found pleasure in watching the boys at play and he laughed out loud, forgetting he was supposed to be hiding out of sight.

The boys looked around but didn't see anyone. Alfred decided to make himself known and stood up. The boys were startled at the sight of the well-dressed man who, just moments before had been camouflaged from their view by the mix of grasses. The boys ran under the broken-up boat hull. Turned completely upside down, it made a very good fort in which to hide. The boys sat upon a slab of stone within it, huddled close to each other and kept quiet.

Alfred's feet appeared to them at the gap at the bottom of the hull, which terrified the boys. Then his head eclipsed the sun as it moved above the hole at the top, blocking their view and casting a shadow on them. The boys gasped at the sight of Alfred peering in at them. Realising their fear, he took a step backward. They kept quiet. He showed himself in full at the broken planks which created the entrance and leaned in.

"Hello!" he said, grinning and trying to come across as harmless stranger.

He looked at their dirty, uncertain faces. Their clothes were torn, ill-fitted and soiled. In Alfred's eyes, their clothing was not fit even for costume playing and it was very clear to him that he had set foot into a situation of dire poverty.

The older boy, who seemed about seven years old, wore trousers which were too long and baggy and were tied to his waist with rope. Each leg was rolled up and tied around his ankles, as if they were made for a man.

The smaller boy wore an old jacket with missing buttons and trousers which had tears straight across both knees. Both trouser legs, which didn't quite reach his ankles, were crudely frayed at the bottom. He appeared to be around 5 years of age. Neither of them had shoes on, and the lack of them led to their feet becoming very grubby.

"I'm sorry if I alarmed you," Alfred said. "I didn't mean to."

Their eyes widened, with the whites of them being the only thing which appeared clean about the boys. They remained quiet.

Alfred saw the older boy rubbing his elbow. "Are you alright, son?"

He lowered his arm as if to conceal it from Alfred and replied sheepishly, "A'm fine," he replied.

"Yer just tryin tae be brave," said the younger one.

"Maybe I can help. Let me see it," Alfred appealed, reaching out.

The boy pulled his arm away out of Alfred's reach. "Who are ye?" he asked in a voice now less assertive than he was as a captain, while not wanting to lessen his protective stance for his little brother.

"My name is Mr Henderson. I got a little bit lost on my ship and need some help getting home. Can you help?"

"A'm no a real captain. Ah wis only pretending," said the boy.

"That is a shame," Alfred said. "I could very much use the help of a real captain. Perhaps your parents could help me. Are they nearby?"

The other boy stood up suddenly and held up his trousers which by the bunching of them looked as if they preferred to fall to his knees. He spoke openly to the stranger who now appeared to be not so much of a threat. "A'm Cameron."

"Hello, Cameron," Alfred said.

"'N' this is mah brother, Ewan."

The older boy, Ewan continued. "Is it a very big ship? Kin ah see it?"

"Not today, young man. It is getting late and I am needing your help the now."

Ewan looked down, disappointed. But Cameron, the chatty one, kept talking as he was eager to tell him anything. He pointed down to the cottages. "Mah mummy is right doon there in th' hoose. Dad isnae wi' us." Cameron then looked up to the fields which, apart from a continual slight breeze, laid empty of activity. "Mummy says he's asleep up there on th' hill."

Alfred was curious. "Oh? I did not see anyone there."

"He's deid," replied Ewan.

Alfred was taken a little back. "Oh, I am sorry."

"Ewan's eight years," Cameron added.

Ewan nudged Cameron. "Ye blether too much. Ah dinnae think a'm eight yet."

"Ewan," Alfred greeted him, offering an outstretched hand. "It's a pleasure to meet you."

Ewan looked at Alfred's empty hand. As he had never before been offered a handshake, he was unsure of what the newcomer was doing or what he was trying to show or give to him, as there was nothing in it, so he got up off the seat and left the hull.

"Come along wi' us, we will tak' ya tae Mum." He rubbed his elbow again, brushing off the dust with the drama.

He ran down the hill towards home as fast as he could with Cameron in close pursuit. Alfred followed but lagged a great distance behind them, watching as they disappeared inside a cottage on the right. With his stick

Alfred fought against the strangling, long bunches of grass and stone until he reached a sandy path where he was able to pick up his pace.

When Alfred reached the front door, he stood outside and looked around, fascinated by the wonky structure in front of him, concocted of various shipwreck remnants. As he looked down the path that ran down to the beach he noticed five other dwellings, one to his left and four others behind him. Each of them looked just as tattered as the next. Made from bits and pieces of ships and what ever else may have drifted ashore.

Before Alfred could knock on the door, a round-faced woman opened it slightly and stuck her head out.

"Who are ye? What do ye want?" she squawked.

Her hair was as thick and fiery as her disposition. It was pulled up into a dark ginger bun, quite unkempt and her round cheeks had splashes of brown freckles under a veil of dirt.

Alfred took his hat off and held it to his chest. "Sorry to disturb you, ma'am. I am a wee bit lost. Your sons thought you might be able to help me."

"Ah cannae help ye," she firmly replied.

"Well, could you offer a lost man something to eat, or to drink?"

"Ah said ah cannae help ye."

Wondering if the other villagers would be more helpful, he looked around to see if anyone else was present. With no one around, he withdrew his appeal to the woman.

"Och, never mind. I'm sorry to have bothered you. Good day." He excused himself and turned to walk away.

"Ah am no their maw. A'm th' auntie," she said. As she stepped into the door her plump body filled the space. She pushed her way out of the house and yelled with a fierce bellow. "Caaaait? Caaaait, come th' noo!"

A young woman came rushing out from around the house, wiping her hands dry on her pinny. "What's happened?"

Alfred and the young woman lifted their heads at the same time and their eyes met. She stopped in her tracks and although she broke the stare, his eyes could not let go of her flowing, dark brown hair glistening like strands of gold as the sunlight filtered through it.

She looked at Alfred again and asked, "Who are ye?" Her voice was soft, like a breeze touching a meadow of wildflowers and the sound of it permeated the air like the smell of honeysuckle in spring. Windswept by this, Alfred turned to watch the most beautiful woman he had ever seen.

The two smudged faces of the boys lit up the shadow of a small opening of the doorway.

A neighbour, Morven, peered from behind the wall of his house across the path from them. He watched the conversation with the stranger before rushing off. Then, two women appeared in the doorway across from Cait's, sat down on a lump of stones and stared blunt curiosity.

"Well?" Cait tried to break Alfred's spell.

He clenched his hat tightly, nervously creasing it against his chest. "Yes, ma'am. My boat got pulled onto Iona by the strong currents. It's anchored in a cove. I – I'm Mr Henderson of Greenock."

"What do ye want from us, Mr Henderson?"

"Well, I'm hungry. I could do with a drink and some food, if you have any; if you'd be so obliged to help me, ma'am?"

"I'm afraid we don't have much of anything to offer ye here, Mr Henderson," Cait explained. "We've barely enough to feed ourselves. Now, I have work to do." She turned and walked away, adding, "You ought to return to your boat then, Mr Henderson, before it gets dark. Gae catch a fish."

Talking to her back he continued. "I understand, however, it's a little late for fishing. If you would so oblige me, I could repay you by making repairs of the house and will leave in the morn at first light."

Cait stopped walking away, took a deep breath and looked back at Janet, who stood firmly with her arms crossed, absolutely unwilling to offer aid to the stranger. She walked back to Alfred and inspected his clothes as if to see what else he could offer. His dark green coat was adorned with several embossed brass buttons that caught her eye. His white shirt underneath was finished with a collar and his sleeves, hemmed with lace, poked out of the ends adding a touch of ceremony. The cuffs on his coat were lined with four more smaller brass buttons trailing up the wrist.

"What are ye? A sailor?" she asked.

Alfred then realised the value of his coat in the eyes of the poor female wrecker and feeling uneasy, he played it down by concealing his hands behind his back. "I've come from the new lighthouse offshore at the skerry. Do you know of it?"

"Aye, well, a've heard o' it," inserted Janet.

"Ye don't dress like a lighthouse worker." Cait shifted her eyes up and down his clothes. "You're dressed too smart."

"Do you know what a lighthouse worker wears?" he questioned.

"They're labourers, are they no?" asked Cait, who was both observant and quick thinking.

Alfred felt embarrassed of his achievements and how he outshone the women on a great scale. But he wasn't able to hide his appearance. So, he looked down at his coat and brushed his sleeves with his hands to remove bits of grass.

"What makes ye think we need help with the hoose?" asked Janet.

Alfred saw the boys standing in the doorway, then looked at her. "The boys told me their father is no longer alive. Could you not do with a man's help?" He turned to Cait. "Un – unless you do have a man? A man's help, that is."

Cait grinned coquettishly at Alfred, who stood fumbling for words.

Janet interrupted. "Nae need, mah brother does all th' mending aroond 'ere."

But Cait contradicted her. "I might think of something. Come in, Mr Henderson."

Surprised, Janet looked at Cait. She rolled her eyes and shook her head in objection.

"Alfred is fine," he said.

"I'm no certain of that yet," Cait taunted.

Alfred followed her inside.

Janet peered around the cottage to see if anyone was looking and turned to the neighbours who were gawking.

"Who is tha' man?" one of them called out.

Janet shooed them away. "On ye go, lassies, nothing tae see 'ere. Keep yer gobs shut tight!" She turned away, closing the door behind her.

As Alfred sat in a small chair that rocked from side to side, Cait filled bowls with a stew as it simmered over an open fire.

"It's not a lot, but it will fill yer belly till morning." She pointed to a broken chair on its side on the floor in a corner. "Ye can take that chair to sleep in if ye can fix it. And I cannae feed you forever, so you'll have to make good yer word and leave th' morrow.

"You are very kind," he said as he went to the chair and kneeled on the floor to briefly examine it, tilting it backwards and testing the loose legs.

With her back turned to him, she smiled so that he could not see. "Am I? How do you ken that?" she snapped.

In came Janet from the other room, pushing the curtain to one side. The two boys followed behind her. "Noo tha' yer oor guest 'ere 'n' there's nothing ah kin say aboot it, I'm Janet, and you've already met th' wean - Ewan and Cameron." The boys sat down at the table.

Alfred spoke softly. "I've had the pleasure of meeting the lads, and you, as well, Janet." He smiled at her, watching her blush before everyone. "And you? You have not yet told me your name."

"I am Cait."

"Cait," he repeated, permitting the sound of her name to soak in. "I have one question for you, Cait. What if I can't fix it?"

"Then I cannae give ye better than the hard cold floor," she replied.

Alfred smiled at her grim words as if charm rang out of them. "It just needs a little work on the leg."

As Janet took warm bread next to the fire and set it on the table, she looked on at the two of them and listened intently to Alfred trying to have banter with Cait. Cait put the wooden bowls in a row on the table and filled each one with the hot stew. Ewan grabbed the bread and ripped off a piece. Cameron followed him by yanking off the next part.

"Boys! Don't be so self-serving! We have not yet said grace!" scolded Cait.

"Come th' noo, Mr Henderson, afore it gits cold," said Janet.

Alfred sat himself between the two boys and Janet placed the bowls of hot potato stew on the table. Each one took a bowl for themselves, and finally, Cait slid the last bowl over to Alfred as a welcoming gesture. The women sipped their broth across from their peculiar, yet polite guest. The boys held their bowls close to their chests while their mother and auntie watched Alfred closely with reasonable suspicion.

Alfred broke the silence. "You would make a great captain one day, Ewan."

"Aye?" he asked.

"Aye, you would." he answered, looking to Cait for approval, to which she gave him none.

Cameron burst into the conversation. "Because he's bossy?"

Alfred laughed. "No, because he's responsible for his men. I was a witness to that today."

"Mummy tells me a'm five."

"I was just about to ask if you know your age." said Alfred.

"Aye, but it wasnae your turn Cameron, noo was it?" Janet quibbled. "He's always interrupting, ken."

Cait clasped her hands together in front of her bowl. "Now then. Shall we be grateful together?" she looked at everyone now silenced, bowed her head.

Janet and the boys followed suit.

Alfred bowed his head while Cait led them in prayer.

"Dear God, thank you for this meal, for our good health and all the good fortune which you have bestowed upon us. We pray that you bring in haste the blessing of another shipwreck, so that our lives may continue to be sustained and we may thrive."

Alfred opened his eyes and looked into his bowl of brothy stew in disbelief at what he was hearing.

"We pray this in the name of our Lord Jesus, who is faithful in every way. Amen."

They all repeated "Amen," apart from Alfred who mumbled, in resistance to the prayer, "Memen," and then tucked into the meal.

"This stew is delicious," Alfred commented. "Which one of you has the skills of the kitchen?"

"Janet prefers other duties; when we can get grain, she makes the bread."

"Thank you, Cait, Janet," he smiled. "You two are marvellous, and I am pleased to be in your company."

Janet's pale cheeks flushed with the compliment while Alfred continued.

"So, tell me, this is a small island. How do people survive here?"

"We fish from the sea and use whatever washes up on the shore," Cait explained.

"And sometimes we find a sheep off the hill," Ewan interrupted.

"One does not just 'find' a sheep, do they? They are not wild," he questioned Ewan, sceptically. "Are you farmers as well?"

"And th' men take from th' sailors in th' sea!" Cameron added.

"What's rightfully ours!" Janet shrilled with resolution.

"Nae, Morven told me they tak' everything they can git and even mah trousers came off a sailor's arse," Cameron said matter of fact as he stood to show them off to Alfred.

Embarrassed, Cait hammered at the boys. "Cameron, sit down! You two boys need to learn to hold your tongues. If you have finished your dinner, pray, leave the table!"

The boys slurped up the last of their stew, mopped up the last of it with bread and left the table to go to their room. On passing Alfred's coat which hung on a hook, Ewan pushed Cameron to go and search the deep, velvet pockets. But Cameron, with his hand up ready to slip it inside, looked at Alfred who was smiling at him. Caught with his raised hand he waved to Alfred, turned away and ran behind Ewan to their room behind the curtain. Alfred turned to Cait.

"I don't think there is any need to get angry with them. They are just being boys."

"What would ye ken? Dae ye have bairns?" asked Janet. While Cait looked at him for an answer, raising her eyebrows.

"No, ma'am, Janet. I don't, but I was one once."

"That doesnae count if ye havenae raised a bairn yersel'," Janet laughed.

"I had a son. My wife and the child died at birth," he explained.

Cait looked Alfred with regret of the conversation and tilted her head with pity.

Janet continued to giggle.

In disbelief, Cait turned to Janet and nudged her to stop.

"I'm sorry," Cait said to Alfred.

Janet's sinister sort of wit sobered. "Och how unfortunate," she said with a rather chilly tone. "Ah will gae see to th' bairns." She stood up and went to the other room, forgetting or perhaps avoiding to clear the table.

Alfred looked confused. "I fail to see the humour in what I just said."

"As do I. Sometimes she has an odd sense of what's funny."

Cait stood up and cleared the bowls. As she rinsed them in a basin of water, Alfred found the silence was an opportunity to dig a little deeper into the life of the wreckers, so he quizzed her.

"So then," he asked, "what happens when there's a shipwreck?"

"The men take the boats out and take what they can find."

She looked at Alfred, who was staring at her. She felt his discontent with her vague answer.

"They're not doing anything wrong. The law says they can," she said in their defense.

"Yes, it does, so long as there are no survivors," he said. "But what if there are, what then?"

Cait thought about that for a moment. "Why do ye ask so many questions?"

"I guess I'm just inquisitive, that's all. There's no harm in my curiosity, is there?"

"Well, to speak in truth, I don't know anything about survivors. I've never heard there to be survivors. We use whatever materials we need for building and repairs and sell the rest - anything of value - to merchants. It's all done fairly," she explained.

They were interrupted by a knock at the door. Cait wavered and fiddled with her hands nervously while Alfred looked on, waiting for her to answer it. There was another, heavier knock at the door.

"Would you not like to see who is there?" asked Alfred, curious of her hesitation.

Janet poked her head from around the curtain. Her eyes widened in distress as Cait looked back at her.

Cait opened the door with a swift tug.

The brute of a man that walked in from the dark night had a heavy, bulging brow which governed above his eyes. As he caught sight of the well-dressed Alfred, who remained sat by the table, his mouth turned under in disapproval.

"Hamish, this is Mr Henderson," Cait introduced in a softened, shaky voice.

With his usual good manners, Alfred rose to greet the man. Both men stood as tall as the other, but Hamish had a wide, stocky build while Alfred was trim without being too light or slim. Hamish's squared, heavy shoulders weighed into his thick neck, pushing his head forward. A wind-tossed auburn mess of hair laden upon his head was unkempt under a well worn out brimmed hat.

His jealous glare at Alfred made him feel uneasy. Trembling, Cait was clearly uncomfortable with Hamish's abrupt arrival.

"Who is this man?" Hamish demanded to know.

"He's a guest for the night; got caught in the currents." Cait tried to explain, but Hamish didn't approve of a man in her home, particularly one who would be making God knows what kind of conversation with her and accepting of her hospitality.

"A strange man should nae bade wi' ye," declared Hamish. "He could be up tae nae good."

Cait defended herself. "I believe he's no trouble."

Hamish turned to examine Alfred up and down with his eyes. "I dinnae like th' look o' him."

"He's left the lighthouse," she continued.

Hamish turned to face Alfred. "Who would dae a thing like tha'? Ye git a wage in return for your work, dae ye no? A place tae sleep as well?" he pried.

"Building a lighthouse isolated with all the threats of the sea is an idea for the mad and deficient in intellect. I would not risk my life for it," Alfred replied, trusting these poor folk were naïve enough and lived too remote to not have heard of Bell Rock or Skerryvore lighthouses as they were both built successfully in the seclusions of the rough sea.

Bell Rock was the first to have been completed and was in fact a very well-known achievement in engineering, accomplishing many firsts and establishing new methods of lighthouse building. Most men associated with the sea by then had either read or heard of its triumph.

Although Hamish seemed to agree with a grunt, he still gave Alfred a less than welcome glare. He turned to Cait. "We've th' fire lit fae th' nicht. Th' waters will be checked at sunrise."

"Oh, I give all hope to The Lord," she said.

Hamish stared back at Alfred. "Any lighthoose built fae th' safe passage o' ships puts us oot o' work. We wid be starved tae death 'n nowhere tae gae, nae way to feed oor families. Ah think ye should ken that."

"Of course, I do." Alfred did try to understand but had little empathy for Hamish, and he tried to impress Cait by challenging him. "But does not the business of shipping provide a more profitable trade of food and provision? All without the need for stealing?" he questioned.

Hamish lowered his voice and spoke in a growl. "There is nae stealing 'ere. 'Tis all rightfully oors. If we need yer help th' morns mornin', ye kin be sure ah will come 'ere tae drag ye oot."

"I apologise, but my leg was injured and I would be of little use to you," Alfred explained.

"'Tis yer arms a'm after, nae yer legs. Anither pair makes us mair productive. Then ye will see how solid we work tae feed oor families 'n' stay alive. Then ye had better be gang. Good nicht, Cait."

Hamish tried to pull her in for a kiss, but she turned away..

Angrily from the rejection, he grabbed her by the arm and Alfred stepped up to defend her. Hamish laughed at the two of them, straightened his hat and left.

Cait closed the door and stared at her shaking hand against the door. She put her hands tightly together and squeezed them to try and stop the trembling.

"Right, I'll get this cleaned up and it will be an early night," she said.

Alfred took his plate to her, put it down and held her cold, clasped hands to steady them.

"I'll be alright," she said as she pulled away from him.

Alfred looked up to a half empty bottle on a shelf and peered at it, curiously tilting his head and squinting to read the worn, soiled label. The bottle was a mirky, dark brown-green colour, just like the rum bottles in the crates that the Lady Albatross once carried for trade. The one similarity the labels would have which he tried to make out in the distance of the shelf, was a thin red scroll printed across the left corner of the label. But none of it was legible. Cait saw him looking up at the bottle.

"He just lacks good manners," he said.

"He hasn't had a good upbringing. It was tough for him."

"He's not had any upbringing, for that matter. But you, you are not one of them. I can see that."

"What makes it your business?" she said defensively.

"It is not my business, but you are different, not like the others here," he explained as he looked into her eyes. Cait knew there was truth to his insight. She turned away from him, reached for the bottle, took it down and set it on the table before him. "Come, let's have some. We'll take it with us."

"Where to?" he asked her.

"A place where I can breathe."

She pulled the cork out of the bottle and poured a little of the dark golden fluid into two cups.

"What is that?" Alfred nodded towards the bottle.

"It's rum all the way from the islands," she answered.

"How do you know what it is, with the label torn off?" he asked.

"It was a little clearer on the other bottles we've gone through. The men found quite a stash."

Then Cait picked up a cup and drank it quickly.

Wanting to impress her, he took his cup and poured it down his throat in one gulp but gasped from the bite of it. She smiled, trying not to laugh at his watery eyes and refilled her cup, downing the rum again without a flinch.

"Follow me," she said. She grabbed her shawl and flung it over her where it fell delicately upon her shoulders like linens drying in the breeze. To Alfred she had both the beauty and resistance of an alluring enchantress. She then passed Alfred his coat and the bottle, and she took the cups. Rotating the bottle towards him, although the glued-on label was sooty and mostly rubbed away, he could see that a little of the thin red scroll in the corner remained. He recognised it was clearly one of his missing bottles. Feeling both startled and relieved, he decided to keep the revelation to himself.

Outside, Cait led Alfred up the hill to the where the children liked to play. There, the ship's hull lay turned over. She led him inside to sit with her on the stone.

It was a chilly and still night and the moonlight streamed in through the cracks and holes of the hull, giving Cait enough light to keep an eye on the stranger. In the dark distance, nothing could be heard of the children or people in their homes, nor of the tiny waves slapping onto the sand and the foam popping and crackling as it was pulled back to the sea. No distraction would interrupt the two as they sat on the slab together. But with the silence Alfred became backward and coy as he was forced to rely on his lack of communicative skills. On the other hand, Cait was in a mood of wanting a friend, someone interesting to talk with, and had made a very forward move by taking him to the hull alone.

She held the cups while he poured more rum into hers, then his.

"I came from a respectable family of weavers in Skye, Mr Henderson," she explained. 'I became *'one of them'* as you called it, through marriage."

"Aye, I knew you were different as you speak less of a Braid Scots."

"And you can gie some braw patter!" she giggled.

"No quite the city lingo, lass!"

To Alfred's surprise, the words flowed smoothly from his lips, much easier than he imagined they would. "Will you call me Alfred the now?"

"Aye, 'Alfred the Now' and no Alfred the Great?" She smiled, cheekily.

He dismissed her compliment. "I'm no Alfred the Great."

"Tell me Alfred, why did you really stop working on the lighthouse? I find it strange that you, an obviously experienced and strong, capable man, would commit to the work, then just leave it – sail awa' home."

Alfred thought about what she was asking. The more he sensed Cait was warming up to him and the familiarity grew between them, the worse he felt about the lie. His quest to find the missing cargo had already been solved; he was drinking it. He was not going to pursue the recovery of only a few surviving bottles, yet he still felt he was stuck, weaving himself deeper into the tale and yet he did not want to leave her company. So, he continued to spin his yarn based on the facts that young Louis Stevenson had told him.

"One storm alone swept away its entire foundation. Not once, but on two occasions. I tell you those workmen will be lucky enough to escape with their lives," he explained.

Cait was fascinated at his explanation. "What will you do the now?"

"I will go back to my home in Greenock, find work on another ship. Tell me, Cait, how did your husband die?"

As Cait didn't answer straight away, Alfred was ashamed of himself for asking such a thing. "No - don't answer that, it is an inappropriate question. I am sorry."

But she was beginning to feel at ease sitting there with Alfred, so she explained "There was an accident on one of the fishing boats. The weather turned. William, my husband, fell overboard into the sea, and his legs got tangled in the nets. He couldn't move them to save himself. He was drowned by the time his brother brought the nets in."

"His brother couldn't save him?"

"No. It was Hamish, William's older brother."

"Just the two of them out at sea?" he asked, surprised.

"Aye?"

"That's unusual," he added.

"Why?"

"Fishermen always go out in a group of three or more, it's a rule," he made clear.

"Well, not that day for whatever reason. And they are wreckers. They lack rules," she explained, passively.

"Although you – you have more sense. I should not have asked. I'm sorry about your husband."

Alfred felt as if he was pushing too hard and retreated from the topic, although Cait was more confident to allow him to continue.

"Are you now?"

Alfred blushed. "Of course."

"That's why Hamish looks after me now. I have no husband; he's always been very protective."

"That all depends on if he is protecting you or if he is pursuing you. There is a difference. The latter could be dangerous." Alfred was not foreign to the cruel behaviour of men as he grew up with one as a father. He sensed from the moment Hamish walked through the door he was trouble and he was eager to know Cait's point of view.

However, Cait knew this already. Immediately she felt embarrassed of her situation and ran her fingers nervously around the cup, not knowing what to say next. She abruptly stood up, reluctant to answer any more of his nosey comments. "I know the difference. Shall we go? You have a chair to fix."

He stood up next to her, bumping his head on the roof of the hull. Moaning in pain, he then pressed his hand upon it.

They looked at each other for an instant and she fret at his little accident.

"Are you alright?"

"Aye."

In that silent moment under the soothing glow from the stars, the warm rush of knowing swarmed around them. The night now felt enticing and opportunistic. She, the lone woman with no prospects, felt safe in Alfred's company. Their connection was level and their words were natural between them. It had been so long; it was as if she had never before spoken from her heart.

Similarly, he had not had the company of a woman in the years following his wife Fiona's death. His loneliness disappeared like it had never existed and he longed for the night to continue.

Cait lifted her cup and took a drink. He looked up into the sky, noticing it was alit with stars.

"Speaking of Skye, just look up there at those stars." He pointed to the night sky through the same large hole in the hull where he had scared the boys earlier that day. "Terra incognita."

"Terra incognita, which one is that? Is it the bright one?" she asked.

"No," he laughed lightly.

"Dinnae laugh at me."

"I'm not laughing at you. It just that I find you –." and a fear of rejection froze his ability to say what he wanted to. "I could teach you much about the stars, if you would like me to."

"I would."

"So then, let me start here. Terra incognita is the place where no one has been. All of it, the spanse, the whole of the sky. I have spent my life sailing under its light and darkness and yet it still fills me with wonder. Now, look at that bright star again." He pointed to the brightest star. "Do you see it?"

"Yes."

"That's Polaris. In the entire northern hemisphere, every sailor is guided by that one star. That's because it does not move in the sky and being as such, it is the one star which is reliable; the most dependable source in which to navigate."

Cait stared in amazement. "Like you?"

"Sorry?" Alfred asked, a little confused.

"Are you like Polaris, the dependable one?"

"Perhaps I am." Facing the sky, he continued to explain. "Actually, Polaris is three stars which look as if they are one."

Cait interrupted. "As in the Holy Trinity?"

"Exactly like the Holy Trinity. In the southern hemisphere, sailors are guided by a cluster of bright stars called The Southern Cross that we can't see from here."

Cait moved in closer to him to see better. As her shoulder met his, he clutched his fist tight in anticipation and began to perspire. She smiled at his clumsy demeanour.

In awe of the stars, Cait looked up as if she had never noticed them before. Observing her gaze and curiosity, Alfred looked at her beauty with a desire and unmistakable hunger inside him that he knew he would not be allowed to quell.

"You know a lot about the stars," said Cait.

"It is my responsibility. If you look straight down from there, you'll see the plough."

"A plough?"

"Yes, if you draw a line between each star, from that one to that one to the next."

Cait burst into laughter, amused at the connecting of the stars to create an image, "I see it!"

"In French, they call it a *casserole* - a saucepan."

Cait laughed out loud, her eyes grew wide, her mouth dropped open, and she looked at him. Baffled and yet perfectly curious, she replied. "Is that so?"

Alfred smiled at her amusement and was greatly attracted to her inquisitiveness. He looked into her eyes. "Just so."

"You know a lot of things – 'tis nice," she said.

Alfred blushed at the complement. "Someone once told me that everything changes once the stars come out."

"If I may attempt to ingratiate you - with some reservation, of course - I would say you're like a breath of fresh air," said Cait.

Alfred didn't know quite what to say in response to her outward flattery but attempted to return the compliment. "I suppose you must know a lot about weaving."

She was beginning to read and understand his awkwardness and accepted it. "Yes, well I did once. But I don't suspect you want me to teach you weaving as much as I enjoy learning about the stars."

"No."

On a hill not far from them, Alfred saw a bonfire growing in intensity. "What's the purpose of the fire?"

"When we have enough wood scrap and grass has been collected and dried, the men make a fire. It imitates a lighthouse beacon. And if we are lucky, a ship will see it from the distance and wreck on the rocks."

Alfred was astonished yet tried to speak calmly in reply. "That is brutal. Hamish's idea?"

"Have pity on him," she pleaded.

"Why should I?"

"Some people never know love. He is one. They live their whole lives believing that love is only that which relieves sexual desire, or an obsession or duty and they never know sacrifice or deep passion. But it is the only kind he knows. It is a rather lonely prospect, I think. Don't you agree?"

Out of a feeling of discontent with the question, Alfred took a moment to think about the subject he had built a wall around: intimacy. It had been a long time since he had felt love or experienced tenderness. It was a difficult topic to discuss, but in order to prevent Cait from waiting in silence, he quoted the Bible.

"Yes, I do, and *without patience, kindness and truth, there is no beauty in love; those other things are empty.*"

"I've known it, the beautiful kind of love," Cait replied, openly.

"As have I."

"There are times, days that I can still taste it, crave it, am controlled by the lack of it. Is that not what grief is, though, just misplaced love? When someone you love dies, you dinnae suddenly stop loving them. Those emotions are trapped inside your heart as if imprisoned, with no one to express them to. That in itself is the grief," Cait confided.

As she unknowingly thrust at his emotional vulnerability, the fortress that Alfred built himself began to quiver. He felt exposed and wanted answers. "It feels like punishment. So, what is left for people like us, left behind to grieve?" he asked.

Whilst Cait took a swig direct from the rum bottle, Alfred leaned into the shadows to hide his exposed pain.

"For some, love hits them over the head like lightning." In the silence of the night, she clapped her hands together loudly.

Alfred jumped.

She laughed at him and took another drink. "Are you alright?" she asked. But he was caught up in her uninhibited articulation and the easy chemistry between them. Infused in her allure it was almost too much to bear.

"I just wonder now … " his words tried.

"What?"

"If it really does strike twice," He took another sip from his glass, trying to bury his words in case she did not reciprocate.

Cait finished her rum. "Come." She left the hull. He took the bottle and his stick. She slowed her pace so he could catch up to her and together they went back to the cottage, avoiding being seen in the glow of the bonfire.

.oOo.

Alfred slept peacefully in the chair which had its leg held tightly together with bindings of twine finished with an impressive harness hitch knot.

In the other room, Ewan awoke from Janet's snoring. As he lay there, he thought of Alfred's coat and the temptation to go through his pockets. He nudged Cameron awake in urgence. Ewan slipped out of bed quietly and pulled his little brother out into to the doorway, pushing the curtain aside. They watched as Alfred slept in the chair and their mother lay peacefully beneath a layer of blankets against the opposite wall.

He pushed Cameron over to Alfred's coat, which was hanging on a hook to the right of their door, to check the pockets. The youngster felt around the inside of one of them, but it was empty. He looked to Ewan and shook his head. Ewan motioned Cameron to take a brass button from the coat, but Cameron did not want to, in fear of getting caught. Ewan pierced his lips tightly together to warn his brother and pushed his fist into the palm of his other hand, showing him the repercussions, which would follow if he did not do as he said.

The wee child tiptoed over to the table, took a knife from the chopping block and crept back to the coat, watching every breath and any movement from Alfred. Suddenly, Cameron tripped over a chipped slab and the knife slipped out of his hand, falling to the stone floor with a clang. Well and truly startled, he pulled himself inside the dangling coat to hide. He stood still, arms frozen to his side and Ewan crouched down on the floor with his hands folded over his head whilst Alfred stirred in the chair. Ewan took Cameron by the arm and yanked him out of the coat. With his eyes wide open, Cameron stretched his short arm across the floor, picked up the knife and with quick and voracious strokes pillaged the button off the coat, threads exposed, and ran into his room with the spoil.

.oOo.

Early in the morning before sunrise, shouts and metal banging from outside awoke the community.

"All men rise! All men rise this morn! Shipwreck! Shipwreck!" came the call.

Alfred clambered out of his chair and opened the door to see the people rushing out of their cottages and Hamish yelling and clanging pots loudly. Six men gathered around the small fishing boats and began to push them off the sand.

Hamish spotted Alfred at the doorway, ran to him, and grabbed him by the arm.

"What is this?" Alfred demanded, clutching his sore head.

"You're coming with me!"

"But -!" Alfred hesitated.

Hamish pulled him out of the doorway and Alfred swung back to reach in and retrieve his stick.

The men filled the boats, sails went up, and with lengthy oars they rowed for added speed to get out to sea. Alfred took a cramped seat and watched on as they slowly bobbed away from Iona. He hid his anxiety as the men struggled to catch wind in the sails and fight the incoming waves. He could have showed them how much more beneficial their efforts would be and get the boat moving more quickly had they remembered to bring the anchor in fully. However, it was making him sick with the anticipation that they might find wreckage, so he opted out of any conversation and let the anchor drag through the water to slow them down.

Inside the boat, he noticed the sad condition of the ropes. They were worn out and the entire length of them heavily fringed. He could vividly remember his days when he was a young man and in punishment his father forced him to repair the ropes, inch by inch. The wreckers would have no one there with the knowledge to do that nor the ability or access to buy the new cotton strands for grafting them, strengthening them and in turn prolonging the rope's life.

He looked up at the sails, inadequately repaired in patches. The stitching would rip out of the old sailcloth already weakened by age if given a forceful enough gust of wind. Their only hope would be to find a shipwreck in which to replace the sails completely.

In that time spent sailing slowly out to the rocks and observing their lack, he warmed ever so slightly to the needs of these people. He began to understand how they had a 'must do' ambition, how they must endure by taking from the sea for their continuance; that people like this were the survivors of this world.

Alfred was in fact not. He was the inheritor of a profitable business and could look after his home and health. Often his business was risky, but nonetheless, it was profitable. He was not immensely wealthy, but had a house, not one which had a splintery, cracked hull for a roof, but one which was covered in durable slate. The roof kept the inside of the house dry and the heat from the fire contained within its four walls. He had clean clothing and someone to wash it for him, to dust and polish the furniture which, often unused and in excess, sat quietly upon clean rugs. He did not have to dig for peat, harvest wheat and bake his own bread. There was food aplenty and rum if he wanted. But he did not like rum, he preferred the taste of whisky and how, when he swallowed, it covered the back of his throat with a soothing warmth as it passed. After a few sips the sting of the alcohol tasted like honey. He had all he needed; this was his level of wealth and now, being on the Isle of Iona he was learning another level.

He looked back towards shore where up on the hill the smoke from the last of the bonfire lifted into the air, his judgement melted and softened. As did his heart as he thought of Cait. She deserved better than losing her loving husband and being left behind to live out her life in hardship. And in her solitude, she opened up to him as if she had been muted. Alfred had seen a side to her which was hidden from all others - a beautiful, unopened flower who waited for the sun to shine on her and allow her to blossom to her heart's content. Under her toughened surface, it was clear to him that she was a kind hearted woman, desiring to be loved and a soul so worthy of being cherished.

.oOo.

Born on 1 March 1849 in Portree, Isle of Skye, Cait's parents, Hugh and Gail Thompson worked as textile weavers in the mid 1850s as sudden demand for tartan began to surge. Much of their fabric was sold to Scottish tartan revival enthusiasts from the south in England. Although many businesses above England's border had taken advantage in the Industrial Revolution, the western Highlands had not yet been fully submerged in the phenomenon. So, many isolated weavers did not benefit fully from use of more modern machines, and instead continued to use their old methods using hand looms which was much more time consuming. Down south, power looms and other machinery were now being widely used. This kept the high-quality fabrics at a low cost, as new dyes and alternative ways of printing on textiles were being discovered.

The Thompson's business did well in this new desire for the trade, selling hand woven wool to dressmakers, kiltmakers and for interior decoration such as upholstery and curtains and window dressings. But working on their own was time consuming. So, over time they employed six other men and women to meet the sudden trade burst and trained up their three young children to be skilled in the same craft, pushing their production to the limit.

Each of the girls was given a drop-spindle when they were young in age. With it, they learned to spin wool for use in knitting hats, jumpers and socks. It was common practice for young girls and women to use hand-spun wool from home in the Western Isles.

Cait did not grow up a privileged child, as the money the family made was reinvested into new machines in order to catch up with the growing demand of handmade tartan knits, which they did. Their gift to Cait was teaching her to work the looms from aged seven and she became skilled in her duties to the family business. Her two younger sisters were expected to follow suit as soon as they each reached the same age.

As she grew she got bored of the monotonous work of the heavy looms and complained vocally about it. This did not please her parents, who thought ignoring her would be more beneficial than to sack their daughter whose talent had very much become an asset to them. But this proved to be an unsuccessful method of discipline, and Cait looked elsewhere for stimulation and for a bigger dream to follow.

Finally, she made herself redundant to her parents by quitting the family's enterprises after a heated falling out. She felt that she was mistaken by her parents for a disrespectful rebel. So, she exiled herself from them by packing her luggage with her few clothes and her drop-spindle and travelled to the shores of Tobermory on the Isle of Mull to live with her Auntie Eilidh, her mother's sister.

Eilidh kept the house while her husband Angus worked as a fisherman. Having lost a young child some years before, they never had any other children of their own. They believed they were not well equipped to look after a child, particularly one who had her own strong headed ideas, so they treated Cait as an adult guest and expected her to look after herself and make good use of her time. And Cait did. Instead of helping with the clothes washing, sewing and needlework as many young girls her age were doing, Angus insisted that Cait work on the docks where she was of better use. She was required to stand long hours joining the older women, learning to salt and pack fish. Every Saturday she would accompany the women to the market to sell them from a stall. The women on the docks were all wives and daughters of the fishermen, or "fishwives" and "fishlasses" as they were often called.

Once the fishing boats returned to shore from a long morning of casting and hauling the nets, the men offloaded them onto the beach. There, the fishwives carried them in baskets to the docks. They were left in charge of the morning's catch while the fishermen restrung any damage to the nets before returning them to the boats to repeat the task early the following day.

The process of curing the fish involved sorting them by type, the majority of which was haddock and mackerel. After this was done, the women descaled each one and removed the entrails from their bellies using a sharp knife to cut through the tough, white skins. Each fish was placed on a generous layer of coarse salt, side by side with salt between each one. More salt was added on top, then another layer of fish went on top of that. This was repeated until the barrel was full. The stack of fish was finished with more salt before the barrel was sealed tightly.

The barrels were opened the next day and the mackerel taken out of the salt. One by one they were strung up with twine and left hanging overnight to dry.

The day she met William MacLeod, Cait was at the local fisheries delivering her uncle's preserved catch to the market. William was there to sell shipwreck loot to a merchant he knew. Anything else that was not purchased by the merchant was set up on a table at the market. He was expected to sell all of the goods before returning to the Isle of Iona.

Cait had left one of the fishwives in charge of selling the cured fish and wiped her hands on her apron while she went in search of some leeks. Eventually, she came across William's table. She did not notice him as she sifted carefully through his interesting pile of spoils.

But he cleared his throat to get her attention and murmured, "You're too lovely a lass tae smell o' fish."

She looked up at him and gasped.

"E'er seen trinkets lik' these?" He held up broken pieces of a ship instrument.

Cait was startled at his remark and leaning on the left of his table, she fell into it, threw the table top off balance and sent it and everything on it crashing to the ground.

William wanted to catch her but did not want to be seen grabbing a woman's arm, so he could only watch in disbelief as she fell. He did, however, offer her his hand to help her stand back up and when she did, he forgot to let go of her soft fingers until she had to ask for them. Immediately intrigued not only by the young woman's looks but also her agility, he introduced himself. She was very aware that having to work with fish every day infused her clothing with the smelly odour and so she smiled and backed off. Cait rushed back to her stall, forgetting the leeks she was sent out to find.

In the days following, William remained in the market. Several times he attempted to make conversation with her, but Cait tried to discourage him from getting too close and avoided passing him. He knew where to find her, though, at the other end of the market across from the wagon filled with sacks of oats. Her restraint only served as fuel to William's fire and soon he was enthralled with her every move and forgot about her fishy odour, or perhaps he was blinded to it by love.

Eventually, after days of uneventful confrontations, he managed to ask to Cait to join him for a walk home at the end of the day. The fishwife she stood with at the stall pressed her to go with the eager young man. Cait was fascinated with William's wrecker lifestyle and in turn, he thought she was a beautiful dream. He begged to see her again and promised he would ask for her the next time he was in town.

Just three weeks had passed when William could not wait any longer and went to Tobermory to find Cait. After staying several very cold nights on his boat and meeting Cait at her stall at the market during the day, William was finally invited into their home for a meal. He cleaned himself up by bathing in a bucket of cold sea water. When he arrived at her house, he put on all airs to become the gentleman he thought he should be and of course to impress Eilidh and Angus.

This was the first time William had entered a house of stone that didn't seep of cold air. Without question he admired the glass windows, comfortable chairs and large cooking hob. It didn't occur to him that these were not wealthy people even though the home was decorated. Compared to the way in which he was accustomed to living, it was the most prosperity he had ever seen. But in his heart, he knew that he would not be able to provide better for her. And perhaps his graces at supper may not have measured up, as when he was taken aside by her uncle after the meal, he was discouraged from pursuing her any further.

William was indeed tremendously disheartened at this prospect and returned to his ship to sail back to Iona the next morning.

However, Cait saw beyond her family's limits, and she went to see William the following morning to implore him to stay. As she reached the moorings, William, just a few minutes before, had untied his boat. With only a little wind available, his sails failed to fill and part way and his boat sat still. She ran after him calling out his name in desperate tears.

He could not ignore Cait's shouting pleas for him to come back. Her cries for him to reconsider her love and of going with him to Iona to make a home together took little convincing. His inability to resist her appeals stirred him to throw her a long line in which to pull him back in. He tied up his boat to the mooring and faced Eilidh and Angus.

The pair were inseparable from then on. Having now committed, they were eager to discover more about each other. She had a hunger for adventure that urged him to take chances and gave him a purpose. William longed to be looked after. He had an amiable twinkle in his eye that sparked every time he smiled at Cait. They were the lid to each other's pot and although Eilidh and Angus felt strongly against Cait's choice, she reminded them she was not their daughter and could not be told. However hesitant they were, Angus resigned and gave Cait away to William in marriage in Tobermory the next day.

She packed her few things in her leather strapped luggage and said farewell to her aunt and uncle. Together, Cait and William took his small fishing boat westward round the coast of the Isle of Mull to his home on the tiny Isle of Iona, where her life would be forever changed.

In her first year on the island, Cait found all her joy in William, as there was little else to find joy in a life of poverty. Soon to follow were their sons Ewan and then Cameron. On the shores of Iona, she was one of nine women, many of them were widows to the sea and were left to form a shared kinship of child rearing. The seven remaining men had the tasks of fishing and retrieving loot from the shipwrecks and took the young boys with them out to see so that they would be trained up from an early age.

Rum, timber and clothing were the usual loot found by the wreckers. Other findings but less often available were sailcloth. They were not very savvy people, as most of the alcohol was kept for their consuming pleasure. The remaining haul which they could not use for mending or building was taken to market to sell in Tobermory.

Hamish was often drunk from the alcohol stash, as were the other men and when he was, he was loud and vulgar. His attraction to Cait was an obvious one. When he was full of the drink, he didn't keep his feelings secret, and always made her feel very uncomfortable with his long stares and coercive attempts to get close to her.

Hamish had a high resentment of his younger brother who, out of the three siblings, was not only the sole inheritor of their mother's good looks, but his kindness and decency were innate. Hamish had a lifelong misunderstanding that William was the favoured one, so in return, he bullied him, punishing him with Will's every good deed.

When the boys were younger, William had an eagerness to learn, was more socially interested among the men and had an outgoing spirit that Hamish lacked. In stark contrast, Hamish was dour, bad-tempered, short on restraint and lacked the acumen and common sense that his younger brother possessed. Because of this, as a child he often appeared lazy and lived up to the lack of expectations his parents had, doing the minimum work required of the young men in the community and kept to himself. When he was in their company, he had little or nothing of interest to say. In short, Hamish was dull.

His skills, however, in building and mending became evident in his teens as did his physical strength in particular. His desire to prove his strength increased more as he grew up. He chronically sought the praise of his dissatisfied father, but his quest was never realised.

Hauling wrecks to shore was always a group effort for the men. Large, heavy items which could not be pulled up on board were left to be dragged behind the fishing boat, slowing down its return to shore considerably.

As Hamish's body matured through into his late teens, so did his stamina and discontent, both in equal measure. In a short time, the trawling to shore was led by him. It made him feel manly and this fed his pride, eventually resulting in a conceited attitude and a belief that his physicality could get him anything he wanted.

When Cait appeared on Iona, Hamish was attracted to her strong will. Cait was one thing he couldn't have. She was discovered and wed by William and this gave Hamish even more reason to hate his brother. She was careful around her new brother-in-law, as he was a gruff, heavy-handed lad whose company made her feel uncomfortable and she had learned in the early days that with him there would be no luminous and stirring conversation. So, she made a conscious effort to keep her distance from any accidental unattended contact, although Hamish often succeeded at making clumsy confrontations all his own.

William wasn't daft about Hamish's growing fancy towards his wife, though. He spent much of his time shielding her, but he could not be present every minute of the day. She didn't want to stir a rift between the two brothers, so she kept silent about Hamish's accosting in William's absence and stuck very close to the other women, with whom she felt protected.

Occasionally, arguments broke out between the brothers in Hamish's cottage next door to Cait. Their sister Janet lived with Hamish and she often left while the two men fought it out. She joined Cait in hanging out the wash on the line or prepare a meal, anything that would keep her away from the feuding duo. Together Cait and Janet could hear the men bickering and they could only just make out some words or phrases such as "yer ain," "jealous" and "one day soon," and when William came home, he was properly shaken up.

Day in and day out, William had to cope with the lingering fear that Hamish may eventually lose all control, cause harm and have his way with his wife. Because of this, he and Cait spoke between themselves about escaping back to Skye with their sons. They would take the smaller, lighter of the two fishing boats before dawn one day in the spring. It would still be dark in the mornings in March and after then the nights would become mostly daylight. If they were to escape before the middle of March, the early morning hours would be dark enough to not be seen.

The journey was meant to take them around the north coast of Iona, sail around the west coast of the Isle of Mull, pass the Isle of Eigg, Rum, through the Cullin Sound and finally, up through Loch Slapin in Skye. At the craigs of Torrin, they would find temporary shelter with her cousin Christopher and his family until the weather was suitable enough to carry on through the Cuillin Hills to Portree.

As March was another three months away, they had to remain a functioning part of their community. Work within the circle of women was physically draining and as long as the day itself was. After the morning's catch arrived and the men straightened the nets on the shore, the women would take the fish away from the beach, organised them by types of fish of which the varieties were seasonal. The women then spent the day gutting the fish through their soft under side, leaving the heads and tails on. Once the fish were partially cleaned, they were laid in barrels or crates and packed in salt . Cait had the fishlass experience of Tobermory behind her and showed the other women of Iona the more efficient ways of curing fish.

Auld Elsie, the wife of Murdo, was the only woman who could not help. She was old and housebound with arthritic hands and hips, rendering her inoperative. Her crippling pain meant that she was completely dependent on the other women of the community for peat and washing of clothes and linen. When the sun was shining, her daughter would help walk her down to the cove to sit. There she would sit and enjoy some conversation with the women who busied themselves with the fish duties.

Enough fish were used for themselves and stored for use over the harsh winter months, should the men either not fare well in the harvests or not be able to go out into a rough sea. In the off chance, if there were times of an overabundance of fish, they were cured and taken to sell at the markets in Oban and Tobermory along with any shipwreck loot which may have been acquired. With their earnings, they were able to buy more salt and twine for curing. At times of a more profitable market trade, they might even have had enough money to buy leather to repair boots.

One late December morning at sunrise Hamish, who had been up all night and was stinking of alcohol, came around for William to go fishing. The two of them took the boat out alone, and when Hamish returned within a short couple of hours pulling the boat close to shore, he shouted for help. Everyone in the community came running to see what the matter was.

Leaving young Ewan to look after his crying wee brother Cameron, Cait ran down to the shore. But she couldn't see what was going on in the commotion with the people blocking the fishing boat. Standing knee deep in the water there were cries and screams amongst the women. Naturally, Hamish shouted for Cait as the men lowered a lifeless body from the boat. Confusion and fear took over her mind and body as she shoved her way through the villagers. She waded lifting her dress, but as it got wet it immediately took on the weight of the water. She moved slower and slower the further out she went and the deeper the water became around her knees. When she reached the boat her greatest fear was realised. William lay in the water, feet tangled together in the fishing net, dead.

She held her stomach as if her body would give way to vomiting. Her knees weakened and buckled from underneath her. There she sat, immersed up to her underarms in the crystal clear, ice cold water. She panicked and tried to remove the nets tangled up in his legs, screaming in vain for the others to help her. She held her husband's body close to her while she cried and rocked him in her arms.

Hamish was full of the stories of the sequences preceding William's death and bragged of how he had made a heroic attempt at saving his life. But he also explained that by the time he pulled William in, it was too late. Never mind the blow present on William's head, or the bruises and gash to his mouth. Hamish had a reason for each trauma and told everyone that those things happened because William hit his head when he fell overboard. "Och, th' dangers o' living on th' sea," he would say.

However questionable the incident remained, William was dead and Cait was stranded on the small island in a tiny community with two young children, amidst the very problematic company of ship wreckers, hagglers and thieves, possibly even murderers. She had nowhere to escape to.

Cait did her best to keep to herself and work among the other women. Janet, who had been living with Hamish, eventually moved in with Cait to help with the boys.

It was thought to be an odd thing that for so long Janet would choose to spend her life living with her brother and sharing a one-room cottage. However, it was well known that there were not so many choices of men for her, although there were several choices for Hamish among the widows, if anyone would have him. Neither one of them lifted an eye to a suiter within their own people. So, they chose to stay as it was, where they had been since they were born.

Behind closed doors the community raised an eyebrow over this arrangement, but it wasn't altogether unheard of among the poor because it was a case of needs must. People had to sleep where they could feel safe and be warm. In this case, they were careful not to voice a dubious opinion, for doing so would only provoke anger from Hamish.

More vulnerable than ever, Cait and Janet demonstrated that they were unable to altogether provide for themselves and the children. Fish were at times few depending on the season, the digging up of peat and carrying the heavy loads home to dry across the grasses and thick bushes of heather was exhausting. It didn't take but a few months of struggling like this before the dark shadow, known as Hamish, closed in on Cait. Because she continued to refuse him, he decided to make her a proposal.

Hamish did not offer to provide food for everyone in Cait's house next door. In addition to this, he would make house repairs as long as he could have his way with her. For four weeks she ignored him spitefully. She regarded his bids as nothing short of bribery and knew that she deserved better treatment. After all, she was raising his nephews and she thought that he ought to show some kindness to help feed them. But it was very clear that Hamish possessed no goodness or tenderness for the sake of charity, not at least family.

Although Cait tried to disregard Hamish, her family faced starvation. For the survival of her and her boys, she caved into his filthy demands. It was some relief, at least, that his deed was a quick one, however unpleasurable to her it was.

For Cait to get through this, she had to close off her emotions. She hardened her empathies until, over time, her state of mind was complete numbness. It was the only way she could brave the act and prevent feelings of self hate. In fact, she cleverly funnelled all that hatred into Hamish and moaned to him feverishly when he was having his way. He misconstrued this as gratification, but Cait was simply detonating the bitterness and loathing bottled up within. She learned to close her eyes to spare herself from looking at his miserable face and washed herself well between her legs afterward. As the months passed, Cait got accustomed to the routine and it became common trade with Hamish. But she had two rules for him: never wake the boys from their sleep, and secondly, to not come over to her inebriated.

And so, there was food to eat. Cooked and smoked fish on the table for everyone, and potatoes from Hamish's own patch. Ewan and Cameron didn't have yet the skills to catch fish from the sea, and there was no one willing to teach them. The only thing that they knew was that Uncle Hamish was dropping off food.

Had he been a better, more generous individual, Hamish could have done so much more for the young brothers. Ewan wanted to learn to fish and was keen to be taken out on the boats with the men just like the other boys were. Ewan and Cameron were naturally curious and were left to learn by watching and listening in on the conversations between the fishermen. The two young boys would often sit together on the beach very near the men and overhear what they could of their various stories - complaints about the state of their nets and matters of women, which the boys didn't quite understand. As an innocent child, all Cameron craved was the affection of Hamish. Cameron tugged at Hamish's trouser leg but would be pushed aside. His affection was never reciprocated, and after several attempts and rejections, Cameron learned to not bother anymore.

The boys were Cait's first priority. On Sundays, she would take them to a wood cross further up the hill and taught them their lessons as she read to them from the bible given to her by her father. There, she would visit William's grave and quietly and calmly to herself pray, pray for mercy.

.oOo.

As the boat ploughed through the water, the noise of cawing gulls was unrestrained. Alfred looked ahead at the birds, who were swarming in circles above a vaguely visible lump in the distance. They had sailed out southwest from Iona where only the point of Mull, in fact Erraid, could be seen behind them. The colony of gulls had flown the distance out to sea for a reason. And, as the boat approached them, the clearer the reason became.

Waves cut through bobbing planks of wood. Several birds occupied the tops of them, busily plucking at the debris. Mobs of gulls swarmed around in the air as if encroaching on a kill, screaming incessantly and diving downward, fighting their competitors over something worth all the piercing hostility.

The men arrived at the mess in the sea. Much to Alfred's trepidation, there it was before him, the shipwreck, spread out in a dishevelled carnage. In his mind, he thought, judging by the sheer lengths of the floating timber, that it was quite a large ship, at least one hundred feet in length. It had been spewed all over the devilishly sharpened black rocks.

Alfred was dismayed. There had been no storm the night before. Instead, it was deliberately caused by the actions of men in the name of survival. How could this be something that God would fulfil – a prayer for catastrophe which would result in the death of innocent people? To Alfred, this was not the God he knew, the God of love but also of wrath. But wrath itself is not a reckless outrage. Rather, it is a just response to the opposition and resistance to God's Holiness. Alfred was not convinced that he would convert the men's hardened hearts otherwise. So, he closed his eyes and prayed for them and repeated the words, "Father, forgive them for they know not what they do."

What little was left, whatever they could salvage – timber and rigging on the mast was gathered and pulled into the boats. On the other fishing boat, one of the wreckers tried with all his might to pull the boots off a dead body while another searched his clothing. Rigid and heavy with water, the boots would not come off. Angered at this, he swore at the deceased and kicked the body away. The wreckers all laughed.

On the boat with Alfred, there was a lot of ruckus at the starboard gully between his companions: Hamish and his comrades Morven and Murdo, who was the elder of the men and less able as a deckhand. Although he had little responsibility physically, he always tried to do his bit and share his knowledge.

A sailor from the wreckage survived in the cold water, but only barely. He was shivering with cold as he held on to a piece of floating wood and mumbled in French.

"Prends l'argent mais m'aidez. Je vous prie de me sauver," his voice strained.

"Henderson!" shouted Hamish, "We'll need yer useful arms over 'ere!"

Alfred stepped forward to offer his hand to help the man up. Soaked with water, and weak from hunger, he was going to be very heavy to lift.

Hamish had other ideas. He leaned over the gully, reached down, grabbed the poor fellow by the hair and forcibly pushed his head under the water.

"Go on lad, be now deid at th' hands o' a Mackenzie!" he laughed with his teeth clenched.

Alfred was aghast at this and yelled back at him. "Stop! What are you doing?"

"Finishing 'im!" answered Hamish.

"No! Why would you?" shouted Alfred, confused. "We must help him!"

With his fist still grabbing hold of the man's hair, Hamish turned to address Alfred, demanding of him further. "Go on, ye drown him, push him under; I want tae see ye dae it! Make a man oot o' ye!"

"No, I won't!" At that, Alfred held to the rigging with one hand while he leaned over the boat's edge and tugged at the soaked jacket on the man with the other, releasing him from Hamish's grasp.

"He must die so tha' we can tak the loot!" Murdo insisted.

"Do you know what you're doing? You're in breach of the law!" Alfred said to Hamish. At that, Alfred turned to the men in the boat in an appeal for help, but Hamish scowled and warned them from taking sides.

"Git this useless man bairn awa from me!" he said.

Morven and Murdo pulled Alfred away while Hamish took hold of the struggling sailor and again pushed him below the water, this time holding him under. The sailor had no chance of survival with Hamish perched over him like one of the savage gulls, and the man's arms wavered about, hitting and splashing the water. He tried with every last effort he had within him and struggled with every bit of his life until he drew his final breath beneath the sea. His lungs filled with the cold, deathly liquid and his strength was no longer enough to fight off Hamish and keep his life.

Alfred could no longer restrain his temper from a flare up. He wriggled out of the grips of Murdo and Morven, stood forward and shouted at Hamish. "The bible tells us, 'You desire and do not have, so you murder! You covet and cannot obtain, so you fight and quarrel!' So, I ask of you Hamish, who are you that you would take life?"

Hamish let go of the dead man, who slid under water momentarily before bobbing back up again. Hamish squared up to Alfred. "Ah may no be weel read like ye, Mr Henderson. But ah tak wha' has been given tae me. Tha' is ma blessing from God! Noo sit yersel doon!" And he shoved him back into his seat.

While Morven and Murdo were holding Alfred back, Hamish pulled the drifting dead man back upside the boat, turned him around on his back and quickly searched the sailor's front pockets. Under his jacket he found a French Lefaucheux revolver secured inside a holster. He pulled out the pistol and without being seen, promptly pushed it inside his own coat to hide it.

Morven saw what Hamish was doing and had seen the pistol. He joined Hamish so that they could continue to search the sailor together. In his front pocket, they found a tiny, wet portrait of a woman and a small pouch of coins, which they took out before pushing the body away. It sank as it drifted out.

All the while, Alfred sat at the other side of the boat, sickened and enraged at the perversion of law and virtue and the complete lack of empathy he just witnessed. He was angry that he was powerless to stop it. All he wanted to do was lash out his anger on Hamish and fight him. But given Hamish's strength, Alfred could see that he would be no match for the ogre, who was filled with far more hate and muscle than he was.

Hamish opened the little sack and poured the coins into his hand for the others to see. The pieces of silver slipped between his fat fingers and jingled onto the deck, bouncing and rolling in all directions. Hamish howled with the men. “Ha!” Hamish sputtered in Alfred's face. “Ask ‘n’ it shall be given tae ye!” The other men laughed back.

Alfred returned to the island feeling completely troubled. He could think of nothing else apart from the insane incident he had been witness to and thought it would be a bad idea to see Cait again in his current state of mind.

As he walked to shore and strode as quick as he could past the cottages, he was on the brink of a messy rage and needed to let it loose. He hoped to God Almighty he would not be seen by the beautiful Cait. Instead, he would make his way to his awaiting ship in the cove and go straight home.

Cait was there though, outside her cottage. On her knees, she turned over clumps of peat to dry in the sun as he walked up from the beach. She watched as he stomped past her. Feeling invisible to him, she stood up.

“Weren’t you going to say good-bye?” she called.

He continued to walk on, his mind full of disturbing conviction.

“Alfred? Alfred! What’s wrong with you? Do you not see that I am here?”

Her plea grabbed his attention and he stopped. He could not look at her, instead at the ground and then, as his eyes watered, he looked up to the sky for an answer. He looked down again and the tips of his shoes shuffled around the dirt, not knowing what to say, or if he ought to turn around and carry on walking away. She knew something terrible was at hand.

“Oh, dear God, what has happened?”

His words were jumbled. “I don’t – I just can’t – the man, the sailor – I ... ”

She took him in her arms as he squeezed his eyes shut and his face turned red trying desperately to hold himself together. And as he leaned into her and pressed his hand into his eyes, his silent tears dripped onto the back of her skirt.

"Come, come in," Cait insisted.

She took his hand and as he dried his face, she led him inside the cottage.

Ashamed that Cait had seen him expose his emotions, Alfred said nothing to her. She fed him kippers, poured rum into a cup and sat with him, not asking anything.

As she went to take his empty bowl, he was disappointed at his inability to converse like a man, and only spoke a resigned, "Thank you."

"'Tis nae trouble at all."

"No, I mean for not asking. Thank you."

In her forgiving nature she replied, "Is it not so that your passions are at war within you? I might imagine what is troubling you, but I will not ask if it's not my business to. If it was, I am sure you would tell me."

Alfred looked at her sun-peached face and nodded. "You are of a good heart."

Little did he know she was not as virtuous and wholesome as she appeared. But he wished to protect her and decided it was best that she remained in the dark about the fishermen's wicked goings on and was content that he had done the right thing by not telling her the details of the morning's event.

He wanted to touch her face, but he stood up to go. In the doorway of her cottage, he put his hat on while she looked at his missing button space and touched it.

"You really might find some less tatty clothes, Mr Henderson. I mean, here we take whatever we can get, but someone like you can do better."

Alfred looked down at the bare button threads and then up at Cait, whose face had drawn in close to his. He swallowed hard. "Maybe what I have before me is as much as I've ever needed."

She blushed.

With Cait at an unusual loss of words, Alfred continued. "It was nice to have met you, Mrs Cait McKenzie, and to be the receiver of your warm and kind hospitality."

"I would not have you leave without complimenting you for fixing my chair," she said, "and for showing me the saucepan in the sky."

Together, they smiled at the previous night's memory. "There is so much more to learn about the stars," he said, being somewhat hopeful.

"If we should meet again, then you must teach me more." She stepped back before her heart would lose control and leap into his soul.

"Fair thee well, Cait." And he waved good-bye.

Hamish saw him leave from a distance, and he watched on as Cait smiled girlishly at Alfred. She saw Hamish's glare and dropped her elation for fear he would punish her for being over hospitable to another man or perhaps he would avenge Alfred. She turned around ever so quickly and shut herself inside the cottage.

Just then, Morven approached Hamish intent on holding him accountable. "Donnae think ah didnae see tha' pistol ye stuffed in yer coat this morn'."

"Wha'd ye mean?" challenged Hamish.

"Ye ken. Just mak certain tha ye add it tae th' loot bag fer th' prosperity o' th' community."

Hamish took Morven by the throat and forced him against the side of the house, giving it a shake as he threatened him.

"Wha'ere ye think ye saw, ye dinnae. Get it oot yer heid right noo, or ah will dae it mysel' wi' this." He made a fist and showed it to him. "Is tha' clear?"

Not able to breathe, Morven nodded his red face. Hamish shoved him out of the way. He fell to the ground, rubbing his neck, coughing and catching his breath before scrambling to his feet and running off.

.oOo.

Cameron and Ewan ran after Alfred, wading through the sweeping coastal grasses, hollering after him.

"Wait! Are ye leaving, Mr Henderson? Where ye gang?" they called.

"I'm going back to my ship and going home. You boys be good for your mum and take care of her."

The boys caught up to him.

"Why are ye gang so soon?" asked Ewan, glowering.

Alfred stopped, turned to the boys and stooped down to address them. He inspected the fishing string, which was wrapped methodologically around Ewan's arm, tiding all the string into a loop.

"I have work to do. Do you boys think you can do me a favour?"

They both nodded. "Aye, what is it, Mr Henderson?" they asked.

"Do you think the next time you say your prayers, you might just pray for the men at sea?"

The boys looked puzzled.

"Let me explain. At times, the sea is rough and dangerous, as I'm certain you two already know."

The boys nodded.

"The vulnerable people who work at sea might need a prayer sent their way."

The boys were still confused, so Alfred went on to explain. "The Bible tells us *In God's mercy he does not put an end to them or abandon them, for He is gracious and merciful.*" Then Alfred took a tone of authority. "Good young men, do pray for their safety and well-being. I implore you."

"Okay, Mr Henderson," Ewan replied resolutely.

"If ye think we ought tae," Cameron added.

"Good lads. Now go home to your mother."

Cameron quizzed Alfred without hesitation. "Do ye like her?"

Alfred smiled. "Sure, I like her. How do you mean?"

The boys looked at each other and giggled. "Will you come back?"

"I don't know. Are you inviting me?"

"Aye!" they shouted, and they ran off laughing. "Good-bye!"

CHAPTER 5

Oh to what extremes o'er me has this lady,
She's weather'd the nights and all judgement of lately;
She tires my duties she swims through my mind,
I sail o'er the North Sea yet too drained to gage tide;
Tho' I work long for my means, so my purse grows in bulk,
Heartache treads the heather upon which she does walk.

Anonymous

It was a cloudy day at the Greenock docks. There was a lot of hustling about of ships' crews and dock workers and a crowd of people queued up to board the Aemelius.

One by one, they each gave their details to Alfred before boarding. He was seated at a table with a pen and ink well and several papers with a list of names. He checked each one as they gave him their information. The folks were mostly women and children, some men and everyone was as full of as many pieces of luggage and trunks as they could carry.

The next passenger stepped up to Alfred.

"Ticket?" he asked of the young man.

The man showed him his ticket.

"Name?" Alfred asked.

"Campbell. John," he replied nervously.

"Age and place of birth?"

The young fellow paused before answering. "A'm eighteen. Rogart, Sutherland."

"Hmm." Alfred thought he looked young for eighteen, and the young lad's hesitation made him suspicious, but as there was a long queue of people waiting, he let it slip. Knowing that the young lad was from the northern Highlands, there was a possibility he might not only be lacking in education, but also the birth records from his parish.

Alfred looked into his innocent face and could that see that he was shaking with anxiety.

"You've come a long way, son," said Alfred.

"Aye, Sir. There's nothing left o' th' Highlands any mere," replied John.

Alfred nodded at him indicating for him to move along.

"Tapadh leat," John thanked Alfred in Gaelic. He took hold of his luggage and walked swiftly up the gangplank to board the ship, eyes aglow with anticipation.

As the excited and eager commotion of the crowd took over, Alfred could barely be heard asking the next passengers. "Ticket? Name? Date and place of birth?" he shouted out like a bookmaker standing among the crowd at the horseraces.

Finally, all the passengers were boarded and Alfred walked up the gangway. The steam engine rattled as it started up and black smoke shot out of the chimney pipe. The sails were hoisted, the ropes were untied at the dock and the ship gently parted Greenock. The raised cotton sheets rattled steadily as they filled with a rising wind from the southwest. They were off.

The voyage went smoothly without bad luck or event as the weather was ideal and by the early afternoon Liverpool began to come into view from the sea. As they moved in closer, Alfred was amazed at the number of tall sailing vessels, steam ships and merchant ships at the port. His amazement quickly turned to diffidence as he looked at his own seemingly shrinking ship in comparison to the much greater ones ahead.

Tosh saw this and was quick to soothe his concern. "It's astounding, isn't it?"

"Aye, Aemelius is as small as the Consolation in comparison," replied Alfred.

Tosh grinned. "You will get accustomed to it after a few trips. We shall keep this route going until that lighthouse is built."

At the Port of Liverpool, the last of their passengers disembarked with their belongings of luggage, baskets and trunks. Unwinding inside the captain's cabin as Tosh arranged the navigational charts alongside him, Alfred gaped out of the window at a large passenger ship across the dock.

"One day, you – we - could sail emigrants, double or triple the numbers of today. We could plan a route to the Americas, maybe further such as New Zealand, in a ship like that," Alfred commented.

"Don't get ahead of yourself, son," Tosh warned. "The west coast of Scotland is our route to navigate, just as your father began to do. That's where you'll have your success. Leave long cargo shipping to the big boys."

Alfred thought back in time. "Ah, yes, my father."

Tosh replied, "He was a fairly good man. Must I remind you of that?"

"Was he? What I recall of him was not so fair," said Alfred. "You will need to remind me again of how he was a good man."

Tosh sighed. "We all have our faults."

"Some more than others."

"Aye, Alfred, but don't let his past dominate what he did good in his life," reminded Tosh.

"His misfortune was his is loss of memory in the end. Do you recall?" asked Alfred, as he avoided talking about his father's disgraced past to save himself the distress.

"The wedding ring," Tosh began to laugh lightly.

"Just when I needed to present it to Fiona, he didn't have it," said Alfred.

"It should have been in my possession, seeing that I was your best man."

"He didn't trust anyone. He never did; he insisted on doing everything his way or he would make a complete fuss about it the rest of the day," Alfred said. "Only as he grew older, his memory decreased, but his cantankerous behaviour magnified. He was fond of you, though. His mistrust wasn't to be taken to heart."

"Aye, it was a day we wouldn't soon forget. How are you doing with everything - you know," asked Tosh.

Alfred thought about that question and wondered if it would have any benefit if he were to divulge to Tosh how his chance meeting with Cait had left him with a desire that he had closed off to all women since Fiona died. It was an emotion which may not ever have had possibilities to be fulfilled by a wrecker woman, no matter how beautiful. Yet, he could not refrain from thinking about her; that she was fatiguing him with the constant running around inside his head and a lack of appetite which only added to his pining, making him sick with want.

"Distracted," answered Alfred.

Taken by surprise, Tosh queried to it being a positive or negative distraction. "Distracted? Should I feel glad for you?"

There was a pause. One moment of it was by Tosh who would be surprised if Alfred was able to portray enough charm with which to enchant a woman.

For Alfred, his momentary hesitation was embarrassment that a woman could make him feel such a way – a little less in control of himself.

"Is it a woman?" Tosh asked.

Not wanting to discuss it in detail, Alfred answered simply, "Potentially," and turned his head. He would have to repudiate the thoughts of her, as he was beginning to lose concentration and focus required for his work.

Tosh smiled. "Ah, I see, the essence of the complicated female is eating at your heart." He grinned and patted him on the shoulder. "Long may it last, my friend."

Alfred changed the subject. "Young Stevenson thinks I ought to consider writing in a journal."

"Much like my captain's journal?"

"Not exactly. Similar to what he writes, day to day thoughts, only not necessarily as dramatical or in the poetical style as he writes," explained Alfred.

"Alfred Henderson, the author," announced Tosh as he raised his voice aloud pretending to make an important announcement.

"Only personal thoughts. He says writing them on paper might be good for my conscience."

“Your conscience is already fixed in your principles and morals. But if for the sake of your peace you can gain from doing so, then there is no harm.”

“I am very sure my peace is the intention,” Alfred revised.

“And in case you inherit your father’s memory,” said Tosh, with a large hint of scepticism. “A drink and a wink?”

“Aye,” Alfred nodded to the offer of whisky. “I do think how beneficial it would be if I could write down my past then conveniently forget it all or set it afire; as if it had gone up in smoke or washed away.”

Tosh took the whisky bottle from a drawer and poured it into two glasses. He passed a glass to Alfred and made a toast.

“Slàinte mhath,” said Tosh.

“Slàinte mhath,” echoed Alfred as their glasses clinked.

They drank a long sip and Alfred turned back to the window to look outside at the tall ship adjacent to them. He lifted his glass to it and finished the dram.

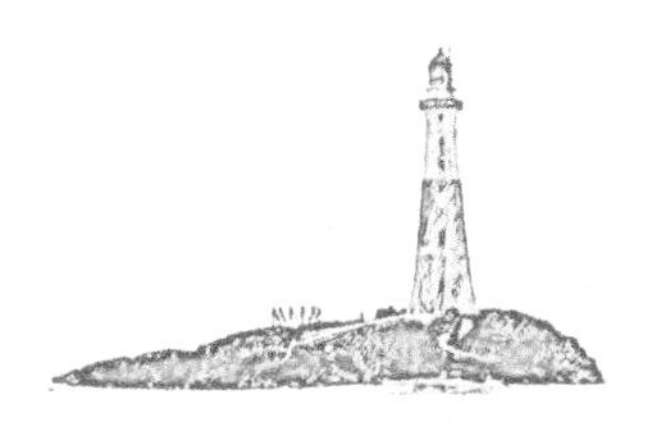

CHAPTER 6

A ship is a breath of romance
That carries us miles away
And a book is a ship of fancy
That could sail on any day.

Victorian, unknown author

Louis stared out into the Inner Seas of the West Coast of Scotland. On the tiny island of Erraid under a mackerel sky, an effect in which the clouds pattern rippled across the heavens as if ribbons of sand under the fading tide. Louis adored watching them. He daydreamed as he sat atop the Wishing Stone. This stone, about a metre and a half wide, rested in the grass on top of the hill above a sandy cove towards the west of the island. The rock was surrounded by a ring of water, much like a moat, and made getting on top of the rock tricky for the less than agile. But Louis had worked out a method to get onto it without getting his feet wet. He got used to jumping up to the stone, straddling it and working his arms legs around until he could lift himself up into a sitting position.

It was Louis's quiet place where he would often disappear to and think about his life; the conflicts concerning his career versus family and contemplate the faults of religion. He yearned for travelling to a warmer country, one which would ease his chronic coughing. He even began dreaming up a scene for a story on the beach below the stone on which he sat.

He went as far as giving the characters their names. As his mother's maiden name was Balfour, Louis thought this would be a good name for the main character. And what of the real life Scottish soldier and Jacobite, Alan Breck Stewart, portrayed as a hero by Sir Walter Scott? Or some of the other characters to one of Louis's favourite stories, the Appin Murder. In this was the murdered royal agent rent collector, Colin Roy Campbell and his accuser James Stewart, relative of Alan Breck Stewart. Because Alan avoided capture for the crime, James was convicted and hanged simply because he was Alan's relative and a penance was due.

Louis's memory of reading the stories of these men became alive within his head once again and he thought of how he might weave them together in a story all his own. As it happened, investigations at a later date revealed that Alan Breck Stewart was innocent. So, the death of his relative James was unnecessary. Perhaps Louis could change the outcome of the past simply by including the characters' names within another story.

Unlike Sir Walter Scott's romanticised interpretation of Alan Breck Stewart, a soldier who returned to serve in the French military and fight against the British, perhaps Louis could make him a likeable character by turning himself in at the end. Or maybe that twisted notion was just beyond belief. Whatever stories Louis concocted, he felt fulfilled and free doing so atop the Wishing Stone.

With his eyes shut, Louis closed off the world in front of him and disappeared. He floated away into his own dream like zone, his imagination soaring in full flight of fancy. His mind reached far out to sea like a soaring albatross. After a while of exploration, Louis dived into the great, darkened, blinding depths as deep as the albatross plunges to seek after its prey. Then he shot straight out into the air with such tremendous power that he felt a spray of water. He emerged from the fictitious fantasies with a jolt and opened his eyes. The rain had begun to fall. So deep were his thoughts, he failed to notice the downpour and he was drenched. But he remained seated as the rain continued.

Along the rocks by the beachy cove below him he imagined a man, soaked from the sea and laying on the shore. The man awoke to the sound of fishermen in their boat sailing past. Fatigued, he stood up rather unsteady on his legs and waved zealously to them for help. The fishermen looked to the lone man and laughed at his situation and sailed onward.

Louis liked the idea of this: a young man on a journey, escaping the sinister plan of one ill-regarded uncle, a shipwreck leaving him to survive in the elements of weather, hunger and conflict to find his way home.

The winds had again picked up. Louis smiled at the story in his mind. And the faint sound of the workmen on the ship returning from the lighthouse broke all concentration. Lacking in sufficient clothing in the rain, Louis began to feel a chill and his cough set in. In his rather fragile state, he coughed deeply as he slid down from the stone, just clipping the edge of the wee moat with his heals and he walked back towards the village.

.oOo.

In the damp, bookless, toyless room where the boys and Janet shared sleep, Ewan busied himself by rearranging a rather numerous and bulky collection of pebbles which he put into a small, carved wood bowl. Cameron stood at the window and ran his finger over the bumps of the shiny, stolen button. At a closer look, Cameron discovered that the button had three raised brass legs and he was filled with curiosity about them until Janet opened the door and interrupted. He slid the button into a space at the corner of the window and dashed under his covers.

"So, mah dears, wha' have ye in mind fur storytelling th' nicht?" she asked.

"Tell us a story aboot pirates who tak' o'er a ship that's stowed oot o' gold," urged Ewan.

"Again? Is there anythin' else which interests ye?" she challenged.

Cameron begged. "Nae, Auntie, it's mah turn tae choose!"

"Your stories are boring," said Ewan. "Ah want tae hear a story aboot a ship wi' an enormous loot o' gold 'n' silver coins all th' wae from Spain, 'n' they smash upon th' black rocks, 'n' we can see th' coins shimmer oot at sea from 'ere, 'n' when th' pirates ..."

Cameron interrupted. "Nae, it's mah turn. Ah want tae hear somethin' differen'!"

Janet conceded. "He's nae wrong, Ewan, it's his turn. So then, Cameron, wha' kind o' story dae ye want tae hear?"

Cameron became excited. "Tell me a story about th' three-legged man."

Ewan snickered. "Hahaha a three-legged man! Has he five eyes as well? Ha-ha 'n' one hundred fingers?" he laughed again.

Cait appeared in the doorway to hear to the story. She dried her hands on her pinny, leaned against the door frame and crossed her arms, listening to the conversation.

"Now Ewan, dinnae poke fun at yer brother's story idea. Tell me more, Cameron," enquired Janet.

"No *a* three-legged man, *th'* three-legged man. Ye ken, Mister – th' man who came tae see us. He has a green coat 'n' three gold legs," the five-year-old Cameron tried to explain in detail to his limited, cynical audience.

Without Cameron seeing her, Janet noticed the button on the window. She went over to pick it up while Cameron talked.

"Mr Henderson? He doesnae have three gold legs. He has one leg just like th' rest o' us, 'n' a crooked one 'n' a stick," explained Ewan.

Janet slipped the button into her pocket.

"But no, ah saw him, he has three gold legs!"

"Enough!" huffed Janet. "Ah will tell ye a story boot a man wi' a stick, but ye mustnae gang roond making up such fibs! Do ya hear me young man?"

The wee boy was upset to not be heard as he was chastened. "Aye, auntie, ah hear ya."

"All right then."

Janet sat down upon the end of their bed, her wide derriere taking up half the length. The boys bent their legs to give her space. She thought for a moment before she began her story. “Once, miles fae here, o’er th’ hills ‘n’ beyond th’ lochs, there was a shepherd wi’ a golden stick, who tended tae two hundred seventy-seven sheep."

“Two hun- that’s almost three hundred sheep! Och!" Ewan interrupted.

Cameron looked disappointed as it wasn’t the story he wanted, but she continued telling it, making it up as she went along, and the boys listened.

“Aye, he had th’ most sheep in a’ th’ Hielands!” she continued. “’Twas rumoured by some that his golden stick was th’ reason why he had so many sheep. They said if he tapped it against th’ edges ‘o th’ burn at sunset, anither sheep appeared at sunrise, as if by magic!"

“Whit’s magic?” Ewan asked.

“Och, weel, magic is wha’ happens -” Janet nodded to Ewan’s collection of pebbles. “When ye expect a bird tae fly, but shud yer stones fly, that wud be magic.”

The two boys were glued to her wild tales and Cait was amazed at her ingenuity to stretch the imagination. Janet continued, “Well, ye ken one morn’ when he was oot in th’ braids ...”

.oOo.

Alfred knocked on Tosh's front door with a letter in his right hand but being impatient he slapped the letter into his left hand in beats, then back to his right hand. Unable to contain his news, his impetuosity thrust him to knock again and again.

Tosh opened the door and Alfred, taking off his hat, tried to speak. However, the MacIntosh household had excitement of their own and a craze had developed therein before Alfred's arrival.

"Alfred, come in, come in," welcomed Tosh.

"Hello Alfred," Marion chanted, "It's hen and broth for our supper tonight. Tosh, why don't you serve him a drink while we wait for the bird to cook."

"Hello Marion, Tosh," Alfred greeted. "I received a letter today from Mr Stevenson." Hardly able to get a word in and knowing his news was drowned out by their joyous pandemonium, Alfred was greeted politely, however hastily.

"Who? What?" Tosh asked, pushing him into the drawing room.

Lois came bursting down the stairs in great excitement, interrupting. "Father, did you tell him yet?"

"No," replied Tosh.

"Tell me what?" asked Alfred, as he slipped off his coat.

"Tell him now, Papa!"

"Not yet, Lois. He only just arrived! Let him take off his coat and have a seat, for goodness' sake!"

"Tell me what? What is it?" Alfred asked inquisitively.

"Let me pour you a whisky, my good man."

Alfred interrupted. "I as well have something to tell you!"

Lois giggled.

Tosh was annoyed at her and gave her a disapproving eye. Tosh exhaled deeply.

Marion came towards the drawing room. She looked in from the hallway and called out to her daughter. "Just settle down, Lois, you won't be a good bride to any man if you have no control over yourself."

All of a sudden, Alfred and Tosh lost their cheerful tempo and the good mood around them came to a distressing halt.

Alfred looked from Marion to Tosh, then back to Marion. "Bride? Tosh? Is this true, is Lois betrothed to Douglas?"

Marion and Lois looked to Tosh as the head of the family and depended on him to offer up a credible answer. One which, with careful handling, would hopefully softly buffer Alfred's delicate heart.

Tosh faced Alfred. "I did. Look, he's young, just finished his studies, and he's working for his father now."

Alfred pressed his lips together and pushed the letter into his coat pocket. "Oh, so it's because he's educated."

Once again, speaking out of place, Lois piped in. "Alf, I'm sorry, did we upset you?" At this, Lois was ignored, as this was now a matter between the men.

"Come Lois, let's leave them," instructed Marion. She took Lois by the arm and lead her out of the room as Tosh raised his voice in order to justify himself. "Douglas lives here! He is present, with both feet on the ground and he can look after Lois properly!"

"And I cannot? You know that – you know me! Have I not proven myself to you all these years?" Alfred slammed back.

"Yes, yes, of course you have. You have never needed to prove anything to me. You are a fine man, but it is not about that. You are a sailor, a merchant. It calls you, sometimes for weeks at a time, and it is fact, son, that you have age against you. I don't want that for Lois, to lose her husband at sea and the father of her children, and to be resigned to live her life as a widow. She deserves more than that."

Knowing that this engagement would have been a plan in the works for Tosh and Marion for some time, Alfred felt betrayed. He had no other prospects for marriage, nor introductions which could be fulfilled.

"But it's acceptable for you to do exactly that to your own family, is it?" he added.

"My father left me for the sea and never returned. I was just a young lad. I don't want the same fate for my grandchildren; the same mistakes and consequences to be repeated," Tosh explained.

Alfred replied defensively. "Mistakes. I do apologise, I got it so wrong all these years. You are like a brother to me. You are my family. This is my family. After all we have been through, I feel as if I've just been discarded."

Alfred took his coat and pushed his arms back into it, straightening out the collar as he left the house. He stood outside, leaning against the house to take some time to think. Momentarily, Tosh joined him and leaned back into the wall beside him.

"We are not discarding you. You will always be family to us. Surely, you can understand, can you not? I want something different for my daughter as you would, as well."

Alfred rubbed his face with his hands. "It's not that I feel as if Lois is exactly right for me. She is much too young, and she is not serious minded, you must admit."

"Oh, now you tell me she is not the woman for you." Tosh alluded to Alfred's flat excuses.

Alfred continued. "I am agreeing with you. At times, I admit I am lonely; I miss Fiona very much. Sometimes I don't think I've any point in anything. Then there are times that I don't even think about her, then something out of the clear blue sky will suddenly remind me of her – her laughter. But I cannot remember her face unless I see a photo and I feel shameful just for forgetting."

"This means you are moving on. You should not feel any shame, because what happened was not your fault. It was out of your hands. It was a part of God's plan."

"Was it God's plan for Fiona and our son to die, with no chance for a life? Is God so cruel to lay that upon my heart and her family's for the rest of our days? I don't accept that God is all the fury and fire that we are told to believe – a god that is meant to be the giver of life and of love and forgiveness cannot be the same god of malice!"

Tosh interrupted strongly. "No, but He is a God of mercy, and your wife and that child needed help at that precise time for the distress they were in. They were not meant to survive, and God gave them His unfailing mercy in the end. Don't you see? It wasn't about you; it was all about them."

"Look at us, Alfred. Marion and I have lost all of our other children and we made it through. It wasn't easy, but we did. We pushed forward and found a way to move on. We survived. That is what you are as well, Alfred, a survivor. You need to let it go. Fiona, the baby, your father. You are not meant to live in the past. Live for today and tomorrow. Discover what God's purpose is for you."

There was a pause between the two men. Tosh had said what needed saying and Alfred needed time for those words to sink in.

Then Tosh added, "Marion and I pray for peace in your heart. If anyone deserves to love and to laugh again, you do."

"How do I do that?" Alfred asked.

"You will find a way, Alfred, it will come. Take it one day at a time. Just like we did."

Marion opened the door and called out to them. "The supper is ready. Come in now and say grace for us, will you?"

Tosh waved to Marion before concluding their conversation. "Now, what is this letter you have?"

Alfred had forgotten about the letter altogether. "What? Oh." He took out the letter from his coat and unfolded it. "It is from Mr Stevenson. Do you recall I told you about the young lighthouse engineer at Dubh Artach?"

"Yes, I do. What does he say? How is progress? Do tell me he sends good news," said Tosh.

"The building is showing progress, but there is still much work."

With reluctance in his voice, Tosh asked, "So, is there a possibility to pass this year?"

Alfred looked more closely at the letter, and turned it over, hoping he had missed reading that part. "He does not say that."

"We cannot take any risk in assumptions." Tosh's excitement deflated.

Alfred replied. "I shall return to see the young Mr Stevenson in person. It will also keep my mind off – off this."

"Oh, just be happy for her," Tosh nudged.

"I am, genuinely, infinitely. Both for Lois and her 'educated' groom."

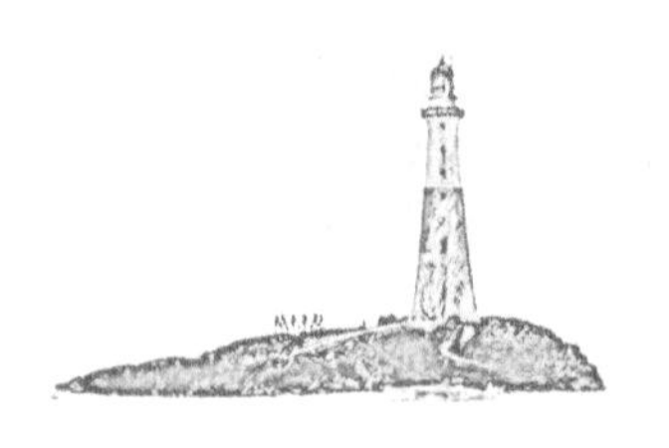

CHAPTER 7

I go to the edge to ground myself,
Shifting sands beneath move me not
I am swallowed, disappearing into myself;
Only the innate awareness remains
The water, it wanders over
It knows what to do
I wait,
It rises over me – washing, caressing the pain, fear,
all which dwell within the shadow;
This holy crux of the earth expurgates my soul
Basting me in atoning salt
And the sea song nourishes my mind
I listen,
Between the soft beating of chants
and drumming of waves
I am baptised, granted a new pulse,
And rejoin the disordered world.

Anonymous

Cait wished a good night to Janet and kissed the foreheads of Ewan and Cameron as they lay warmly tucked underneath the blankets on their bed. In the same room,

Janet went to her bed, a simple, elevated bench made of a wooden board. It had a thick blanket placed on top of it which she slept on and pulled another blanket over her. Cait took the lantern with her.

Outside the cottage, Hamish rested against his house, edging his way towards full obliteration by the rum. His arm swayed as he stared at the ground and the near empty bottle dangled through his swollen fingers, the little bit of liquid and a muddy brown sediment sploshed about the bottom of it.

In the main room, Cait blew out the flame inside the lantern. The wood in the fireplace had reduced to a dark red glow, so she dropped another log on top to keep the heat going for a while longer into the night. In the dark, she prodded the log with a metal poker, pushing it to the back of the fireplace in order to give it the most heat, then propped the poker up against the wall as the moisture in the new log let off a whistle and steam.

She sat herself on the bench, kicked off her old, tired boots and placed them neatly beside it. She then pulled a blanket over herself and with a heavy sigh, slid deep down into it to fall asleep.

Seeing the cottage go dark within, Hamish decided to make his move. He dropped his bottle, he then careened over to Cait's door, pounding on it and fiddling noisily with the handle, trying to free it open.

He banged and shouted, "Let me in!"

Desperate as to not wake the boys, Cait rushed over and lifted the latch, shushing Hamish as he pushed his way in past her. The smell coming off him was overwhelming. She used her hand to shield her nose and made an embittered face as the stench of dead fish and alcohol floated in with him as if he had carried around a haar all of his own.

The boys heard the commotion and tried to take a snoop at what was happening. They watched, worried for their mother, who was obviously ill at ease. Janet awoke and from behind she pulled them back into their room, closing the curtain.

"Shh! You'll wake the boys!" Cait whispered.

"Ah dinnae gie a damn boot th' bairns, A'm here fer ye," he spat.

"No the now, Hamish, you're full of the rum. You reek of it."

Hamish grabbed her by the arm and pulled her in to his chest, kissing her madly and sloppily, making her face wet. "Ah just want tae git full o' ye, Cait. Ah love ye."

Cait tightened her lips and tried to fight him off and finally wriggled out of his grip. "No, Hamish, I said NO!"

"Come noo, a'm gang tae have ye while th' bairns sleep," he beseeched as he stumbled over her. "Ye'r mines!"

"I am NO yours. I don't want you, nor do I love you. NO! Stop!"

Hamish stepped back and slapped Cait in the face. She fell backward, hitting her head against the wall. She held it with her hand to ease the pain then looked at her palm. There was no blood, but she did not allow the pain to keep her from defending herself.

"Look, ye dreadful slag. Look wha' ye made me dae!" he blamed.

In the glow of the moonlight, Hamish saw the brass button shining on the table. He set his rum bottle down, took the button and put it in his pocket. Cait grabbed the fire poker. While his head was turned, she made an attempt to fend him off. She stared at his leg and with sheer, focused fury, in one go she drove the poker straight into his thigh. It was a graze less than what she had hoped for. Nonetheless, he grunted. Her eyes peeled open with fear, and she waited terrified of what his response may be and how he would retaliate.

He took hold of the poker and tossed it behind him, seized the sleeves of her white undergarments and threw her down to the ground. He met her on his knees. Cait kicked and pushed him, but he was much stronger than her, and as he forced her dress up, he untied the waist of his trousers. He laid his heavy body on top of her frame and rhythmically thrusted himself against her, all the while smudging her face with his wet lips and licking her neck much like a savage beast.

Cait grimaced and tears streamed down her face whilst she forced herself silent as to not disturb the children, whom she thought were sleeping. But they were awake. Janet kept them in their bed, humming a tune all the while to cover up the woeful moaning in the other room.

In a very short minute, however feeling to her much like an eternity, Hamish stood, did up his trousers, one leg now torn and bloodied by the wound. As his passion and numbness were provided by the rum, he had forgotten all about it.

"See it as payment fer keeping ye 'n' yer bairns fed. The sooner ye admit that ye love me, th' easier it will be. Ye'll see. Althoogh, yer a fierce yin, Cait. Ah dae fancy a good fight wi' ye," he laughed.

Hamish wobbled out of the cottage and slammed the door shut. His leg now began to pulsate and ache with the wound. He clenched his teeth as he held the lesion tight with one hand, tripping over stones and the clumps of drying peat that Cait and Janet had laid out, and he made a general mess of their tidy work as he hobbled home just a few metres away.

Cait stood up slowly. Feeling dishevelled, she wiped her tears and took a cloth from a bucket of water. She rubbed the blood from her hands then cleaned her face and neck with the cloth and scrubbed vigorously between her legs, as she had done many times before. But now she had enough. With her fingers trembling, she straightened out her murky, tangled hair and pulled it back out of her face. Then she sat down in Alfred's chair to catch her breath, get her head together and try to find some peace of mind.

The only feeling she had for Hamish was revulsion, and she loathed herself even more for the duty she had bound herself to, although she had tried to appear impervious to this.

She took a firm hold of the arm rests and ran her hand under the seat of the chair. Cait thought about him sleeping peacefully in her house that one night. She closed her eyes and imagined she was touching a part of Alfred, perhaps caressing his arm. With her hand she explored where he had dabbed the now dried mass of gluey compound weeks before and she ran her fingertips round the twine which still held the leg to the seat. She sighed. She longed for him, the handsome lighthouse worker with the pleasant masculinity and protective nature. The man with the knowledge of all the stars in the heavens, who was also somehow able to touch the emotions trapped within her heart which she had interred along with William.

Cait thought of his green coat with the fancy buttons that she had previously mocked before and now in her mind it suddenly seemed very smart and desirable indeed. She sat there, in Alfred's chair, crying for reasons anew; to be given a chance with him, if only the lighthouse worker would have reason to sail back to Iona again. As she compared what his life might be against the one she was currently living, that of an exhausted coastal wrecker widow and mother, she found some strength suddenly emerge from within. Her burden was heavy, but her fresh aspirations were full, and she cracked a tiny smile to herself before she burst out in laughter, because in the hideous grime of that night, she felt a new sense that courage was within reach. Whether it was to find a love for living, or to be freed by love once again, she was going to win. Whatever Cait was overcome with, she was ready for it, and yet would have to be full of patience whilst she devised an operable plan.

.oOo.

The resented haar was rolling over the coast and visibility diminishing with every minute as the Consolation arrived on Erraid. Duncan secured the boat to the iron fixtures along the mooring and helped Alfred ashore.

By evening, the low cloud had settled with the dusk and stuck itself to the island for the night. There was an eerie stillness in the air, the fog as thick as stew and not a seagull was heard. The only sound was footsteps; the crunching of sand and grinding of pebbles under foot. Then, a figure cut straight through the fog. With the luminous lantern that accompanied him, one would know that the steps were those of the watchman.

It swung, alternating with each step, the little enclosed flame unphased by the motion. He walked past the cottages, stopping by each one to light the tobacco pipes of the men who waited outside for him.

Inside Louis's cottage, he, Alan Brebner and Alfred joined in a meeting about the lighthouse and drank their beer rations together.

"We will soon close the project down for winter. Even when the structure is complete, we will still need time to assemble the glass lens, and of course, everything is dependent on good weather," Alan explained matter of factly.

"I see," said Alfred, not wanting to add any complication by complaining.

"All the while," Alan continued, "the commissioners are pushing this work so that it will be finished before the weather once again turns on us."

Alfred exhaled, frustrated that a whole winter would have to pass before any more progress would happen. He was keen to end his contract with the passenger ships in Liverpool. He tapped his fingers impatiently on his leg, trying to hold his tongue.

Alan collected his papers together.

Louis abruptly spoke his thoughts on the matter before Alfred could. "We are doing our best, Mr Henderson. But I beg for your confidence in us so that we can finish our work without interruption."

"Indeed, Mr Stevenson, I have no doubt. My only concern is for the safety of my ship and her passengers on board. This time it will be lives, not rum at stake."

"Understood," Alan added. "In which case Mr Stevenson here shall keep you informed by letter of our progress."

Louis nodded in agreement. "Aye, of course I will."

"Very well. I thank you," said Alfred.

"Not at all. I am glad we can be of some service to you. And, speaking of service, tomorrow is Sunday. Will you join us for church?" asked Alan.

"I am certain I will find much pleasure in doing so."

"Good night, gentlemen", Alan bade them.

He nodded to both Alfred and Louis before disappearing into the haze outside. Alfred turned to Louis. "Tell me, Louis, do you have a family to which you will return when this is all realised?"

"I will leave here for Edinburgh tomorrow. My father, mother and cousins await my return."

"Do you have a plan after you return?"

"The plan is that I will return to Edinburgh University where I must submit my dissertation on Dubh Artach. I may receive my qualifications as an engineer. Even without the desire to."

"What then? Will you continue to build more lighthouses or seek another engineering capacity?"

Louis looked into his glass for a moment and swirled the beer around thinking about his answer. "I am doubtful this is my destiny, rather it is my father's. My path still lingers in considerable question."

Alfred admired Louis's response and his ability to challenge the cloth from which he was cut. It prompted Alfred to admit something he had never said out loud before. "I understand this. If not a ship merchant, perhaps I would have instead practiced to become an advocate."

"Hmm, an advocate. That is something I have never considered."

"The law interests me. It's changing and growing within its own realms, yet it keeps everything correct and orderly, which is something I find appealing. Law challenges whilst remaining stable."

Louis laughed. "Perhaps that's why I have never considered it either until now."

Alfred was amused. "Don't fill your head with too any ideas! It sounds like much work for someone who clearly enjoys and finds satisfaction escaping into storyland. But if it's your wish to fill your purse, then you will make a good engineer, Louis."

"How will I know?" Louis questioned. Alfred took the hourglass from the table. "Watch this. Just as these sands pass through the hourglass, they won't fall for eternity. And neither will your dilemma. For where your passion is, invest in that for your future. It's the only way you will live fulfilled and without regrets," said Alfred. As the sands continued to escape to the bottom of the glass, he looked over to Louis who was shuffling notes of poetry into a pile.

"Women?" he asked. "I have plenty of interest in them."

Alfred smiled. "There is no guarantee in them, nor is that any way to fill the purse – quite the opposite. Love is but a fleeting moment. Whether it is to please your father or to please yourself: Advocate? Author? Sure. You will be a success in whatever it is you choose."

"And you, Alfred, why do you not find contentment in your life as a ship merchant?"

"My father planned my occupation long before I was born; I was trained up in it and it suits me. I must continue to make a success of it, so that one day, if I have a son, he too will have an occupation. It is all I know. Just as the Stevensons will make a success of this lighthouse. It's in your blood." Alfred thought for a minute then continued. "But you also need grounding. Truly, a wife would give you that."

"Do you know this?" Louis stood up tall as he was intrigued to know more about this man who shared such compelling conversation and he pressed him for more answers.

"I do, but to my misfortune she - Fiona - is no longer in this world. Take my advice, when you find a suitable wife, in the beginning your heart will spin without control. But a good match means that when the flutters disappear, you will look after one another well."

"Are you ready to find another?" enquired Louis.

"I am old now, but if the Lord so desires it to be."

Louis jumped excitedly. "Ah, you see! Why the Lord? If you so desire it, then surely it is up to you to seek after her! Does not the Lord Himself say, 'Seek and *ye* shall find'?"

"Yes," Alfred responded calmly, "but marriage is a union brought together by God. I do not desire to live only for myself, nor do I have much opportunity to meet a respectable woman."

"So, you will wait perhaps many years for a thin wafer of chance for that to happen?"

"God will create an opportunity. Take the lighthouse, Louis. It is a beacon guiding the way for a man and his ship for the reason of a safe passage, correct?"

"Indeed," Louis said suspiciously, as if he knew he was being led into a trap.

"God works in the same way. He is the light unto our path. If you follow it, you cannot go wrong."

"Well, Alfred, you have explained it well. I cannot find an argument in your analogy. I suppose, then, I shall live my life guided by an invisible God and hope for the best."

"Life is short," Alfred commented in a firm tone. He set the empty topped hourglass on the table with a thud. "Don't let yourself run out of sand."

.oOo.

The lighthouse craftsmen and their families were all sitting close together with their heads bowed inside a small onsite makeshift chapel, held in one of the cottages. Some of them were kneeling in prayer, prostrate on the floor. The room was quiet apart from the constant squawking of overhead seagulls outside in the search for their own daily bread. Then, the silence in the room broke with the words from Alan, who led the congregation.

"Let us end the service with our guided prayer," he said. He looked down at the table-come-altar at a sheet of paper from which he read the prayer which was written by Robert Stevenson earlier in the century and selected as the official prayer by the Northern Lighthouse Board.

"Our enemies we beseech thee to forgive and bless. Bless us, even us also, O our Father! Give us thy grace in every season of trial; give us thy protection in every hour of danger. Prepare us for the dispensations of thy Providence; prepare us for the discharge of duty; prepare us for the inheritance of the just. And may grace and mercy, and peace from the Father, the Son, and the Holy Ghost, be with us forever. Amen."

Everyone echoed, "Amen."

Alan lifted his head, as did his congregation. "Please open your new hymnals to number 37, *Hail the day that sees Him rise,*" and he led the tune. All the men, women and children in the cottage stood to try and sing along as best they knew how.

.oOo.

Cait and Janet spent the morning digging and collecting peat from up in the boggy fields, muddying their boots and trimmed edges of their long dresses. The bare bog showed the evidence of the many collections of the past from the few islanders, with its shallow pit quarried well through. Some had made stacks of bricks and left them aside the edges of the field to let partially dry before retrieving them on another day. This lightened the weight of them due to the amount of water they held. However, it was to Cait's insistence the bricks were taken home on the same day to prevent anyone from stealing the fruits of their back breaking labour.

The women cut the bricks in the soil with broad-edged trowel-like shovels that had a short stick attached and a wide handle. They lifted each brick from the wet field and as they had no basket in which to put them, they bundled them together in a long stretch of cloth. This was lifted on to their backs which then crossed around their waists twice before being tied in the front.

"This much ought to keep us going through winter, I reckon," Cait told Janet with confidence.

"Aye, if we're canny," replied Janet. "Let's git this lot dried oot."

Together, under a grey sky, the women walked the lengthy path home with the cool, clammy peat bricks, that dripped down the backs of their skirts along the way. Janet huffed out of breath as she attempted to compete with Cait's steady, faster pace.

"Ah cannae keep up wi' ye, Cait. Ye'r far mair capable than ah," shouted Janet as she lagged behind by several metres.

Cait continued walking, partly ignoring the whines and partly distracted by her own thoughts and planning.

"Cait!" shouted Janet.

"Eh? What is it?" Cait called back and looked at her with an agitated glare which should have told Janet that she was tired of her growing more and more into a complaining, annoying hag.

"Dae ye no listen tae me anymore? Ah cannae keep up. A'm tae auld fur this!" she said with frustration and a gathering anger.

"You're not too auld, you just eat too much of the bread. It slows ye down."

"Aye, weel, ye 'n' the bairns dinnae tak near enough o' it. Better 'tis eaten by me then goes tae waste!"

"You make far too much of it just to please yourself, Janet. Don't worry; we spend every waking hour together like we're attached by the hip. You know your way back; you don't need to keep up with me. The sooner I get hame and take this load off my back, the ever more grateful I'll be. I reckon you will feel the same way."

Janet puffed away. She lifted her soiled, thick skirt layers through the tall island grasses so she wouldn't trip over it, though the back of her skirt dragged along, rubbing the mud further into the threads, staining her clothing. Her back ached against the already strained laces of her corset, which had no margin left to stretch.

Every breath inflated her bulging bosoms and tested the worth of the laces, until one foot became entangled in the tall grass and she tripped, plunging face first. She growled to herself. Weighed down by peat on her back, she struggled to sit up, angry at Cait for refusing to acknowledge her gloomy state of mind.

Cait had no time for that. She had to get back to the boys and give them their reading lessons. So, Cait ploughed onward, not looking back. Janet continued to complain from the growing distance between them. "Th' bairns ought tae be put tae work in th' peat, sae they should ... "

Approaching the cottages from the top of the hill, Cait saw Ewan and Cameron fishing from the rocks below. She shouted over to them. "Did you catch us something for our tea, boys?"

"Nay mum, nothing yet," Ewan called back. Cameron got excited to show off, "Ah caught this oot o' th' sea!" he giggled, proudly holding up a dripping clump of seagrass and waving it.

"Aye, well unless it's breathing and flapping about, I don't want it. Time to come in for your lessons."

When she reached the cottage, she bent over, untied the cloth sling and carefully released the peat bricks onto the ground, one by one. She stretched her arms out over her head to relieve the muscle cramps. So that they would dry in the sun, she spread the peat out evenly on top of a pair of spindles which sat just off the ground with stones underneath. Minutes later, Janet came toddling down the path, panting and tripping over herself from fatigue. Cait chose to pay no attention to her drama.

Ewan and Cameron sat on the rocks fishing with their twine dangling lifelessly beneath them. They stared into the water, mesmerized. The little lapping waves tweaked at the wet strings, carrying them, lifting and pulling them to the left with the gentle undercurrents.

"We ought tae gae hame noo," said a bored Ewan.

"Aye, but wha' fur oor tea?" Cameron conceded.

"Uncle Hamish wull gie us a mackerel."

Ewan stood to gather up his twine and wrap it neatly into the loop in a method that his father taught him. He started by holding one end in the palm of his hand then pulled it under his elbow, then back into his hand, down to his elbow and repeated it until it was fully gathered up.

Cameron watched Ewan do this and tried doing the same with his bit of twine, however with a little less finesse. Ewan stopped midway as he was distracted by the men pushing out the two fishing boats from the beach.

"There they go again," he said. "One day whin ah graw up, which wull be afore ye, ah wull be a man 'n' wull push th' boats oot 'n' gae fishing with th' men."

"Aye, ye might be a good fisherman by then," Cameron replied.

"Aye, a'm gang tae be so good th' fish wull be jumping at me tae tak them hame tae be salted!"

Cameron laughed at the silly image Ewan had stirred up in his head.

Hamish was on one of the boats with fellow wreckers and fishermen Munro and Morven. The youths falsely felt a sense of safety in their distance between them on the rocks and Hamish on the boat. Immature and so lacking greatly in self-control, they could not resist shouting insults to him, the man they despised for hurting their mother.

"Ah hope ye git lost at sea!" shouted Ewan.

"Aye!" joined Cameron.

"'N' n'er come back!" Ewan called out in a bold whim.

Hamish turned to face the boys, stiffened his closed fists and pinched his lips as if to warn them. They gasped, but as the boat was beginning to sail out, Cameron thought he was safe and hurled more unpleasantries to their uncle.

"The three-legged man is gang tae git ye! He'll come back; he'll dae it fur Mummy, he loves her!" cursed Cameron.

Even Ewan thought that slight was going too far and he nudged his brother with his twine-looped elbow to stop. The boys went quiet and Ewan saw that Cameron hadn't yet mastered looping his fishing twine, so he put his down to help his wee brother.

"Ye dinnae reckon we could git lucky th'morra 'n' actually catch something fur once, dae ye?" Ewan hoped.

"'N' give th' biggest one tae Mummy," Cameron said with satisfaction.

"Auntie Janet could eat th' biggest one!" Ewan giggled, and Cameron laughed out loud.

"She could eat a whole whale!" Cameron amusingly added.

Suddenly, Cameron's head was jolted backward. His blonde locks were grabbed from the back of his head.

"Ye filthy scoundrel! Ah wull shaw ye wha tae gie respect tae!" rumbled the familiar deep voice from behind.

The boys turned to see that Hamish was standing over them. He had jumped off the fishing boat and ran up the bank to give them the terrifying surprise.

They screamed. Ewan, fearing for his life and not knowing what to do, ran off, falling over as he looked back in horror to see Cameron being carried off over Hamish's shoulder towards the boat. Ewan ran toward his mum. She heard his cries from the distance.

"Mum! Mum! 'Tis Cameron! Hamish has got him 'n' he's gang tae kill him!"

Cait stood up from the peat pile in a sudden, gripping dismay. "Where is he? Ewan show me! Ewan!"

His fear locked him into a closed box against all possible practical thinking. He stood, staring at his mother who was by now frozen with perplexing anxiety which creased her otherwise soft alabaster face. The pair of them stared at each other in a petrified space in time, when all of a sudden Ewan broke free from the spell and cried, "Run!"

At this, Cait, too, was released from the clamp of fear, and ran as any fiercely protective mother would to the aid of her young. She sprinted as fast as she could towards Ewan, who was running toward the beach.

Pounding his little fists into Hamish's back, Cameron tried to get Hamish to release him. But with one easy swing Hamish mercilessly passed Cameron onto the awaiting boat to Morven, who took no care of the lad. Hamish climbed into the boat and as Morven held a squirming Cameron, Murdo adjusted the sails and Hamish took over from Morven. They were taking him out to sea.

Cait and Ewan heard Cameron's faint screaming from the boat but couldn't see him. Cait was frantic. She ran into the water whilst Ewan whimpered from the shore, pacing back and forth and feeling inadequate to help.

On board, Hamish gathered bits of fishing net and held it up as if to tie up Cameron's legs with it. Cameron screamed at him and Hamish slapped him in the face, knocking him fearfully silent.

Hamish whispered to Cameron, "Ah dinnae ken who yer mother's three-legged lover is, but a'm gonna shut ye up, just like ah did yer father."

Panicking, Cameron who was terrified beyond measure, sobbed. "Ah made him up, it's just a story. Ask Aunt Janet!"

Now hip deep in water, Cait grabbed the stern of the boat, latched on and tried to pull herself up. As her many layers of skirt were soaked through, the wet, weighted clothing kept pulling her back into the water.

Morven grabbed Hamish's attention. "Hamish, look, 'tis Cait!"

Cait had not heard what Hamish had said to Cameron, because she was occupied with losing the battle to climb into the boat.

Hamish turned to look at Morven, then Cait. He laughed perversely at her efforts. "Ye coming fishing today?"

She screamed at him. "Give me my son! Hamish, give me Cameron!"

But he continued to laugh at her. All at once, the cloudy skies opened up and a heavy shower of rain came down, battering everyone and dousing Cait over the dry top half of her. With this added hindrance, she could barely hold on to the edge of the boat.

Disgusted by his lack of empathy, she began to cry and swear at him. "You're off your head! Pure evil you are!"

Claiming no empathy for her, he aggrieved the woman he said he loved. "Just like a slag, a cheap prostitute, begging fur yer meal. What is it worth tae ye, Cait? Ye cannae stop wi' me, or you'll starve tae death, ye ken?"

"How dare you!" she spat back at him.

"So, wha' are ye gang tae dae, eh?" He knelt down to her. "Who is yer lover?" he demanded. "Tell me, or else th' boy goes in th' water."

"What? I don't know what you're on about." she replied. "I am going to take my son now and take him home, even if I have to starve to death, our deal is off. Do you understand?" Her voice grew into a low, authoritative rumble. "Give him to ME!"

"Ye coudnae git back tae shore noo tae save th' pair o' ye," he jeered.

His sarcasm only fed her desperate plea. "GIVE HIM TO ME!"

Hamish took Cameron and lifted him up. With one swoop, he tossed her little boy overboard like rubbish. She screamed hysterically. How could he do this – to his own nephew and his sister-in-law who still grieved for his brother and clearly painstakingly toiled to provide a suitable life for their sons.

In a flash, Cait instinctively plunged into the cold water after Cameron. Innerved with trepidation, Ewan watched from the shore while Janet arrived at the beach with the speed and agility of a sea mussel.

Cait felt around under the waves, arms lashing about blindly trying to touch him, to reach him. Her wet clothing slowed down her ability to move quickly under water. She came back to the surface and gasped for a quick breath before throwing herself back under the surface. Finally, within the rain-stirred sea, she bumped into Cameron. She grabbed his clothing and lifted his head out of the water. With difficulty, she dragged him along to the shore, and Janet waded in to meet them and to help them out.

Cameron gagged and coughed out for his breath whilst Cait cradled him, crying. Together, burdened to their heavy clothes, they shook uncontrollably with the cold.

Hamish led his crew out to sea whistling a fanciful tune. He didn't look back to the emotional mess he had created and harboured no sentiment as to what he had just done in the minutes prior.

.oOo.

As the sky cleared of its showers, the Consolation anchored in the remote cove at Iona. With his stick in hand, Alfred stepped from the ship, his boots splashing in the shallow water. The sun peaked out from the afternoon's passing haze and he was in a positive mood. As he walked across the marram grasses along the coast towards the wreckers' cottages, he took in his surroundings with an acute awareness. He listened to the finches sing from within dried teasels and spied the oyster catchers, who were spread out along the beach below pointing their bright, orange-speared bills over the shallows. He was both eager to see Cait so he might to test his heart and in turn, he had to know if there might be any feelings from Cait for him.

Alfred arrived at the hilltop by the cottages. He walked down the path to Cait's house, took a deep breath and knocked on her door. Janet opened it with a downturned face and her tone was dispirited.

"Mr Henderson. Ah wasnae expecting nae visitors today," she said.

"When would you ever expect visitors?" he asked, perplexed.

Janet looked around outside to see if anyone was watching. It was clear. "Come in. We mist nae let anyone see ye. Come, quickly."

Alfred took his hat off. "Why not? Janet, what's the matter with you?"

She pulled him inside by the arm with a sharp tug, which caused him to trip over his stick on his way in.

When Alfred caught his step and looked around, he was completely taken back by the atmosphere - the sad ambience within the thin walls of the house. It felt very drafty and cold with the rain. he noticed there was no fire alight in the fireplace and no wood or peat piled next to it. In fact, the house was dark, damp and bare.

Then a terrible thought came over him. "Tell me Janet, has Cait taken ill? Good Lord has something happened to her?" he beseeched.

Janet assured him. "'Tis nae Cait that causes oor distress."

From behind the curtain of the bedroom Cait walked in to greet him. Her long hair was unbrushed, roughly tied back and strands hung loosely out of place. She made an appearance of little effort and her face looked gaunt and fatigued. Infused with surprise, she pulled the strands out of her face and tucked them behind her ear. But she was too tired to question his visit or find the words to defend the state of the house. Instead, she greeted him with a concerning smile.

"I apologise you are to see me this way," she said.

"What has happened? What has happened here?" An immense sense of compassion came over him. All he wanted to do was to hold her, to keep her warm, to release her from her onus which had consumed her beauty and happiness. He longed to be her hero and to take charge of any of the problems that possessed her.

Cait sat down on the bench, and Alfred joined her. Janet disappeared into the boy's room.

"'Tis Hamish. He's been around to violate me, helping himself. He is the devil himself and he's fearsome," she declared, stammering her words and wrapping her arms around her body.

"Cait, if only I could help."

Cait stood up, nervously fiddling with her pinny ties. "He's hurt Cameron, as well. He nearly died." Cait began to cry. "If Hamish sees you here, he will come after you, too."

Alfred tried to sound gallant. "He won't hurt me."

"Don't be so irresponsible, Alfred. He's a monster. He's dangerous - he tried to kill my son!"

Alfred moved in to console Cait, wrapped his arms around her and held her to his chest. His nose nestled in her hair which to him smelled irresistible and he closed his eyes as she shed her tears.

"Shhh, it's alright, I will protect you. I'm here now." He said as he stroked her arm. "Why don't you have the fire going?"

Cait looked over to the corner of the room where the stove sat cold and empty. "We've been soaked with weeks of rain and have no more peat to burn."

"Where are the bairns?" asked Alfred.

Cait led Alfred into their bedroom. The boys were sleeping whilst Janet sat at Cameron's side. She dipped a cloth into a bucket of water and squeezed the excess out before laying it on Cameron's head. His face was red with fever and he was covered in a dirty wool throw. Cait and Alfred stepped back out.

He paused a moment to think. "The poor lad."

"'Tis been nearly a fortnight and he's still burning with the fever," she trembled.

"What have you got to feed him?" Alfred asked.

"Boiled nettle is all we have the now," Cait said, knowing it was not sufficient.

"Cait, he requires a doctor's help, and fast. I can get him out of here and take him back with me. He hasn't got a chance if he stays here. You should come, too; all of you," Alfred insisted.

This was the chance Cait was praying for, and she was ready to accept his offer.

Eager to help, Alfred persisted. "My ship is in the cove with my men; the housemaid will call for the doctor to visit him tonight, whatever time we arrive."

Cait was alarmed. "But what do you know, you're a lighthouse worker! Where is this doctor, men, a housemaid – and what ship? Who are you, Alfred?"

Alfred took a breath. Cait had not known that he was a ship merchant, a successful and prosperous trader in rum and sugar and provided the safe passage across the North Atlantic for thousands of people. He realised that by telling her the truth about himself now, he was risking every chance he had with her. But without it, he would not be able to see her again. He had no choice but to come clean.

"My honesty with you has failed me. I'm not a lighthouse worker, I'm a ship merchant. Before that, I worked on the Isle of Man on a steam packet. That's where my leg was injured, in the engine room. There was a fire and I tried to put it out. My leg was burned badly, and well, it doesn't bend as it should. That is the truth."

Cait touched the row of buttons on his coat, and for a moment she felt compassion. She ran her thumb over the space where one was missing.

"I don't understand. Why would you be so untruthful to me?" she asked.

"Because - we don't have time for this, Cait."

"Och, but we do! You must explain! Time has escaped us and my thoughts have been only for you and to survive! And what for? You are only a deceitful man," she confessed.

Taking Cait by the arms, he pleaded with her. "Do you trust me, Cait?"

"I have lost all reason to!"

"You must! I see that you are afraid and uncertain, but you have no other choice, and you must listen to me."

"Must I!" She pulled her arms away from him and folded them in defence.

Alfred looked at Cait in surprise at her reaction. He, too, had been thinking only of her. He composed himself quickly so that he could give her some assurance. "This is my story, Cait. I have two ships, no, I *had* two ships, both left by my father for me to manage. One of them was wrecked on the black skerry last year, not far from here, the place where they are building the lighthouse. Along with the ship, I lost my crew and a cargo full of rum and spices."

Cait looked around in disbelief and her anger escalated. She compared him with Hamish and now he was just another man wanting a woman at his disposal. She felt sick and so, in a bitter retraction she pursed her lips and pushed him away.

"So, that's why you came here, to find your rum? You lied to me to get something! You are no better than Hamish! He, too, uses me, just as you did."

She reached for the bottle of rum which she'd hid under the chair that he had fixed. "Here!" she said. "Take it back with you!"

"Now, wait a minute, that isn't fair. You need to understand. My ship, and everything on her, was a great loss to me."

She interrupted him. "You dare tell me about loss? Who are you to do so when I have lost my family, my home and my husband? Is this not greater than some – some rum?"

Alfred continued to try to persuade Cait. "I did come here to find what was mine! And I found it, didn't I? But, still, I did nothing. I didn't take it away from you. I may have found my cargo here, but I didn't know I would find *you!*"

She shouted in return. "Well, I am not cargo! I, for one, am not yours!"

Cait turned her back, exasperated. The silence set in and the mood darkened.

"I think you should just go. I've been made a complete fool of," she concluded.

"A fool? You're anything but. Don't you see, Cait? You are the real treasure here, the reason I have come back. Trust me – trust me now. I must take Cameron. I know a good doctor, the best in Greenock. If I take him now – right now, he can see to him as early as the morning. You neYver have to speak to me again if you so wish. But how else is he going to have a chance?"

Knowing that Alfred was right, she turned to him and in finding no other excuse to dismiss him, she looked into his eyes.

Take him, Alfred. Take him and look after him, make him well. if you can bear it, do this one thing for me. But I I will not be going with you", Cait stammered.

Alfred reached out to touch her face softly with the back of his hand, but she turned her cheek away. His heart was full of conviction. In order to quench the greatest assurance a woman needs and to calm her desperate fear of losing a child, he whispered assuredly, "I will look after him, I promise."

Wrapped as snug as he could be within the worn-out blanket, Janet passed Cameron to Alfred. It was then in the light that he noticed the many holes which weakened the old blanket. He placed no judgment on the two women for their lack of necessities, for they had none.

As he went, Alfred lifted Cameron onto his shoulder and took his stick into the other hand. He could feel the heat of the fever against his neck as in the cold air the steam was rising off the sick boy. Cait leaned in to kiss her son and she and Alfred paused to look at each other. There was a longing stillness between them, and for Cait, a desire to trust Alfred, but she pushed them onward. Alfred then hurried up the hill bound for his small ship in the cove.

Cait did not forget the promise she had made to herself to leave, but her pride had now foiled her opportunity to escape. She tried to keep a tight grip of it as their distance grew further and she began to lose sight of them. The little bundle Alfred was carrying waned smaller and smaller before disappearing altogether over the hill. *'He will have to come back*, she thought. *He has my son.'*

CHAPTER 8

Talk not of love, it gives me pain,
For love has been my foe;
He bound me in an iron chain,
And plung'd me deep in woe.

But friendship's pure and lasting joys,
My heart was form'd to prove;
There, welcome win and wear the prize,
But never talk of love.

Your friendship much can make me blest,
O why that bliss destroy?
Why urge the only, one request
You know I will deny?

Your thought, if Love must harbour there,
Conceal it in that thought;
Nor cause me from my bosom tear
The very friend I sought.

Robert Burns
Love In the Guise of Friendship

A large Victorian building, used as a workshop for the production of the lighthouse lamps, was located at Baxter's Place on Leith Walk in Edinburgh. Inside the busy workshop, a room swarming with a team of men pressed and fitted the lenses into housings for the lighthouse. A steel structure was fabricated into what would become lantern panels which would rest above the tower's gallery. The dome cupola was then made to fit on top of the panels. This was a process in which the dome was beaten and welded for the glass panels to fit into perfectly.

It may have been freezing outside, but the large room was hot and full of activity. The ovens smouldered with fire for melting and enormous, long troughs of water for cooling the glass and metal. Billowing puffs of steam and the deafening hammering of shaping steel filled the room and escaped out to the open doors at Greenside Lane. This was no longer the space it originally started out to be, which was for manufacturing simple fittings for lighthouses for the Northern Lighthouse Board.

The Stevenson family reputation had grown since the early 1800's when Louis's grandfather, Robert, began to innovate light designs, including his own reflectors, rotation and shuttering systems. The acknowledgement he received for this kept him immersed in a bustling business. Robert took on numerous engineering projects which included the construction of roads, bridges, harbours, canals, railways and aids for river navigation. In addition, the movable jib and balance crane, which were necessary for lighthouse construction and used during the

Dubh Artach building project, were also Robert's invention .

.oOo.

Cameron was in bed where a doctor attended to him. He pressed the skin on the boy's arm for changes in colour or spots, checked his temperature and listened closely to his breathing. On the opposite side of the bed, Alfred sat, holding Cameron's hand.

Ede brought in a tray of tea and set it at the bedside table next to Alfred. The curtains were drawn closed and although the room was kept warm with a fire, the darkened space gave it a sombre feeling.

After several minutes of observing Cameron, the doctor finally spoke. "He still has the fever, though it is not as high. I'll return in a couple of days. He'll need to continue to rest." He took his bag and turned to leave.

"Thank you doctor," said Alfred. "Ede will see you out." He didn't quite know what to talk about with the young boy, as he had not had experience with children before. So, Alfred opened an old book of his own and began to tell him about it.

"This book is called *Tom Brown's School Days,*" he said. "It was published in 1857. My father gave it to me when I was a lad to try to encourage me to read more."

"'N' did ye?" mumbled Cameron.

Alfred shook his head. "Rugby was never my interest."

"Rugby?" Cameron asked, curiously. "What's tha?"

Alfred realised that he had probably not hear of many social sports. Cameron was not only limited by his young age, but that he knew nothing of the world outside his secluded cove.

"Don't you play games of sport?" enquired Alfred. Cameron smiled, "Aye, we hae games we play lik' tossing big stones, but that's more fur th' men. We play agame wi' twine on oor fingers called Cat's Cradle; Mummy taught us that. 'N' we play pirates. Ah lik' tae play soldiers, bit Ewan doesn't wantae, so we dinnae play it much."

"I mean, games with a group of children."

"Na?"

"Well, rugby is a ball game, played between two teams, with twenty people on each side," said Alfred.

Cameron's eyes lit up. "Twenty? That's a lot!"

Alfred explained, "It's even more than twenty, because altogether twenty and twenty makes forty men playing together."

"Forty! We dinnae have forty, nae even counting all th' women." Cameron looked better already, at least for a few minutes as he listened to Alfred talk about all the men who ran on a field fighting after a leather ball in a barbarous attempt to steal it away from the one player who had possession of it, whilst everyone collided into each other into a heap.

Alfred attempted to draw out a comparison of rugby to soldiers. "Imagine there is a war of soldiers. There are forty soldiers in your army and forty in the enemy camp. But usually, one group outnumbers the other."

"How is that fair?" asked Cameron.

"It's not, but when there is a war, both sides gather up as many men as they can to fight against the other army. Anyway, the ball is the one thing everyone in rugby wants, right?"

"Ah guess sae," answered Cameron.

"Yes, it is. Whereas in war, the one thing everyone

wants is possession of a country."

"Who wid want something as big as tha'? 'Tis enough fur Mummy just tae wash th' claes 'n' look after me 'n' Ewan. A whole land seems a lot tae look after," Cameron said, innocently.

Alfred giggled to himself. "Aye, you're learning a lot, son. It's all about man's egoistic desire. In other words, they get greedy, then they send other men out to fight for them, as their want is bigger than their ability to fight for themselves."

"Ah dinnae ken ah lik' rugby," Cameron said decidedly.

"I was talking about war," replied Alfred.

"Wull ye read th' book tae me noo?" Cameron asked.

Alfred then began to read and noticed how much he enjoyed doing so. The first few minutes were rather enough for Cameron as he yawned before the end of the first paragraph. Alfred continued to read on and as quickly as Cameron fell asleep, Alfred escaped into the pages which told about a young boy at an English public school. The story revealed the difficulty he faced during his early attendance, as he was the subject of bullying and yet also of friendship. So thrilled was Alfred at the story he never noticed Cameron had long drifted off into a deep slumber.

When he had finished reading, he looked up at the sleeping child with the feverish rosy cheeks who seemed to be lost in the big bed. Alfred watched him as he thought about the life that Cameron had just come from and how much more he could benefit from staying in Greenock. Alfred straightened out the duvet and tucked the side of it under the mattress. Then he leaned over and gave Cameron a kiss on the forehead before blowing out flame of the bedside lamp.

.oOo.

It was early evening and a letter which had been delivered that morning waited all day on the hall table for Alfred. He noticed it as he came in through the front door. It was addressed from *RL Stevenson, 17 Heriot Row, Edinburgh.* Without haste, he took it to his desk in the next room. Slipping an intricately carved whale bone knife into a corner of the envelope, in one swift shave he sliced it open.

"To Alfred my dear friend and muse,
I spent some time pondering over our discussion we had when we were together at Erraid. Those shifting sands of time have given me fond remembrance of my mother's own father, once a minister in Colinton. He has not been alive for many years, yet with fondness I recall his teachings, not of his services but in the space of our company together, of faith and perseverance.

My father's father, Robert, I did not personally know as he died only months before my birth. Although, I have grown up with all his jewels of knowledge from my family through his journals and I have myself witnessed the craft of his engineering feats. With Dubh Artach my greatest hope is that my father and I are doing my grandfather a just service with what is being accomplished there.

All the lessons of my youth have grown into the lighthouses of the world in which I live and from where I draw comfort. They are the evidence that hope will shine brightest where it is darkest, when I may be of most need; in this I am grateful, and to you for gifting this revelation to me.

Yours sincerely,
RL Stevenson

.oOo.

Outside Cait's cottage, she and Janet busied themselves with the sun dependent chore of hanging up laundry for drying. Seeing as this time of year the weather up and down Scotland's west coast could change within each hour from rain to sleet to sun then return to rain again, the linens were often resoaked before they dried. Usually, clothing was taken indoors to be hung by the fire to dry and the same heat was used for bread baking, cooking porridge and heating water. Whatever hung by the fire absorbed all of its odours - peat, wood and fish.

"Next time the men trade at Oban, we ought to exchange our share of loot for some reading books," started Cait.

"Who's gonnae read? Ye'r wasting yer time, hen. There's nae need fur tha 'ere. The only advancing required 'ere are th' skills o' th' sea 'n' land," Janet said, disapprovingly.

Cait disagreed. "The bairns should learn some proper things; it's necessary, should they ever leave here."

"Leave Iona!" laughed Janet. "No likely! 'N' what dae ye consider tae be proper?"

"Aye, reading and writing," Cait defended. "Sorry, hen, I cannae see that happening. It's survival tae feed ourselves oot 'ere. But if th' men agree, which they wilnae, who is going tae teach them?"

"I am capable," Cait said, and Janet laughed again.

"Aye, I am!" defended Cait. "I have taught them the alphabet already. They will read, ye will see." Cait pointed at Janet. "Then I will teach ye."

Janet laughed out loud.

"Aye, I will!" Cait giggled. "You will be my best student." Just then, Hamish showed up looking very angry and walked straight up to Cait. He stuck out his hand, showing her the brass button.

"Ye been stealing?" he demanded.

"Whatever do ye mean?" she asked, refusing to look at him.

Hamish shoved the button in her face."This! After th' loot sacks went tae th' traders, ah found this in yer hoose."

Cait's eyes met the button but then she continued her work, ignoring him.

"Ah would be certain one o' yer precious wee bairns stole it," he said.

"Nae, they wouldn't," Cait defended them.

Janet went to have a look in his hand.

"That's mines. Did ye tak' it fae this hoose, Hamish? Pity on ye!" Janet scolded.

"You'd better pray ye'r nae lying. Ah dinnae tak' tae weel tae traders," he said.

Unafraid of Hamish, Janet snapped back. "Ah dunnae tak' tae weel tae thieves. Noo gimme mah button 'n' shove off!"

She ripped the button from Hamish's hand and gave him a hard stare. He mumbled under his breath. "Feisty ole woman, eh?" He kicked the ground, looked at Cait and smiled, displaying his few remaining, black teeth.

Cait looked at him for that moment and showed her distaste. "Don't bother yourself, Hamish. After what you did to Cameron, you'd be smart not to show your face to me ever again."

"You'll regret ye said tha', pretty woman."

"I won't."

"Gie it a day or two, when ye'r starving. You'll be begging a' mah door." He walked off.

Cait swallowed hard. She had depended on him to feed her family since William had died. His disingenuous act of mercy had a hefty price for her to pay, to which she could see no end.

Janet passed the button to Cait and said, "It's off Mr Henderson's coat. Wee Cameron had it." Janet sighed. "It gies me such pleasure watching him squirm fur a change." Janet pushed the clothesline up with a stick, planted the end of it into the dirt and the laundry caught the wind. "'N' dinnae ye let him git tae ye," she added. "We've git enough food tae last a wee while."

Cait looked up at Janet. "And then what?"

.oOo.

Cameron sat at the dining table at Alfred's house, where he drank tea from a china cup and clumsily spread strawberry jam across the top of the bread and his fingers. As he licked it off his skin, his cheeks also became pink with the sticky confiture. His diminutive, little legs dangled from the chair under the table as they swung back and forth carefree over the floor. Ede sat at the end of the table, showing him how to spread the jam evenly and smoothly over the bread using a knife, something Cameron had never held before.

Ede attended to him by spending time teaching him other basic table manners. "Not like that, Cameron. Don't grab the knife, hold it just like I do. Now watch me do it again," she instructed.

He watched as Ede exaggerated the steps to make the point clear. She took the knife elegantly into her right hand, laid it perfectly horizontal on its side over the bread and glided it all the way across, spreading the jam evenly.

"Don't hold it upright like this," she said, as she held the knife in her fist pointing the tip to the ceiling. "You will be seen as someone not having good table manners."

"What if na one is looking?" Cameron asked.

"Oh, they will be, just when you think they aren't!"

He copied as she did, although still managing to spread the jam over his thumb and couldn't resist licking it off.

"Better, much better that time, but don't lick your hand at the table. Instead, wipe it with your serviette; that's what it's there for."

"Serviette?" he asked.

"Your table napkin, dear boy."

He looked at her as if she were speaking another language.

"The linen on your lap. The napkin?"

"Ye said it's called a serviette."

Ede's patience was beginning to waver with the challenging boy.

Cameron continued. "If ah clean if off, then ah will be wasting it. A'm no allowed tae waste. Mummy says we cannae afford tae waste 'n' it's no polite."

"Yes, well, for the sake of good table behaviour and when you're in the presence of others, you can wipe your hands," she insisted.

"If a'm no in th' presence o' others, can ah lick it?"

Ede sighed as she gave in, leaning her chin into her palm. "Alright then."

Alfred came into the dining room to inspect Cameron's newly fitted clothes.

"I see you're dressed in your new clothing. Stand up for me, son and let me see how it fits," he said pleasingly.

Cameron scooted off the chair, stood prostrate facing Alfred, and wiped his hands on his new trousers.

"Now, don't do that, you'll get your new trousers all dirty!" Ede scolded.

She poured some water from the jug and onto a towel, ran to Cameron to wipe his clothing and hands while he contentiously grumbled under his breath. Alfred tugged at the little sleeves and shoulders, squaring the fit. Ede wiped the jam off Cameron's face while he squirmed.

"Now, that's better," Ede commented, inspecting him up and down.

"Right, son. It's a good fit. You look like a proper sailor. Now, do you remember what I told you about the rigging?" Alfred asked, helping him into his new coat.

"Stay clear," he answered.

"That's right. And why is that?"

"Ah might git all tangled up in th' rope 'n' hang upside doon."

Ede gasped, "Alfred! You'll put the fear of God in him! Now you two boys go and mind yourselves!"

"A little fear will keep him out of mischief. Come now, son, let's go." Alfred turned to face Ede. "Fare you well."

"Goodbye, Ede," waved Cameron as Alfred led him out by the hand. In a flash move, Cameron ran back to the table, took the last wee bit of his sticky, jam spattered bread and ran back to Alfred with it. He looked at Ede who inhaled in dismay and stared frightfully down her nose at him.

Cameron grabbed Alfred's hand for protection and together they walked out. Cameron looked back at Ede, chewing on the bread and licking his fingers.

In the cooling, blowing wind and masses of seagulls catching the current overhead, Alfred walked Cameron along the Greenock docks. He nodded a "Good morning," to all the familiar men he had known for years. They tended to their fishing boats and cargo ships tied up at the docks. The pair arrived at Aemelius and past the end of the queue where the last few passengers were boarding via a gangplank and railing. Cameron was taken back by the immense size of the ship, gazing up to the top of her masts.

"This is giant!" he exclaimed.

"Giant?" answered Alfred. "Just wait until you see the ships in Liverpool. They're almost twice the size. Enormous!"

"Giganticnormous?"

Alfred laughed. "Yes, gigantic...normous."

Tosh waved from the deck to greet them and noticed Cameron kitted out, nodding in approval. "Well, now, this is quite a change! Don't you look the part, young man, " Tosh remarked.

"I thought the sea air could do him some good and keep him busy learning how to sail by watching the men," said Alfred.

"There's a lot to learn about sailing, young Cameron. So, it's best you stay out of the way. This is a big ship with plenty of danger."

"Aye aye, Captain MacIntosh," Cameron replied as if obeying orders.

A young sailor waved and nodded to Tosh, who then turned to Alfred. "It appears the passengers have all boarded, so let's set sail."

Tosh commanded John, "Gallagher, ready to set the sails."

John shouted the order. "Men, set the sails! Set sails!" The steam engine started up with a roar and black clouds of smoke puffed out of the pipe. The crew rushed around the deck. Some scrambled up the masts to unleash the sails whilst three other men untied the mooring ropes and pushed the hull out at the bow. With one leg they straddled the dock and the ship until the final moment before their diminishing balance determined when they were to jump aboard.

Cameron turned to Alfred. "Ah wish Ewan was 'ere tae see this."

Alfred looked down at him and put his hand on his shoulder. "I know, son, I know. Today it's just me and you."

.oOo.

Cameron was below deck seated with the passengers and watched on as two of the children played a game with cards.

Alfred went down below and swarmed around the crowds of people looking to find him. He spotted his little head, rushed over to him and grabbed his shoulder.

"Cameron, come quickly! I want you to see this!"

Alfred scooped him up and carried him over the passengers and scrambled up the stairs to the deck to watch as they sailed into the mouth of the Mersey River. It had started to snow, and Cameron stuck out his hand to catch the snowflakes as they fell. Alfred looked at each one as they melted into his warm palm.

Not being able to see very far in front of them, the minutes passed as Cameron stood next to Alfred, who was fixed upon the white mottled horizon, deep in thought. He had the ship and a house, but still he felt that something was missing. He could give the little boy everything he needed, yet he wondered how long it would be until he as well disappeared. Still, Alfred was curious as to why he even cared so much or how, in the small space of his own head, it was possible to question everything in his life. All his quiet thoughts allowed a gutter of negativity to run fluidly out of control.

With a shiver in his teeth and his eyes wide open, Cameron snapped Alfred out of his trance, yanking on his coat. "Mr Henderson? Mr Henderson, don't ye think th' snowflakes look like little stars? They twinkle when they melt."

Cameron lifted his hand up to show Alfred the wet drops.

"I do think they look like little stars. And they fade quickly like that light over there," Alfred pointed to a lighthouse ahead as they neared Liverpool.

"Whit's that?" Cameron asked.

"That, son, is the New Brighton Lighthouse. Watch it closely, it has a light pattern all its own," Alfred explained.

Cameron stared at the tower. It flashed a white light.

"Did you see that? There will be another flash, then a red one.

"Ah saw that," said Cameron, gazing and waiting for the next white light. Then it happened. "Ah – ha! There it is!" he giggled.

The next few minutes were occupied with a game of watching the lights flash until Cameron began to ask questions.

"But how come is that there, in th' water?" he asked. Alfred told Cameron the story of the Lady Albatross and how it had crashed into the rocks and how everyone who was on the ship was lost at sea. There were fathers, mothers, brothers and sisters on board. He also explained how the lighthouses all around Great Britain were of great importance.

"The men inside the lighthouses keep the fire lit in the lamp to make sure the ships out at sea are safe, even though they may never see them pass," Alfred explained.

"Just lik' ye, Mr Henderson," added Cameron.

"What do you mean 'like me'?"

"Aye, well, yer as weel lik' a lighthouse keeper because ye keep everything bright."

Alfred didn't quite understand how a child could see that. "I do?" he asked. "How is that so?"

Cameron explained. "Ah think that ye and Mummy are always shining bright on th' ootside while ye hurt on th' inside. 'Tis yer job."

Alfred was stumped. "You are very observant, young man."

"Noo ah ken what a lighthouse is. It's where th' gulls gae wi' th' poems; Mummy told me all aboot it," remembered Cameron. Then he sang a song:

Ah want ma light tae shine, oh shine like th' sun
But all ah have tae gie is a verse tha' lights when sung;
How do ah send th' poems tae th' lighthouse - och me!
A'd roll them up fur th' gull tae ferry oot tae sea.

Alfred' eyes glazed over as he grasped how minor his troubles were compared to many of the people around him.

They sailed into Liverpool Port. The snow changed to a drizzle and at the sight of the busy harbour, Cameron was for once speechless. It was full of large steamers and tall sailing ships mysteriously coming from and going to God knows where, all built for navigating the world's oceans. The sounds of thousands of people bustling about brought tremendous excitement, as the smoke hovered in the air over the city staining the sky with dark blotches of grimy greys and browns.

"What do you think?" asked Alfred.

"They're very big, 'n' thare ur sae many o' them!"

Alfred looked at Cameron affectionately as the boy stared into the port, then he pulled the wee lad close to him and laid his hand on his shoulder.

.oOo.

Tied to the docks at Liverpool, Aemelius rocked slowly and quietly in the pink and blue sky as the sun was slipping off over the horizon. All of the passengers had long disembarked to board larger ships which would soon be en route to exotic continents like North America, New Zealand or Australia.

The ship was secured, the ropes tidied, the sails had been rolled up and tied onto the masts. The crew had trickled away to the local pubs for the end of day pleasures of drink and women, but Alfred was left behind to search for a missing Cameron. He frantically ran around the ship becoming more worried that he may have left with the passengers.

"Cameron!" he called aloud as he searched down below deck, then again, but louder, "Cameron!" as he searched the closets and bunks to no avail. He searched the deck, then to the bow where Alfred stood and rubbed the back of his neck, worried as to where the lad could have gone. Then he heard a faint whistle. The tune was unknown to him and carried the sweet, soft tone of the high notes of a child.

Alfred followed the tune to a locker hatch at the bow and tapped on it, to which the whistling ceased and then a faint call peeped out from below. "Aye?" Alfred knelt down and opened the hatch of the rope locker, where three feet down in the centre of a pile of neatly wound rope sat Cameron quietly playing with Tosh's brass quadrant.

Breathless, Alfred collected his nerve and asked him sternly, "Cameron, what are you doing down there? I've been looking all over for you."

Alfred's authoritative approach failed to rouse Cameron. Instead, with the lantern light now pouring into the rope locker, the boy looked up at Alfred with his big blue eyes gleaming. Alfred softened to him. The boy perhaps lacked manners and discipline but craved discovery, which Alfred understood.

"A've been 'ere - where it's warm. A'm gang tae be a sea captain one day, just lik' Captain MacIntosh."

"Well, that would be fine, but you mustn't make me worry."

"Because ah could play wi' all his toys," he added.

"To him, they are more than toys. They are important instruments of navigation."

Cameron looked up at Alfred, confused. "Eh?"

"They help him sail from place to place. Without them, he would get lost. A bit like you."

"But a'm nae lost. A'm right here." Alfred smiled at Cameron's innocence. "How can you see down there in the dark?"

"Th' light comes through the cracks, just lik' in th' play hull at hame, where ah kin hide awa' from Hamish."

"Don't let the sailors or Tosh hear you whistle on their ship."

"How come nae?"

"They're superstitious and believe it will bring bad luck."

"They're what?"

"Superstitious. It means they believe in a lot of things they shouldn't do – that if they do certain things then bad things will happen. One of those things is whistling. Another is setting sail on a Friday, especially not a Friday the 13th of any month – and definitely no bananas on board!"

"What's bananas?"

"It's a type of food. But tattoos are good luck."

Cameron's eyes popped wide open. "Och, th' drawings on th' sailors!"

Alfred nodded. "That's right."

"Ah saw some o' th' sailors with tattoos on their arms - a swallow, anchor, star 'n' a big ship. Where are yer tattoos, Mr Henderson?"

"I don't have any. I'm not so superstitious. Come, son. I want you to meet some friends of mine. We've been invited for supper, and you can put your new table manners into practice. Pass me the quadrant first."

Cameron passed Alfred the instrument, then he took Cameron by his small hands and pulled him up out of the locker.

"Wait, Mr Henderson," he said, having a jolt of revelation.

"What is it now, Cameron?"

"Ewan whistles a' th' time. If it brings ill luck, then that's how come he ne'er catches any fish!"

"That is quite possibly so," Alfred said, considering his perspective. Or maybe he's just a bad whistler."

.oOo.

Inside John Gallagher's small house, a short walk from the port, his wife Anne and their four children were all conversing in the kitchen. After a knock on the door, John opened it to Alfred and Cameron, speaking in a jovial Irish accent.

"Welcome! Come in, Alfred. Do you remember my Anne? Anne this is Cameron, the little lad I told you about."

Alfred took his hat off and nodded to Anne. She smiled and turned to Cameron.

"Well, well, just look at how handsome you are, Cameron. Come in and meet our own youngsters." She turned to her children and listed each of them as if recalling the varieties of flowers in her garden. "This is Joseph, he's ten, Kerry, she's nine, Kristen, she's eight, and Aiofe, just turned seven last week."

Cameron turned to John. "Yer th' sailor on th' ship?"

"I am, indeed, young man, and this is my family."

"Are ye fearful o' ship wrecking?" he asked.

There was a pause as John looked at Alfred then back to Cameron. "Not if we all know what we're doing."

"Why dae ye talk funny?"

John smiled at Anne and then to Alfred, who decided to stop Cameron before he embarrassed them further. "Cameron, don't ask so many questions!"

John began to dance around. "Oh, like this, you mean! That's because I'm a jolly leprechaun from Ireland! This is how we leprechauns talk and jig!" Then John entertained Cameron and his children by telling a limerick.

"There was an old man with a beard,
who said, 'It is just as I feared!
Two owls and a hen,
four larks and a wren,
have all built their nests in my beard!'"

All the children laughed out loud. "Tell me anither!" shouted Cameron.

"That's enough, Cameron," insisted Alfred.

Anne turned to Joseph, "Joe, why don't you show Cameron here how to play your new game?"

"Yes, ma." Joseph took Cameron by the hand and led him outside. The other children followed behind, skipping outside to the street, lit by a gas lamp.

"Mind your mother when she calls you in for supper!" shouted John, closing the door behind them.

The girls shouted back, "Yes, Papa."

"I'm sorry for all of his questions," said Alfred.

"Ah, it's no bother, that's what children do. The little lad, he's curious and learning about the world."

As Anne stirred the pot, she leaned back to the men. "John tells me he's from the Isle of Iona. What is his family like? What do they do on Iona?"

"Oh, well, his mother comes from a weaving family on Skye, and his father is dead."

"Are they farmers then?" John asked, as he placed a jug of beer on the table.

"Not sure there's anything else to do up there except farming and fishing," Anne said. "Only ship wreckers were thought to live there. Or monks," she added, laughing at the improbability of either, as monks hadn't lived there for centuries.

Alfred's face turned to stone, too ashamed to answer, as he stared at her and then John. The answer was obvious. The room turned silent as they both looked blankly at Alfred, and John nervously tapped the tip of his fingernail on the table in hope someone would talk.

John couldn't take it any longer and decided to interrupt the tedium. "Oh, Christ please tell me they're monks," he pleaded.

"There is a community of poor ... it's small," Alfred tried to soften the blow. "But Cait, his mum – she's different. Very different. She's not like them."

"Alright, say no more Alfred, I accept that," Anne interrupted.

John turned to Anne curiously. "You do?"

"I'm sure it wasn't her choice. Women don't often have any choice. I didn't."

"Didn't you? With me?" he gasped.

She nudged John. "With us, of course I did. But I am saying, don't judge other people." Again, she nudged him to break him from his shock.

John began to trip over his words. "I wouldn't - I'm not, God forgive me." He dropped his head in shameful respite and made the sign of the cross over his chest.

.oOo.

Early the following morning, Aemelius was under sail and on her way back to Greenock with a good cargo of hops. Railway lines were not to extend to the Highlands for another two decades, so the delivery of goods was often loaded and mixed up with passengers, to avoid ships returning empty.

The sea winds turned gusty by mid-morning and by noon they were strong enough to fill the sails all the way to Greenock with much of it weather side and tacking, or going from one tack to the other, passing head to the wind. This caused the ship to roll deeply into the swelling waves.

Above deck was a dangerous place for a small child. So, when the decks began to take on water, Alfred took Cameron down below and made him lie down in a bunk.

He comforted Cameron while he cried, "A'm afraid, Mr Henderson."

"Shall I tell you a story?"

"Aye."

"Please," reminded Alfred.

"Please?"

The ship rolled hard as the starboard side dipped, then lifted high again as the port side was submerged.

Cameron screamed, "A'm afraid! Mummy! Mummy!"

Alfred spread his arms out as they rolled again. "Of this? This is nothing! Oh, you are safe here, it's just some waves and wind. You will get used to it. We have to trust in God and in all the men who are working on deck."

"Is God workin' on deck, too?"

"Ummm – yes, of course he is."

"How come we should trust them?" asked Cameron.

"Because they're negotiating with the wind, so that you and I will be safe."

Cameron was confused. "Whit does that mean?"

"Negotiating? Hmm. Think about the time when Ewan wanted to play shipwreck, and you were getting tired of the same game, so you suggested another game?"

"Soldiers!"

"Yes, that's the one. You 'negotiated' with him to try to play something else that may also be interesting for him."

"But how ur th' sailors daein' that wi' th' wind?"

"Well, with the sails, they take a little wind, then they let some out. Then they keep doing this as they need to. It is all to keep the ship moving steadily along. I have complete trust in them and so should you."

Cameron turned pale. "Can they ne ... nego ..."

Alfred steadied him on, "Negotiate."

"Negoshate wi' th' waves, a'm gang tae be ill."

Cameron held his mouth closed while Alfred found a bucket and stuck it under Cameron's head.

"Here, use this."

Cameron vomited, cried, spat and cried some more. Alfred took a cloth from his pocket and wiped his face clean, then with an indisposed look, he put the dirty cloth back into his pocket.

"Why don't you sleep now?" he insisted.

Cameron pulled the blanket up over his shoulders and leaned into the pillow. As if making his last confession on his death bed, he asked Alfred a question. "Can ah tell ye something, Mr Henderson?"

"What is it, son?"

"Mah Uncle Hamish, he's a bad man, nae lik' ye. Yer nice. Also, ah miss mah mummy. Can she come tae oor hoose?"

Alfred was taken back by this and thought about it for a moment before he answered, "If she wants to."

"Ewan 'n' Aunt Janet, too?"

"Aye, if they want to. I'll do what I can, son. Now, get some rest."

"Can ah tell ye something else?"

"Yes, son, anything."

"Ah took yer button," Cameron confessed.

"Oh, I see," Alfred was perplexed, not really knowing what to say about the matter.

"Ah cut it off yer coat wi' a knife."

"When did you do this, son?" asked Alfred.

"When ye were sleeping in th' chair. Ewan dared me."

"And how did that make you feel, taking something that belonged to someone else?"

Cameron got excited. "Ah felt very brave doing it!" He looked up into Alfred's warm, weathered face and touched the lines on the edge of his eye. Suddenly, this made him lose his smile, as he thought the wrinkles made Alfred look sad. Cameron slumped down lowering his voice. "But, after that, ah felt bad. That's how come a'm telling ye noo."

"Well, I believe you are most brave for telling me," replied Alfred.

"Are ye gang tae punish me?"

"I will teach you how to sew and you can mend my coat by putting the button back on it."

"I want ye tae teach me everything."

Cameron smiled and closed his eyes. Alfred stood up and paced the floor, rubbing his neck and getting wound up having to stay put with the lad, as he thought he would be needed on deck. So, he left the room and just outside the door Tosh was standing there waiting for him.

"He's going to sleep. Poor lad's been sick."

"Careful ole boy," warned Tosh.

"Of what?"

"You're getting very close to that wee lad."

"And?" All of a sudden, Alfred was defensive.

"And he doesn't belong to you."

"No! But what does that matter?"

The conversation turned heated as Tosh hit on a sore subject. Alfred paced the floor steadily. He felt a plethora of emotions surge through him, heating him up from within like fresh kindling on an open fire.

"He will be going back to his mother. He can't replace your own son and ... "

Alfred snapped back. "And? And don't you think I know that? Where is this coming from, Tosh?"

"I don't want to see you get hurt, not again."

"That lad needs a father, a positive man that he can look up to. No, wait I know what this is. You don't want to see me happy, not for even a day!"

"You know there is no truth to that! It isn't about me, it's about you not disappointing the wee boy not letting his mother down, and simply doing what is right for everyone!"

"I would not let her down. And how is this not right? This has everything good about it."

"Is that so? Tell me, what will he do with his fancy clothes and big dreams you've filled his head with when he has to return to a life of excruciating poverty? You're giving him all these good things just to take them away again. Tell me, what good does that do him?"

"Of all people, I thought *you* would understand." Alfred stormed off.

"I do!" Tosh defended.

CHAPTER 9

The Sun now rose upon the right:
Out of the sea came he,
Still hid in mist, and on the left
Went down into the sea.

And the good south wind still blew behind,
But no sweet bird did follow,
Nor any day for food or play
Came to the mariner's hollo!

And I had done a hellish thing,
And it would work 'em woe:
For all averred, I had killed the bird
That made the breeze to blow.

Ah wretch! said they, the bird to slay,
That made the breeze to blow!

Nor dim nor red, like God's own head,
The glorious Sun uprist:
Then all averred, I had killed the bird
That brought the fog and mist.
'Twas right, said they, such birds to slay,
That bring the fog and mist.

The fair breeze blew, the white foam flew,
The furrow followed free;
We were the first that ever burst
Into that silent sea.

Down dropt the breeze, the sails dropt down,
'Twas sad as sad could be;
And we did speak only to break
The silence of the sea!

All in a hot and copper sky,
The bloody Sun, at noon,
Right up above the mast did stand,
No bigger than the Moon.

Day after day, day after day,
We stuck, nor breath nor motion;
As idle as a painted ship
Upon a painted ocean.

Water, water, every where,
And all the boards did shrink;
Water, water, every where,
Nor any drop to drink.

The very deep did rot: O Christ!
That ever this should be!
Yea, slimy things did crawl with legs
Upon the slimy sea.

About, about, in reel and rout
The death-fires danced at night;
The water, like a witch's oils,
Burnt green, and blue and white.

And some in dreams assured were
Of the Spirit that plagued us so;
Nine fathom deep he had followed us
From the land of mist and snow.

And every tongue, through utter drought,
Was withered at the root;
We could not speak, no more than if
We had been choked with soot.

Ah! well a-day! what evil looks
Had I from old and young!
Instead of the cross, the Albatross
About my neck was hung.

Samuel Taylor Coleridge
The Rime of the Ancient Mariner, Part II

Alfred walked Cameron over to the new Greenock Academy for a pre-registration meeting. It was a short walk on Inverkip Road, past the fields and Greenbank House then to the Academy on Nelson Street. The large, stone building displayed its fancy main tower to the front which, just right of the entrance, resembled a chapel embellished in glass.

Alfred talked to Cameron about his busy schedule. "The morrow I will have to leave Greenock again."

"When weel ye come back?"

"Captain MacIntosh and I are very busy now. We may be away some weeks."

"Ah donnae want ye tae gae awa'," gloomed Cameron.

"Ede will look after you and take you to school until I come back."

"Dae ah have tae go tae school? Kin ah just gae hame tae mah mummy? Ah lik' being wi' ye, but a'm wantin' tae gae hame."

"I'm too busy to sail you back home the now, son. Wait until I return, then I will take you home."

Together they jumped up the shallow steps of the main entrance, Alfred being as playful as the six-year-old. Once inside the hall, they were greeted by the rector, who shook their hands.

"You must be Mr Henderson. How do you do? And this wee chap, well, you must be Cameron. I'm Mr Montgomerie, the rector.

"Mr Montgomerie, how do you do?" greeted Alfred, who composed himself as an adult of a responsible nature.

Cameron remained silently full of nerves, unsure of what was going to be expected of him. The rector showed them into his office.

Mr Montgomerie started the conversation. "So, I understand you would like to register your son here into our primary school?"

"Yes, that is correct," Alfred replied.

"And how old is he?"

There was a brief pause as Alfred thought about it. "Five?"

"A'm more than six!" insisted Cameron.

"Six? Yes, six," blushed Alfred.

"His date of birth?"

Alfred and Cameron looked at each other for the answer. "Well, it's May – the first of May." He winked at Cameron. "Isn't that right?"

Mr Montgomerie was puzzled. "You don't know?"

"Aye, that's right, Sir," piped in Cameron. "A'm six th' noo."

A stern look came over the rector's face as his lips tightened. "You may address me as Mr Montgomerie when you do not speak out of turn."

"Aye, Sir, Mr Montgomerie," repeated Cameron, softly. Mr Montgomerie turned to Alfred. "Mr Henderson, I will need further personal details about you and Cameron here." He handed Alfred a form, then faced the young boy.

"And do you know what we do here, Cameron?" Afraid to answer the Rector, Cameron suddenly sank into a shy manner. He looked up at Mr Montgomerie with his head dropped and shook his head, shyly.

"We are a school, where young boys and girls learn all things of importance: Mathematics, English and Grammar. If, for any reason you are behind in these subjects, then perhaps your father will help you with these subjects at home."

Cameron blurted out "Och, he's noo ... "

Alfred jumped in. "Yes, yes of course I can. Mr Montgomerie, may I have a word in private?"

Cameron waited in the empty hallway in one chair of a row of six, which were placed together side by side, enough to seat a family. Inside Mr Montgomerie's office, he and Alfred discussed the situation of Cameron's family.

"Cameron has an older brother who as well has had no educating," explained Alfred.

"How old, exactly?"

"Eight, nearly nine."

"Would you be interested in registering him with us as well?"

"Yes, but I am unsure when he will be arriving. It's just an enquiry, but would you have a place in your school next term for an eight-year-old?"

Mr Montgomerie thought for a moment. "Mr Henderson, I'm not saying I don't have the places, because I do, only just. This is a public school, with fees. And it is my job to decide if the children have a place here at Greenock Academy. So, where is the other boy attending school this year?"

"Ewan, well, he isn't attending school anywhere, yet."

The rector didn't understand Alfred's vague answers and gave him a disapproving shake of his head. But before he could give his opinion, Alfred spoke up. "Look, I do realise by starting late, he will be behind in his lessons, but I am willing to give him extra help – just until he reaches the same level as the other children."

"Mr Henderson, forgive my enquiries about the boys, but I have a job to do here and the education must meet some requirements. I need to know - do you have the guardianship or the right to educate them? And, of course, do you have the means by which to pay for this education?" he queried.

"Why, yes, on both accounts, Mr Montgomerie." Alfred took the papers handed to him. "I will return with these completed in the next few days. Good day."

"Good day, Mr Henderson."

Alfred turned to leave, but Mr Montgomerie's pompous words irritated him. He turned back around to face him. "Mr Montgomerie, may I make it absolutely clear. I have taken it upon myself to understand the new educational laws of Scotland. No matter whose son Cameron, Ewan, George, Gregor or Fraser is makes no difference to his right to receive an education as established by the new School Board. So, I think you would prefer to make this more amenable by not complicating matters with your careless judgements. Do you understand what I am saying?"

Surprised by Alfred's thorough comprehension, Mr Montgomerie replied, treading more carefully with his words. "I am indeed aware of the rules, Mr Henderson, and I am satisfied that we have a common interest in the children and their wellbeing. So, yes, I do understand. Good day to you."

Alfred gave him a firm look with a nod before taking his stick. "Good day."

Alfred met Cameron in the hall. "Time to go, Cameron." He took hold of his small hand and they left together.

"Whit happened, Mr Henderson?" asked Cameron.

Alfred thought for a moment. "I had to turn the assuming bad luck albatross into the good luck it really was."

"Would that be the same as changing a bad luck whistle intae a tattoo?" he replied, with no answer from Alfred as he was too occupied in thought. "A'm hungry, Mr Henderson. Dae ye lik' Mr Montgomerie?"

"He's no bother to me. He's what we call 'gobermouch'."

"What's goberouch?"

"It's Irish. Mr Gallagher taught it to me. But don't repeat it, son." Alfred smiled.

"'Tis a Leprechaun word?"

Alfred laughed out loud. "Aye, it is!"

.oOo.

On returning home one evening from the long voyage, there was a letter propped up against the lamp on the hall table. Alfred cut it open with a small knife from the drawer and pulled out the neatly folded parchment.

To Alfred my dear friend and muse,

I hope that my letter finds you well in health and well engaged with business in Liverpool. I have received great news that I must share with you. Upon my return to Edinburgh, there was much satisfaction to my family and to my father in particular, as I delivered my paper on the engineering of the Dubh Artach lighthouse to University.

However, so predictable was the situation that once I broke the news to father that I would not earn my living as an engineer, he was disappointed greatly - although not entirely surprised! I would like instead to study law. You did plant that little seed into my mind, which, as you know, is ever restless – and it grew! My grandfather once said, - If you want to live as a gentleman, you must work as a man for there is no dining without a purse.

Father has agreed that I may fulfil this desire as it is indeed a respectable occupation which meets his full approbation, hence I shall return once again to university for my studies. I will, I suspect, continue to write stories as they simply cannot seem to escape me.

In other good news, saving the best for last, the very lamp itself is now in Erraid. Preparing as a hat to top all hats at the races, the new lens will grace the lighthouse and beam twenty miles out to sea!

I shall not return to Dubh Artach to witness the grand event of the lamp lighting, nor see its flame flicker away

in the autumn darkness. Yet, I will be there in presence of mind as this happens and I will think of you and your ship sailing evermore safely.
Alas, may I leave you with this thought; Keep your fears to yourself, but share your courage with others.

Yours Sincerely,
RL Stevenson

Alfred sat at his desk as the sun was taking its time setting into the late summer evening and shone behind him through the window, warming his back. Taking fresh paper from his drawer, he began to write:

My dear friend Louis,
I am filled with gladness for the news of the Dubh Artach light. The day will be celebrated with an imminent departure to Nova Scotia.

This evening with the fine taste of whisky on my tongue I am putting pen to paper in the hope that I will solve my own issue in due course. I have taken to heart your message to me: Keep your fears to yourself but share your courage with others.

Whilst I may be well practiced in keeping my fears to myself, my courage is not easily shared. I have taken on the task of looking after a child which, in the months that have passed, has been both a burden and inestimable joy - Perhaps his own mother will see me as fit as any father and even more as matters of the heart; yet I admit this is where I lack the required courage. I fear I must put my trust in that invisible God! I have yet to write a journal as you suggest, but I have contemplated the idea of self expression with a minor appetite. The page after this is my observation on the obscure subject of snow whose soft powder has been recently distributed to us along the parks and rooftops from Greenock to Liverpool. I pray you read it with an equal measure of enjoyment and humour.

Fond wishes,
Alfred Henderson

After signing the letter to Louis, Alfred unfolded some notes he had taken earlier, pulled a sheet of paper from the drawer and several clean pieces of paper from a stack upon which to write. He then dipped his pen in the ink and copied his notes to the new page.

To the distinguished splendour of Snow its well sculptured forms and incredible advantages for man's use; if you adapt your mind and eyes, you will stop wondering why I should acclaim the most marvellous name of Snow in this little work. For lying hidden here are secrets of smooth management, and as if a painting, things are represented that shape the soul of the man for whom the burden of governing rests heavily. The heavenly origin of each flake and its formal resemblance to the stars removes it from the vulgar masses and sons of Earth; and like Cato once before, it fell a new model of "laws" and messenger of justice from heaven.

He placed his pen down then ran his fingers through his hair, leaned forward so that his tousled curls piled into his hand, and he rubbed his whisky-fatigued face. Rejected, the pen rolled around along the desktop smearing ink. The blotter was ignored, and instead he left the stained paper sitting there on his desk to dry overnight and shifted himself from his desk to the more comfortable armchair in which to relax.

He thought about Tosh's words, and how they had barely spoken since, only in matters of business and planning with charts. That autumn they sailed together with few words, had not shared a whisky after work and Alfred had not been for tea at the MacIntosh house in weeks. He did not have the services of Andrew and Duncan to sail Cameron back to the Isle of Iona as they were called to duty on the busy Aemelius.

Ede and Cameron came into the house together from a walk. She sent Cameron upstairs to change into his bed clothes, and there was a knock at the door behind her. She opened it and there stood a post-boy in his round, boxy shako hat and tunic. He handed her a letter.

"Ma'am," he said.

"Thank you, young man."

She took the letter to Alfred who, in one swift swipe of the whale bone knife, sliced it free from the envelope.

To my dear friend and muse Alfred,

Your letter of snow brought me much pleasure to read! The waiting out of gales has not dismayed the lighthouse workmen and before another winter governs progress, I can, with great pleasure, finally bring you the great news received from Alan Brebner who informs me that the light at Dubh Artach will be shining 1 November of this year 1872. The building of it has been an immense challenge for all of the men, yet the evidence is such that the stone tower will stand proud and be the beacon of safety in the most unrelenting of waters.

I wish you God speed and may He be the guide to the path you so longingly seek.

Yours sincerely,
R.L. Stevenson

Alfred jumped out of his chair, grabbed his coat and hat off the hall hooks and rushed off with his stick into the night just as it began to rain.

Arriving at Tosh's house out of breath, he punched the door ring against the plate repeatedly like the callous hammering of a nail. Marion opened it, frantic with worry.

"Alfred. What in God's name is the matter? Has something happened?"

"No, no, nothing, Marion. I am sorry if I have caused you fear. But I have some good news to share. Is Tosh at home?"

He isn't yet, but he will return soon."

She stared at him with some hesitation, but as he was becoming drenched, she opened the door fully.

"Well, don't just stand there in the rain, come in then and wait."

"I will, thank you." He stepped inside, removed his hat, yet didn't take off his coat. "Actually, I won't stay."

"Why ever not?"

"If you could just give him the news for me that I have received word from Mr Stevenson with regard to the lighthouse lamp."

"I hope there is no problem."

"No, in fact it's nearly complete."

"Alfred, why don't you wait for him and tell him yourself?"

There was a pause from Alfred as Marion waited for his answer. "It's the problem of the boy, isn't it? Come through, we need to talk."

Marion helped him take off his drenched coat and hung it up. He followed her through to the sitting room and made himself comfortable in an armchair; Marion sat herself across from him on the sofa. She served herself tea from a China teapot and offered him some. "Tea? Something stronger?"

"Tea is fine. Thank you."

She poured him a cup and he took the delicate china into his bulky hand and sipped it unceremoniously.

"Look, Alfred, I am going to discuss this with you and I will be clear about it. We need to talk about wee Cameron and getting him back to his mother."

"I know he needs his mother, but I have been occupied with much work."

Marion looked at him with disbelief, raising an eyebrow.

Alfred continued on a more honest note. "Not only that, but I can also keep him safe here and I can educate him – and I'm liking the company," Alfred replied.

"Aye, I can see that. But he must go back to where he belongs. It's not your job to keep him safe or educated, it's his mother's. As well, it's not fair on him if you show him this life just to return him to the world of poverty to which he is accustomed."

"I've heard it all from Tosh. But a child needs an opportunity. What if he does belong?"

"I'm not understanding you," Marion said.

He put his cup down into the saucer, clumsily spilling some of it. "What if Cait belongs here as well?"

"Oh, I see. Are you wanting her here because you think you love her, or just so you can keep the wee boy?"

Alfred looked away, uncertain of how to answer her.

"Aye," Marion said, realising she caught his attention. "Well, you'll be needing to sort those affections out now.

The boy needs to go back before this Cait resents you for taking him. Then you'll lose them both."

Alfred pushed himself back in his chair, trying to make sense of the feelings which swirled around, disorganised inside his head.

"I cannot live in this atmosphere, this suffrage of love as – as I cannot discern between the pain caused by the longing for her in her absence or withstanding and enduring the lust I hold for her when she is in my presence," he explained.

Marion looked at him in surprise and smiled at him. "Why, Alfred, my dear, what a gift you have found!"

"What gift?" he questioned.

"You have found your voice! Such bittersweet emotion can only come from a heart that is capable of feeling; one which is ready to love!" she exclaimed.

Alfred became flustered and uncertain of what his own words had said. He trusted and respected Marion and her point of view as a woman, and no other woman knew him better and the strife he had lived through.

"Never have I felt this way. I do not know if it will be reciprocated."

"Yes!" she said. "Go! I am sure of it! Do your duty and take the laddie back. Go for the sake of discovery! Listen closely to me. You can think of your losses in life as that - a loss. Or you can consider them an opportunity. The choice is yours. Marion took a deep sigh. "We all want someone to love and to be loved in return. No one has forever."

The comment threw Alfred off. He observed her melancholy change of tone. "What are you saying?" he asked.

"You do know, Alfred, I have my own fears. Tosh is married to that ship of yours. One day he will sail away and never return. I feel it in my bones. He is as much a part of Aemelius as the helm itself is attached, and his great skill does not fear me less. Over the years I have learned to accept that I cannot control his fate. Forgive me; I do have my weak and trying moments such as now. Now is not the time to lose yourself, Alfred - to fall foul of something potentially wonderful. Each lifetime is limited, so do not waste it. Be strong and determined; find your purpose to which you must take a chance. *That* is a quality that most attracts a woman."

"Only I'm not very forthcoming with women – not women like Cait. She is both beautiful and intelligent, and this alone makes me rattle with nerves. And I don't know how she feels."

"She must have given you some suggestions or a sign?"

"A sign?"

"A special look with her eyes? A touch of the hand? Why is it that men don't often pick up on the clues we give them?"

"Marion, you surprise me!"

"Go find out. Take the risk, be brave! What do you have to lose:"

"Nothing."

Marion passed a journal to Alfred. "Here, this is from Tosh. Seeing as you two aren't on speaking terms, I suppose he won't mind me giving it to you the now. It was meant as a gift for your maiden voyage to Nova Scotia."

Alfred took the journal from Marion and looked at it. He gently touched the beautifully embossed initials 'ARH' on the front. Emotions fulsomely poured over him as his eyes swelled up like the little puddle of tea in his porcelain saucer, obstructing his view. He thought that he hadn't deserved such a gift, and he was full of guilt of his poor disposition that had caused their falling out.

Marion stood up from the sofa. "I have much to do, if you'll excuse me now. Lois waits for me upstairs. We have a wedding to look forward to tomorrow."

"Aye, we do! Marion. Do not fear for Tosh. He is the best captain I know. I trust his abilities and so should you."

"As you should trust yours," she mirrored back to him. "I speak in truth, Alfred, you deserve more than you think you do."

CHAPTER 10

Oh wert thou in the cauld blast,
On yonder lea, on yonder lea;
My plaidie to the angry airt,
I'd shelter thee, I'd shelter thee:
Or did Misfortune's bitter storms
Around thee blaw, around thee blaw,
Thy bield should be my bosom,
To share it a', to share it a'.

Or were I in the wildest waste,
Sae black and bare, sae black and bare,
The desert were a Paradise,
If thou wert there, if thou wert there.
Or were I monarch o'the globe,
Wi' thee to reign, wi' thee to reign,
The brightest jewel in my crown
Wad be my queen, wad be. My queen.

Robert Burns
O, Wert Thou in the Cauld Blast

It was the day of Lois's wedding to Douglas. The family walked together down a lane to the church under the usual heavy Scottish sky of grey and a swift, cool wind.

There was a traditional order to the group as they proceeded. A piper led the group, and behind him Douglas led his sister, the maid of honour.

Lois was dressed in a white gown whose edges just touched the dust on the ground and as it blew with the gust, her cream buttoned boots underneath were revealed. As she walked following her oldest friend, Alfred, she held onto her large, white brimmed hat. It was tied down with a matching silk ribbon which passed under her chin and then brought back up to the top of the hat and tied with a large bow.

Alfred looked dapper in his black morning suit coat, striped trousers and top hat. He was the best man and Lois walked behind him. The rest of the family were behind Lois, while Tosh and Marion held onto Cameron's hands.

Lois talked cheerfully to Alfred from behind him. "You do know, Alf, don't you, that I am quite grateful that you're here to see me off. It means a lot to me. You're like the brother I never had; as if you are necessary to a special purpose."

At her sweet words, he repaid her with a compliment. "You look lovely, Lois. If I may say so as your 'brother'."

Gleefully, she serenaded him with a poem.

"Clothed in yellow, red and green,
I prate before the King and Queen.
Of neither house nor land possessed,
By lords and ladies, I'm caressed!"

She laughed out loud, and Alfred turned to her and smiled.

"I hope you always remain this way," he commented.

"What way do you mean?" she asked.

"The way you are so enchanting. You are playful and full of joy."

"Och just how you used to be," Lois teased.

"I was never that way," replied Alfred.

Lois recollected. "Aye, you were! Don't you remember, when I was a little girl and together we played? The time I was with you on the back of the big velocipede. How we laughed as you pedalled and we flew over the bumps!"

Alfred smiled. "Aye, you kept falling off!"

"I would like to see that again, you as the old Alf."

"I grew up."

"You grew old."

Lois took the sprig of heather out from the back of her bouquet and handed it to Alfred. "Here ye go."

Alfred stopped in his pace, with the others slowly catching up from behind. She placed the heather into his hand and closed it with a grip of sincere intention. She looked up at him and smiled.

"Take this and make a wish. The heather from my bouquet brings good luck. You need more of it than I."

Lois then took the cutting of heather and pushed it into the buttonhole of his coat. "To smile again. That's my wish for you."

He looked down at the wild, tiny purple blooms which gazed back up to him and a moment later Lois scooped her arm into his, linking them together and she skipped as he ran, catching up to Douglas and his sister.

.oOo.

At Iona, Ewan waded his dirty feet in the crystal-clear shallows, in search for food. He looked around base of the rocks and underneath the green seaweed fixed firmly to the rocks. He pulled off some of the slimy, stringy brown-green algae which waved with the water and stuffed it in a cloth bag. A little crab skittled sideways under another rock. Ewan went to grab it, but the pinchers got him first. Shaking his finger to free the pain, he spotted another creature burying in the sand. He dug into the sand to catch up to it but lost its path. Then he saw a fish egg sack and out of desperation, Ewan pulled it off the rock, shoved it into his mouth and chewed the salty little pouch as fast as he could, squeezing his eyes shut.

The wreckers stood alongside the path by the sea together. They pulled the morning's catch out of the nets into a pile for the women to divide before the men repaired the net twines. From there, the women took the mackerel and hung them up on the broken pieces of twine for drying. Standing next to Hamish, Morven made a brief attempt to gain his favour by sharing his wife's gossip.

"Ye dae ken that Cameron is awa, don't ye?" he asked.

"What are ye on aboot? He's gang tae stay in Mull with some nurse, nae well."

"Ye'v been fooled by those women. That stranger, that man haes taken him. A ship, a doctor, there's mair tae that man than meets th' eye."

"How dae ye ken?" Hamish asked.

"Th' wifey told me. There's na nurse. Ye'v been lied tae. Ah thought it's yer business tae ken."

At this, Hamish grew furious. He pushed Morven out of his face, grabbled around the fish and took a suitable one for his tea. Then he stormed off home. Inside the house, he threw the fish down on the table, took a rag out of a hole in the wall and sat on the stool.

He unwrapped the rag and took out the pistol that he had been hiding away. He felt the gun, exploring the its mechanics, opened the cylinder and slipped the two bullets out. He put them back in, opened the cylinder again and let them slide out into his hand. He repeated this again and again, like he was exploring and learning his way around a woman's body. Only this was a weapon and he likened it to getting what he wanted with Cait. It made him feel powerful over them both.

.oOo.

Cait, Ewan and Janet were at the table eating small torn off pieces of bread that they shared. A banged-up metal jug of water decorated the centre of the table, a damaged relic from a shipwreck.

Midway down the edge of the table was a hole in which a nob had once been placed, and one end of the table had been cut sloping down in a curve, giving it the appearance of having once been a door. According to Ewan's mammoth yet ingenuously green imagination, it wasn't just a door to a cabin, rather it was the door to the captain's cabin on a ship stolen by pirates from far-off shores.

The trio, full of gloom and hunger, sat around the pirate's door without having much to say.

"Mr Henderson says we ought tae pray fur th' men at sea because they are vulnerable. But what aboot us? Doesn't God even ken we're 'ere?" Ewan spluttered out.

"O' course, He does! God is everywhere," Janet answered assuringly.

"Then how come am sae hungry?"

There was silence round the table as the women couldn't disagree that his question was a valid one. Even a young bairn saw the truth in the situation. He huffed at the reticence, stood and gathered up his fishing string.

Cait snapped. "Ewan! No one wants to hear you complain!"

Ewan ran off outside from the sudden, alarming fear of his mother. She was becoming more and more distressed with their situation and the cracks were showing.

Even so, Cait was not about to resume relations with Hamish. The old rumour of Janet's relationship with her brother did cross her mind and she wondered if there would be a chance that Janet would help by returning to him, even for the sake of feeding her family who remained starving before her.

Perhaps Janet had already been making visits next door. Not once did she complain of hunger, nor did her dress or corset need tightening at the waist. She, if fact, seemed rather oddly content within herself and her belly remained satisfied and round.

It made Cait suspicious until Janet looked at her from across the table, jolting her attention. Cait felt repulsed at herself for believing such a thing and she shook it out of her thoughts.

As if reading her mind, Janet took Cait's hand and rubbed her arm to give her some assurance. "Pray fur th' men at sea. How come Alfred would put that thought intae the bairn's heids?" She smirked.

Cait sighed, "Because that's the kind of man he is - or was."

That chilly evening, Cait, dressed in her cloak, walked up the mound to a field onto a simple burial ground and stopped at the wooden cross which marked the place where William was interred. She sat on the ground to be close to him and touched the ground where he lay deep below. Her loneliness was overwhelming and she began to sob. She looked up into the clear sky above, she lifted her head as if to take a closer look. she watched all the stars and saw the North Star twinkling over her.

Knowing what she had to do, Cait lowered her head in self-reproach. She collected her emotions, patted her tears dry and returned to the cottages along the path. She passed her own house and stopped next door at Hamish's. The light shined out from his little window at the front and through the cracks of the side stone wall. Cait hesitated for a moment and looked around to see if anyone noticed her standing there. There was no one. She tapped the door very lightly as she didn't really want him to answer it anyway. The door opened to her, and she entered. Then the house went dark as Hamish's lamp was blown out.

.oOo.

Cameron took a couple of books to Alfred, who waited downstairs in the sitting room. He sat beside him, legs dangling off the sofa, feet pointing inward, and he showed his guardian what he had found on the old bookshelf in Alfred's bedroom.

Alfred looked at each cover. "What have we here? Yes, this is the new book called '*Through The Looking Glass*', written by Lewis Carroll, and this other one is ..." Alfred slid the second book from under the first. "It's not a book, it's my journal."

"A journal?" Cameron asked.

"It's an empty book, waiting to be written in."

"But who wants an empty book?"

"Someone who wants to fill it in with their thoughts." Alfred fanned the pages, creating a little breeze in his face.

"What kind o' thoughts? How come ye dinnae put something inside all by yersel'? Are ye gang to leave it blank?"

As the pages slipped through Alfred's toughened fingers, much like the lapsed chapters of his own life, he passed over a penned note written just on the first page. He flicked back with his thumb to it to see that there was an inscription to him. *"Fellow lighthouse lover and admirer – a possible nucleus for a lighthouse library. Tosh"*

He slapped the cover shut, now disturbed yet wildly curious about the meaning of it all – Cameron's comment and Tosh's inscription.

He whispered under his breath, "All by myself."

Cameron tugged at Alfred, now almost meddling with him. "Mr Henderson, ye can write yer ain story."

This idea awakened Alfred. Cameron's eagerness for a reply was about to lose Alfred his patience, as he had now lost his attention to the boy.

The trepidation swirled around inside Alfred, intensifying with every moment as he questioned everything that happened in the recent weeks. He revisited the past months, putting the pieces of the puzzle together, believing that perhaps they had all been part of some universal plan warning him with implications which demanded to be headed.

The 'what ifs' clouded his mind. 'What if' Marion would one day be widowed? 'What if' writing his own story was a prediction of Tosh's absence in it? 'What if' the lighthouse beacon would not reach far enough to sea for the passing Aemelius? And why had Cait and Cameron entered his life?

He needed to make everything clear; he needed to see Tosh and apologise, hoping that would be what was necessary to pacify, better still, rectify his discontent. He paced the floor and called out loudly, over and over, "Ede! Ede!" until she arrived.

"Yes, Mr Henderson?"

"Look after Cameron until I return; I have something I must do."

"At this hour?"

"Yes, at this hour - immediately!" he shouted.

"Yes, of course, of course," Ede answered, feeling the urgency.

Alfred rushed out of the room, slamming the front door behind him.

.oOo.

Tosh answered the knock at his door. "Alfred."

"Good evening, Tosh," Alfred shuffled his words uncomfortably, searching for the right ones to say. "As you may know, I shall leave in the morning to return Cameron to Iona. Please accept my apology for my unkind words to you. You were right, it was not correct of me to keep wee Cameron longer than he needed to be here. I cannot justify what I have done, only that it was of a selfish nature. I can only hope that something good will come of it."

Tosh nodded, "Something already has."

"Has it?" Alfred was confused.

Tosh continued. "I understand why you feel the way you do about the wee lad. I interfered; I said too much."

"No, you didn't. I need – I mean, I needed to hear it."

"We all fail each other eventually. Even when I fail you, just know you're like a brother to me. I would never make light of that," said Tosh.

That was another odd hint to Alfred, he thought: 'even when I fail you'. Was tosh implying the past or the future? He tried not to panic, but it was difficult to not exaggerate any conclusions.

"I know you wouldn't, and for me it is the same sentiment. You are a good man," said Alfred.

They stood together in the doorway as Alfred continued. "I shall return the day after the morrow in time to join you on the voyage to Nova Scotia. Good evening."

Tosh nodded. "Very well. Good evening."

He watched as Alfred turned and walked away into the dark evening before closing the door. Whatever bigger plan was taking place, Alfred was aware he could do nothing to change it, only surrender to it.

CHAPTER 11

The sun, it rises steadily beneath the lingering clouds
Warming the valleys and lifting the heavy, misty shroud
And with a sweep of its cloak the night creeps in to bury
As to devour the blue sea and the looming black skerry

But the sun it cannot glow within the night
And the moon at times it disappears out of sight
And even the star's own twinkle may draw to a fade
From under the ceil of a flourishing, cloudy raid

But high above the ground a lone tower stands
Giving a sudden bright burst, flashing from the land
It warns of danger at sea yet also of refuge
And within it a man attends, trimming the wick's spent fuse.

Incessantly minding the flame and entrusted to those
Whom in their darkness drifting along they go
Alight is the lamp for everyone who passes
He sees his light, yet not the measure of warmth he surpasses

For behind it he remains, ingloriously giving and tending
Keeping the flame alive, he is both watchful and mending
The wickie sees not that when he lights the lantern
He humbly brightens his own path in return,

Giving a beam of love, of hope, not to forget caring
Cherished by all whom he shines on whether land or seafaring
Of all the world's towers, far mild and meeker
Not one can compare to my own lighthouse keeper.

Anonymous

After a very early start, the Consolation glided effortlessly into the hidden cove at Iona before sunset, without being seen. With his arms full of provisions, Alfred passed a dead hen to Cameron to help carry. Cameron, wearing his new clothes with his fresh haircut covered by a new cap, ran ahead while Alfred managed his stick, the heavy sack of oats and kale over his shoulder. The end of October sea winds blew behind carrying them as they walked across the grasses and thick, purple heather towards Cameron's home.

At the shore, the wreckers were cleaning the fishing nets and tying up their broken ends. As Morven scratched his nose he looked up and noticed a moving figure with a walking stick crossing the hill.

He was afraid to divulge anything to Hamish and decided to say nothing. Instead, he nudged Murdo to look up from the nets and the two of them watched the silhouette of man, whose limp gave Alfred away. Morven became nervous and Murdo tried to calm him. "Steady yoursel', lad."

.oOo.

Cameron had run ahead to the cottage, so that by the time Alfred arrived, Cait was joyously crying over her son.

"Oh, my boy! Look how big you are! And, your clothes, how very smart!"

"A'v been gang tae school, Mummy; ah'm th' best reader o' all th' other children!"

"What? That's wonderful news!"

Cameron passed her the bird. "Here, Mummy, this is fur ye."

"What is this?"

"'Tis a hen!" the boy declared proudly.

Laughing with excitement, she agreed with him. "Aye, it is, it's a hen!"

Cait called out loud to Janet, who was pulling down laundry outside in the wind behind the cottage. "Janet, come quick, Cameron's home!"

Cameron ran to find her, leaving his mum to face Alfred. Janet could be heard fussing over the boy who had been away for so long.

Cait froze as she stared at Alfred, not sure of what to say.

He took off his hat.

In a moment of hysterics, she stepped up to him. "You've kept me waiting, waiting so long! You dreadful man!" she cried and hit his chest with her fist.

Alfred held her by her shoulders, trying to get her to stop. "I know, I'm sorry. I came when I could. I'm so sorry, Cait." Her emotional outburst was so upsetting to him, that he didn't feel as if his presence was welcome and he was unprepared as to what to do or if there was anything he could say that would be acceptable to her. "I'll just go. You don't want to see me, and I don't blame you." Alfred turned to leave.

Cait watched as he walked away. "How dare you leave me now!"

Just then, Janet rushed to the front of the cottage with Cameron, panicking.

"Mr Henderson, come! Ye'd both better come in. Quick, all o' ye!"

She pushed everyone through the front door and stuck her head outside, looked around then closed the door behind her.

Inside, Cait leaned into the table nervously fiddling with the tie on her pinny.

"Th' whole village kens ye'r 'ere. How lang will ye stay this time, Mr Henderson? Ye'll be th' cause o' trouble ye ken."

"Seeing as you've got the lad back, I will be on my way. I don't want my presence to put you in danger."

Cait was confused as to what to say so she turned away. She was tempted to try to talk him out of leaving as much as she wanted to run off with him.

"Nae, dinnae go!" Cameron shouted.

"Cameron!" Cait scolded him.

"But ah dinnae want him tae go!" he cried.

"We should feed ye something first," she said.

Janet blurted her disbelief at Cait. "There's na time fur that fur Christ's sake! Hamish is comin'!"

"No. My men await at my ship; I won't keep them. The longer I stay here, the more of a problem I will be."

Alfred turned, opened the door and walked out. The disappointment wasn't easy to hide and he covered his face like the haar covers the land, unable to lift. He rushed up the hill. Cameron burst out of his house and ran towards him, crying.

"Mr Henderson!"

He tugged on Alfred's coat hem to halt him, and Alfred stopped in his tracks. He took Cameron from under the arms, lifted him up and held him tight.

Cameron snuffled his words behind his tears. "Aren't ye gang tae be wi' me any mair?"

Alfred was touched tremendously by this and embraced him tightly. Cait ran up to them. She was grabbed at the obvious, visible bond they had and stood back.

"Don't go, Alfred. Please." She spoke in a gentle appeal.

"I really must, unless you want – unless you want to -"

"What is it?" she begged to know.

"Leave here; come back with me?"

Cait wrapped her arms around the two of them. "I've waited for you too long. I won't let you go back without me now. Let's find Ewan!"

Alfred took her long hair into his hands and ran his fingers through it as he had dreamt of doing for months. "To see you again after thinking of you for so long and not being able to touch you has created a longing that I cannot ignore. How unnatural it is to have to restrain myself as if I am undeserving of a woman's affection." he said.

"Alfred," Cait asked. "What are you saying?"

The words flowed from his lips as if it was not at all him speaking, but rather his deepest, earnest self. "The uncertainty of your affection for me," he continued. "For what purpose are we brought here as the spirit never ends but neither does, all our lives, the aspiration to love and to be loved, even at my age. The years have ticked past me like the kirk bells of Greenock and I wonder, with much of my life behind me, is it not too late or too much to ask of my faith? To fulfil this one, impassioned desire?" Physically taken aback at his own words, he pushed back his greying locks, revealing the tender look in his face.

Cait looked directly into his eyes and placed her hands into his, holding them tight. Then she clasped his face to hold it still and with complete certainty replied to him, "It is not too much to ask? For I, too, hear the bells ringing."

Cameron looked up at them, clinging to every word. Very suddenly realising their urgent situation, together they took the boy's hands and hurried back to the cottage, locking the door behind them.

Inside, Cait and Alfred talked with Janet, who was not content with the notion that they would leave Iona.

"How dae yoe reckon they'll git oot o' 'ere alive? Hmm? Hae ye really thought aboot it?" she asked Alfred.

Alfred worked to assure her. "Either I leave now - on my own, then later I return for you, or we all go together tonight. I have a plan."

"Janet as well?" asked Cait.

"Of course. You will all be looked after in Greenock."

Cait smiled. "You have thought this through."

"I had to make sure you wanted this as well. I do admit, the sight of you today was soothing for my sore eyes. I've come for you, Cait. It's our time." He looked around the room at Janet and Cameron. "I've come for all of you."

Janet stubbornly contradicted him. "A'm no taking th' risk. Anyway, ah belong 'ere. Iona is ma family. Ah wullnae gae."

"If I try to escape and Hamish finds out, he will kill me and you, as well. I'm sure of it," Cait warned Alfred.

"Not if we're careful. Where's Ewan the now?" he asked.

"He's outside," Cait answered.

"A'm fair certain he's fishing at th' rocks again," said Janet.

"Fishing, again?"

Janet snapped. "Aye, fishing! He's trying tae catch yer next meal so tha' fachan brother o' mine doesn't need tae catch it fur ye!"

"Janet! I would think those words were beyond yourself!"

Alfred tried to calm the quibbling women down. "It doesn't matter now. We better get Ewan back here quickly. We need to stay inside quietly, all together."

"Ah will look fur him; Ah will git th' laddie," said Janet.

Cait didn't agree. "No, I'll go. I'll look less suspicious and I'm faster. Janet, you and Alfred start gathering our things, only what we need to take with us."

Cait ran outside to look for Ewan. The shorter autumn days meant it was dusk early on. She looked down to the fishing boats on the shore where the men were at the nets and called his name around the houses.

While Janet gathered up clothing and pushed them into sacks, it dawned on Alfred that he might just know where to find Ewan. So, he took his stick, left the house and crept towards the hill along the back of the other houses, being careful that no one saw him. He made his way to the play helm and looked around, but there was no sight of Ewan. He then shuffled over to the boat hull, looked inside the big hole and smiled at Ewan as he there sat alone, arranging some stones.

"Am I welcome?" he asked.

"Mr Henderson!" Ewan smiled as he went in for a hug. "Is Cameron wi' ye?"

"Hi pal. Yes, Cameron is home and well. Taller, too. Come, let's go see him."

"Mummy's cross wi' me. We dinnae hae any food 'n' a've still ne'er caught a fish."

"Well, we're going to fix this."

"Eh?"

"Would you like that I show you how to fish?"

Ewan became very excited. "Wid ye tak me fishing? Right noo?"

"There's no need today, as I brought you food. You can eat a meal fit for a king tonight."

Ewan's face lit up with an enormous smile. "A'm sae hungry, Mr Henderson. We're a' hungry; thir's nothing but nettle soup."

Cait ran up the hill and she called out, "Ewan! Ewan!"

From under the old ship's hull the young voice called out. "Mummy, a'm over 'ere."

Ewan stepped out of the hull and Cait took hold of him. "I've been worried about ye."

"But why?" he asked.

Alfred peeked out from underneath.

At the same time, in the distance, Morven was walking along the path to his cottage. He looked up and saw Cait and Ewan standing together. Alfred ducked back inside.

"Mr Henderson is inside th' hull," said Ewan to his mum. "He's gang tae teach me how tae fish."

"Shhh. Be quiet for me the now."

She broke a half smile and a nod to Morven to indicate that everything was normal.

Hamish came out of his cottage with a bottle in hand. Standing pendulously, he snorted, spat then returned inside.

When the way was clear, Cait took Ewan by the hand and together they walked home quickly down the path. Just as she opened the door, Morven appeared from the side of the house, making her jump. She held her hand to her chest and took a breath. Ewan went inside.

"Everything a'richt?" Morven asked.

"Aye?"

"Hamish kens ye'r hiding that stranger."

"No? No, he's gone."

"Ye be careful, he's angry. He's heavy on th' rum th' noo."

"You can tell Hamish he's away now, Morven. Good evening."

"Guid evening," he repeated.

Morven looked around with his prying eyes and saw Alfred's stick propped up by the door.

"Gang, is he?"

She stopped, caught in her lie.

"Whit favours wull ye grant me fur keeping mah mouth shut, pretty one? Ye dae ken a nod is as guid as a wink. A've noticed yer subtleties, Cait." He moved in closer to whisper. "Ah will wait till th' night arrives tae hae yer pleasures."

Cait slapped him across the face. Off balance, he held his cheek and she took the stick and pushed it into his stomach.

"I'll remember your wife if you can't, you disgusting, weak man."

"Then ah cannae promise ye anything."

"You never have before, Morven, and I expect nothing from you now. I swear it, if you speak a word of this to Hamish, your wife will hear of your vile proposition and what your pathetic self is made of. How can you respect yourself if you live to please a beast like Hamish, always pandering at his feet? He has utter control of you!"

Morven looked at Cait as if looking into a mirror.

"That's nae sae far fae yer ain truth, Cait."

He pushed the stick away and walked off.

Cait appealed, "Morven, please!" to which she was simply ignored.

Cait went inside the cottage and closed the door behind her, reeling with anxiety over her conversation with Morven as well as expecting Hamish to come over any minute.

"'Tis dark th' noo. We'll hae tae wait till everyone is asleep in thair beds if we're aff tae leave," said Janet.

"And Hamish? He'll know Alfred's here and will be round in no time! We need to escape now!" stressed Cait.

"We can't sail tonight, the sky isn't light enough," said Alfred. "We'll have to wait till first light in the morning now."

"Surely we could stay on the ship till then'?" Cait suggested.

"Hamish is full o' th' rum 'n' aff tae his sleep th' noo," Janet reassured. "But if he were tae wake 'n' come roond 'ere just tae find us a' missing, he would gang intae a rage.

Alfred agreed to her common sense. "Aye, she's right."

"So, you will come with us Janet?" asked Cait.

Janet nodded.

Ewan went to his mother, hugging her tight around the waist, and Cameron followed just behind them.

"A'm afraid, Mum," moaned Ewan.

Cameron imitated his big brother. "So am ah, Mummy."

Cait tried to reassure them, although she herself was full of angst. It was one of her subtle but strong gifts she had as a mum, soothing her children. "Och, I know, boys, it will be alright."

She looked to Alfred. "You have looked after my son well, and I must find a way to repay your kindness, if only I knew how."

Alfred was taken back by her wanting to repay him. To him, it had been a clear, romantic gesture to which repayment wasn't expected. All that he had hoped for in his awkward, simplistic way was to spark an emotion in return; to know there was a mutual feeling within Cait.

Little had he realised that his looking after her sick child was not the only way to her heart. There was a point where it may have become this way, but somewhere within those months of waiting and with no news of his recovery, she grew to resent him awfully, as Marion warned him she would.

With each sunrise she awoke with yet another absence and craved him less and less as she wondered whatever happened to Cameron. With every passing sunset the emptiness slowly ate away at her hopes. A mother would never be able to resolve the issue of a missing child, unlike she would with an absent man. As long as just one tiny thread of hope was present, she would have kept her heart alive, waiting his return. Cait had forced herself to keep busy from glancing over at the horizon in hope that she might catch a glimpse of a passing ship. She collected all the upcoming winter's peat, taking several trips up to the bog on her own. In the solitude and confinement, she became self-absorbed, which in turn pushed her into a poor mental place of emotional destitution. Janet had had enough of the ghost of a woman who lived in the house, and she coaxed her to be back among the women, taking the duties of washing clothing and listened to their problems of wrecker men as they all sat around to lay the fish in the curing salt.

Regardless, there was no respite for her torture, no relief even for a brief while. Anyone could see the agony that played upon her ageing face; the evidence of her broken heart.

Deep down inside she was forgiving and all of the displeasure that weighed on her heavily was washed clean away the moment the wave who was her wee Cameron rushed into her arms that day.

At the offer of a repayment, Alfred began to doubt himself and wondered if he had gone about pursuing Cait in the wrong way. She wasn't altogether pleased with him, that was obvious. And after all, he was well out of the practice of courting. On the other hand, he wanted to help Cameron in his time of need, and in their time together he had developed a very special relationship with him.

It was a feeling he wanted so desperately to have had with his own son, whom he never got to know. The only glimpse he had had of him was through his tears as he looked into his baby's vacant eyes which would forever forbid the two of them from connecting. As Alfred closed Fiona's and the baby's eyes, he also shut out and closed off the brief part of the life he knew as a lover, husband

and father. Behind his eyes he lived within his very own private prison cell.

"You don't owe me anything," he told her. "It pleases me that you're to come back with me. How could I ask for more?"

"I can start by returning this," she said, as she put her hand into her pinny pocket and pulled out his lost brass button. "This belongs to you. I believe Cameron owes you an apology for taking it. Don't you, Cameron?" She handed the button to Alfred and looked at Cameron in dismay.

He took the button. "He has already done so with his own words, as if a grown man."

Alfred bent down to Cameron and said, "One day, my little sailor, you will earn your own buttons, I am sure of it."

Cait looked to Alfred with a bright smile, as Janet came in with two small cloth sacks of clothing.

"Here we are then, that's th' clothes ready tae go."

"Good," said Cait, smiling. "Let's go dress the hen and get ourselves started on this wonderful meal our good men have brought us."

With an odd sort of pleasure, Janet yanked the feathers out of the hen. Standing next to her, Cait opened the sacks of kale and oats, and the cauldron began to steam with simmering water as the flames danced with plentiful peat beneath it. Alfred took the boys aside and explained the plan.

"Alright boys, this is what I need of you. We all must be calm, quiet, and stay inside the house – and no fighting amongst you lads. We don't want to attract attention and someone coming to the door. Can you do that?"

The boys nodded their heads.

"Kin ah tak' mah stones wi' me? A've git a collection of them," whispered Ewan.

"Have you got a pocket?" Alfred whispered back.

"Aye."

Cameron interrupted. "Aye, but without holes?"

"Aye, one. I turned a knot in it." Ewan showed them.

"Then go fill your pocket with your favourite stones," Alfred permitted.

Ewan smiled.

Alfred raised his voice. "That's settled, men. After supper, we will sleep and then I will wake you just before sunrise and be gone from here before the rest of the village awakes. However, it is important to leave swiftly and without complaint. Am I understood?"

"Aye, sir," the brothers said in sync, looking up to him and fully respecting his authority.

.oOo.

The three sacks of clothing sat at the ready in a small heap by the front door. Ewan, Cameron and Janet slept quietly in the back room while Cait slept in the front room as usual. Alfred nodded off in the old chair.

There was a shuffling sound outside around the front of the cottage. A sudden banging on the door made Alfred and Cait jump. Alfred rushed over to hold her back, keeping her calm.

Hamish slurred his bitterness at the door. "Cait! If that man is wi' ye, Ah will murder th' both o' ye. Cait? Cait, ye owe me!"

This woke Janet and she came running out from the bedroom and stood staring at the front door, waiting for Alfred's instruction.

Alfred put his finger up to his lips. "Shhh," he told her.

The three of them listened fretfully as Hamish shuffled his feet around in the dirt outside. Cait buried her head into Alfred's chest and closed her eyes until the commotion disappeared. His masculine smell and warm body made her feel protected and he surrounded her with a sense of sanctuary, something she had not felt since William. He put his arms fully around her and held her close, encapsulating in his tenderness, yearning for him, his body against hers.

"Don't let me go," she whispered softly into his neck. Alfred's prison walls came crumbling down as her words chiselled them away. He felt needed. Cait laid her head against his chest, breathing softly into him. He felt the blood rush through his veins and exhaled in desire.

Seeing the pair of them engrossed with each other, Janet sighed as if to give a quiet yet strong and vehement expression of disapproval as she shook her head and retreated to the back room to stay with the boys.

Alfred pulled Cait's head up so that her eyes met his as they looked deeply to each other. She felt ashamed of the trouble they were in with Hamish. He kissed her forehead and pulled her back into his chest.

"Cait, that's over."

"Is it?"

He nodded. "Aye, forever."

He wrapped his arms around her tightly as if to squeeze out her bitterness and fear, replacing it with his own affirmation of love.

.oOo.

Hamish kept a light with the fire eating a kipper with his fingers and vigorously ripping it apart from the bones with his teeth before sputting them into the flames. With the back of his hands he wiped his mouth clean, then he dried them on his trousers, leaving oily streaks that matched the others on his clothing. Hamish then swallowed the last of the rum to wash down the fish. He looked at the empty bottle, dissatisfied it was empty and threw it into the fire. But the glass smashed onto the floor and he grunted at the mess of shards in an outburst, standing up and kicking them aside.

He looked at the hole in the wall next to the fire, went over to it and pulled out the wrapped-up pistol. Taking a seat, he disrobed it from the cloth and opened the cylinder to reveal its two bullets. When he tried to stand, he swayed about on his vacillating legs and clumsily took his place in the chair again, fidgeting with the weapon as he thought about his next move. He slipped the pistol into his trousers, closed his eyes and nodded off promptly, gurgling from the back of his throat.

.oOo.

The last few hours of the night were windy but still in the way of slumber, though the silence was not meant to last. Inside Cait's cottage the full house would be soon waking.

One of them, though, Janet, lay awake in her bed. With her eyes half open, she watched as the boys slept soundly across from her. She looked over to the window where the autumn wind seeped in, the clouds were swept away and the stars now shone. She spoke quietly to herself. "Got tae git Hamish tae fix that windae afore winter."

The thoughts of her family leaving Iona were getting to her, making her edgy and she began showing cracks at the seams by bunching her blanket tight into her chest. Janet shared her brother's bad temper, yet had a little more self control. She now became overheated with the growing uneasiness. Laying outside of her blanket, she rubbed her face briskly one moment and gripped her fists the next.

More thoughts filled her head. "Praying fur sailors, ha! 'N' whit was that Alfred thinking, having they clothes made fur a wrecker laddie? Promises, reading 'n' school? Nae likely. Whit else are ya planning fur *mah* kin?"

Full of the twitches, she rose from her bed, restless and festering into a sweat. She made her way to the window and looked around outside, seeing no one. Softly and delicately, her little feet glided her large frame across the front room floor, passing Alfred and Cait who were sound asleep once more – Cait on the bench and Alfred in his chair pulled in close next to her.

Janet stopped at the door. After staring at it for a few moments, she reached for the handle, when a hand suddenly touched her shoulder from behind. She jumped.

"Janet, what are you doing?" Cait whispered.

"Ah cannae sleep; Ah need tae git some fresh air."

"This is not the time. We will be awake and leaving before the sunrise soon," Cait tried to reason with her.

"A'm likely just a wee bit nervous aboot gang. Ah will ainly be a minute or two. Ah wiil stand just ootside th' door. Just fur a minute. Really, a'm fine."

"Shall I go with you?" asked Cait.

"Na, na. A'm fine on mah ain," Janet tried to assure her. "Ye git back tae sleep.

"Fine," Cait stepped aside.

Janet opened the door and Cait closed it behind her, leaving it unlatched for her return. She went back to the bench and pulled the blanket over.

Moments later, there was a low thump at the door. Cait got up to check, but the door wouldn't open. She tried to pull it harder, rattling it and waking Alfred. He stirred, sleepily confused.

"I'm sorry to have woken you," she said. "The door, it seems to be stuck."

"Why does it matter now?" he asked.

"Janet went for some air. She's not sleeping well."

"Could she not have just waited?" Alfred got up and tried the door. "It's locked from the outside."

"That's not possible. It doesn't lock from the outside, only from inside," she said, showing him the latch. Cait banged on the door, hoping Janet, outside, would hear her.

"Janet? Janet!"

There was no reply. They looked at each other, confused.

"Something is wrong. Something terrible, I feel it," she said.

"She's probably just gone for a walk."

"Aye, but she left all sweaty like she had the fever. And why is the door stuck? Alfred, I left it open for her."

"The wind?" He knew his answer was a weak one. "Alright, I will go check."

"How? You can't get out."

"I'll have to force it open," he said.

So, with the remaining embers from the fire, Alfred lit the lantern for some light and returned to the door to try to free it open.

.oOo.

Inside Hamish's cottage he used his lantern flame to light a torch. He held it up and Janet's face glowed and flickered within the warm glare of light as she sat up in his messy bed. She buttoned up the front of her dress. He gave her a shove as he stepped past her, leaving her to sulk on her own.

Janet fell back.

"Aye, ye gae find yer princess while she sleeps in his arms, ye filthy beast!"

On the inside of the door, Alfred was using the fire poker to open it. Looking through the crack he'd made in the door, he noticed that a plank of wood was propped up on the outside, holding it closed. Loosening the cracked wood till it gave way, he slipped his arm out to reach the piece of wood and pushed it aside. When the door flung open, he was taken by surprise to see Hamish standing there.

Hamish's words mumbled through the effects of the rum.

"Ye trying tae leave wi' mah Cait?"

"Cait is a free woman; she doesn't belong to you," Alfred tried to reason with the drunk. "Why are you here, Hamish?"

"Ye leave this island alone 'n' ye wilnae git hurt. But she - she's nae gaug anywhere."

"I believe that is up to Cait."

Hamish bellowed, "NA!"

Alfred tried to close the broken door, but Hamish, still holding the torch, slid his arm in, obstructing the doorway and trapping the flame inside the house.

Cait screamed and the boys came running in to see what was happening.

"Ewan, Cameron, stay back!" Alfred ordered.

The force of Alfred trying to hold the door closed against Hamish's arm made him drop the torch. It fell onto the bags of clothing on the floor, igniting them instantly.

The winter fires had been plentiful due to Cait's efficient collecting of peat all summer. This made the wood of the roof and heather thatch very well dried out. It never crossed her or Janet's minds that it might become a feast for danger.

The fire spread quickly inside the cottage. While Alfred's attention was distracted by stamping out the fire and ushering the boys out of harm's way, Hamish pushed his way in and grabbed Cait's arm, dragging her outside.

"Ye'r comin' wi' me!" he spat.

"No, no I won't!"

Cait struggled to release Hamish's grasp on her wrist, as if it was locked in a shackle. The fire separated her from the boys, who were still inside the house with Alfred. They could no longer see her due to the flames and heavy smoke.

Gagging and coughing, Alfred took the boys by the hands. They skirted the fire, hurried to the door and disappeared into the cold, windy night.

"Where's Mummy?" they cried.

Cait was nowhere in sight.

Alfred had no answer. "I'll check inside. You two stay right here!" At that, he ran back into the blaze while the smoke flooded out of the house. The boys could hear him calling their mother's name but there was no reply. They stood there holding hands, feeling completely hopeless.

With his lungs filled with smoke, Alfred stumbled outside, gagging and gasping for air. Rife with fear, he instructed the boys as he caught his breath.

"Go to the hull on the hill and wait there for me. I will return to get you."

"Where weel ye gae?" asked Ewan.

"I will find your mother. Go there and stay there, under the hull."

As the boys ran hand in hand up the hill, Alfred rushed around to each cottage, banging on the doors, shouting, "Fire! Help, fire!"

The wreckers came out from their sleep to see Cait's cottage disappearing in the smoke. Alfred ran in all directions looking for her, asking frantically if they had seen Cait or Hamish. No one knew where they were. Alfred ran to Hamish's cottage and pulled on the door. He banged and shouted to him.

"Hamish, I know you have her, let her go!" When there was no answer, he kicked the door open, rushed around and looked inside the dark room. There was no one there, so he left.

Up on the hill the boys sat inside the hull. Cameron showed Ewan how the sailors smoke by exhaling the cold air when Janet arrived.

“’Ere ye are! Yer mither has been looking fur ye everywhere this side o’ th’ isle!” she said, happy to have found them.

“Oor hoose is on fire! Mr Henderson told us tae wait ‘ere fur him,” said Ewan.

“Ah ken, he's wi’ yer mum. A’m tae git ye ‘n’ bring ye back hame,” she explained.

“Back where?” he asked, as Cameron looked on.

“We cannae gae hame,” quipped Ewan.

“Tae yer Uncle Hamish's hoose.”

She took them by the hands but Cameron pulled back.

“Ah dinnae wantae gang tae his hoose!” he cried. “Uncle Hamish hurt me!”

“He hurt Mummy, too!” Ewan added.

“He didnae mean tae,” she explained, trying to soothe their fear. “Aye, sometimes he kin a wee bit moody, ah agree. But, at th’ end o’ th’ day, he’s kin ‘n’ he looks after us all, noo doesn’t he?”

“Ah guess so,” Ewan said to his Aunt Janet, then turned to Cameron to show his approval. “Aye, let’s gae.”

“Come quickly noo, everybody is waiting,” she said, keeping the mood sweet. Holding their hands, she led them out of the hull together.

Janet took the boys behind the cottages so as to not be seen by the neighbours, who were busy putting out the fire by passing buckets of sea water, person to person.

She took them into Hamish’s dirty cottage and locked the door behind her. Inside, the boys looked around at the mess of the empty, one-roomed shack.

“Where’s Mummy? Where’s Mr Henderson?” asked Ewan.

When there was no answer, Cameron began to panic. "A'm wantin' Mummy!" he shouted.

"Keep quiet noo, boys. Honestly, they'll be 'ere soon. Just hae a seat."

The two brothers nervously squeezed in close together, arms folded and eyes wide open, knowing something wasn't quite right.

.oOo.

At the shore, Cait was trying to pull away from Hamish, so he slapped her and threw her over his shoulder, laughing as she screamed. He waded through the water and dumbed her into the fishing boat. She fell, moaning against the mast in pain.

"Why are you doing this, Hamish?" she groaned.

"A'm no letting ye leave oor hame," he said as he pulled up the anchor by the rope.

Cait thought about that for a moment, then asked, "How did you know we were leaving?"

"Ye cannae keep secrets 'ere, darlin'. Word gits roond 'ere fast."

"We hadn't discussed it with anyone! Only the boys and Janet knew."

"Och well, mah dear, 'tis oot th' noo."

Then it struck her. It was Janet who had betrayed her. "Janet? She wouldn't - why would she? I need to go find my boys! Hamish, you have to let me off this boat!"

"Thir's na chance o' that. If ye'll want that man – that sailor, 'tis th' end o' ye. A'm gang tae tak' ye oot afore th' sun rises, drop ye heid first in th' sea 'n' watch ye sink just lik' ah did William."

At this, Cait's mouth dropped and her eyes widened. She couldn't believe what he was telling her and with her feet she pushed herself into the corner of the boat to distance herself from his words. Hamish lifted the anchor into the boat.

"You, you - what did you do?"

"Aye, that's right. He could ne'er love ye as much as ah can. He didnae deserve ye. He wanted tae tak' ye far fae 'ere 'n' ah couldnae allow that. 'Noo – noo that ye'r yearning fur another man, if ah cannae hae ye nae one kin. 'Tis as simple as that, Cait. 'N' Janet? Blood's thicker than water, hen."

She was still trying to process his confession. "You killed my William? Your own brother?" His truth hit her as it all began to make sense and she cried out loud in anger. "Is this what love is to you? You cannot hold me as prisoner, Hamish. This is not love! Love is free, love is the beautiful emotion that is equally shared by two people. It is passion. It is not rape, it is not forced, and it certainly isn't bribery of food! How could so much good come from one brother and so much evil from the other?"

Hamish did not answer her. He did not even have the wisdom to understand what she was asking.

Alfred ran down to the shore. He looked around, heard Cait crying and in the glimmer of the moonlight, he was able to see the commotion on the fishing boat. He ran towards it just as Hamish stood in the water to push the boat out.

"Stop!" Alfred yelled.

Cait sprung up at the sound of his voice, waved her arms about and shouted, "Alfred, help!"

Alfred looked at the dark sea before him with much apprehension. He staggered into the water and made his way to the boat quicker than Hamish could push the heavy bottom through the sands on which it was lodged in the flooding neap tide, strong as he was.

When Alfred reached the boat, Hamish grabbed Alfred's stick, tossed it far before the boat like a spear and shoved Alfred aside, causing him to lose balance and fall backwards into the water.

Hamish jumped into the boat. He used an oar to push the boat out and to fight Alfred off with it, brutally hitting him on his shoulder. Alfred took hold of the oar and pulled it out of Hamish's hands.

The boat started to slip easily off the sand as Hamish searched for another oar in the dark. Alfred hit Hamish in the back with the oar which made him fall over onto Cait's legs. She kicked him off, clamoured over the top of him and stood up at the stern of the boat to face Alfred.

"Quick, jump in, I'll catch you!" he called out to Cait.

She was hesitant, knowing a wet dress would pull her under water. Hamish stood up behind her while she took the anchor to throw it back overboard to keep the boat from drifting out. Alfred's eyes peeled open at the sight of Hamish.

"Behind you!" he shouted.

Cait turned to look, and Hamish was coming for her, angrier than ever. She swung the anchor at him, getting the pointed fluke lodged in his shoulder. He fell to his knees and wailed barbarically. Cait froze for a moment in terror not knowing what he might do or if he could retaliate. She was surprised at what she had just done and now she had to get away quickly.

Hamish pulled the anchor out of his shoulder and it shined with his dark blood.

Cait gathered her dress into her hands and jumped into the water, standing thigh deep next to Alfred. Together, they pushed out the boat with Hamish still in it, while he moaned on the floor.

Taking her hand in his, they ploughed their way through the water to the shore as fast as they could. Alfred helped Cait as she laboured in her weighed down dress, which was completely soaked to the core. Similarly, Cait helped him as he limped through the sand and uneven stones, pulling him along as they went.

"We must get the boys," she said.

"And find Janet," he added.

Breathless but still resolute, Cait told him about Janet's betrayal. "No! She's the turncoat. She told Hamish our plan to leave Iona. I am certain it was she who barred the front door."

"Cait, is this so; it's ludicrous!"

"Aye, but it's true just the same."

"Let's hurry onward, the boys are waiting for us up at the hull."

As they rushed up to the cottages to get to the hull on the hill, they could still see the folks outside running around with buckets of water from the shore to the fire, trying to extinguish it.

In order to avoid being seen, Alfred and Cait slipped behind the cottages to keep out of sight, as everyone was distracted by the fire. They hurried up the hill to find the boys were not there.

"I told them to meet me here and to stay put!" said Alfred, crossly.

Worried, Cait cried out for them. "Ewan! Cameron!"

Alfred joined in with his strong, loud voice. "Ewan! Cameron!"

"They wouldn't just leave," Cait said. "I know they wouldn't, not if you told them to stay." She thought for a minute. "Janet! I'm sure she's found them and has taken them. Let's check Hamish's house."

"Why his house?" he asked.

"Where else would she go? There's a good chance," she urged.

"Alright, let's go."

They crept back the way they came, behind the cottages and arrived at Hamish's house. They hid behind it and waited for the opportune moment in which to enter.

The community watched on as the last of Cait's roof burned and fell to the ground. The women returned to their own homes, leaving the men to keep watch that the fire didn't spread to the neighbouring hovels.

Cait stared over at what remained of her home. The hull and thatch roof now lay on the ground as an unidentifiable piece of black char and there was nothing left of the front door or of the carefully organised blocks of peat which had been drying outside to use for the winter.

Alfred placed his hand on her arm. "You'll not need that house anymore."

She nodded, unable to speak.

Quietly they edged around to the front of Hamish's house. Alfred tried to open the door, but it was locked shut, an unusual thing, so Cait banged on it hard.

"Janet, open the door now and let me get my boys! Janet!" she demanded.

Alfred tried vigorously to open the door. "Janet!" he said, firmly, "You can't hide in there. Hamish has gone out to sea and likely not coming back, so surrender yourself."

Soiled with soot and his face red from the heat of tending to the fire, Morven walked up to them. He was clueless to the other dramas that had been unfolding.

"Whit's happening 'ere?" he asked.

Cait turned to him and pleaded, "Morven, Hamish has ruined my house and now Janet has taken my boys. If she's not here, where else might she be? Please, Morven, help me." "If she has them, she wilnae hide them forever. Both o' ye, stand aside."

He banged hard on the door and jiggled the latch. "Janet, 'tis Morven here, open th' door." He pressed his ear to the door and listened closely. "Ewan? Cameron? Are ye in there?"

They could hear the faint cry of the boys inside the cottage.

"Aye," they sobbed.

"That's them inside!" said Morven.

With that, Cait began to panic. "We hear you! We're coming in!"

Morven slipped his fishing knife out of his belt and pried the door until it opened enough to see. They looked inside. Cait burst in but Janet clenched a knife in her hand and pointed it at her, forcing her to stay where she was. Cait gasped and backed off. Ewan and Cameron were still sitting together in the corner of the room.

Cameron cried out, "Mummy, Mr Henderson!"

"Janet! What's the meaning of this?" Cait implored.

"Ye cannae tak' these bairns awa', ah wullnae allow ye. This is their hame!" Janet scowled.

"Home is wherever I take them!" Cait said, defensively. "They're my boys, my family, and it is up to me where they go."

"No, this is a family decision, 'n' a'm th' elder."

Cait tried to reason with her. "Janet, we're all going together – you, me, the boys – to have a better life. Isn't that what you want?"

Janet shook her head. "Ah belong 'ere. Maybe *ye* dinnae, bit we dae. While ye'r off collecting peat all th' day lang, ah look after thae wee boys lik' they're mah ain 'n' wi' me they will stay!"

"Janet ... " pleaded Cait.

Janet began to scream. "Ye married intae this family, this life! 'N' these bairns are a part o' it. Where is yer commitment tae that?"

"Commitment? To insanity? No, my commitment ended tonight when I was told my husband was murdered! Your brother murdered William! And you have betrayed me. I owe your family nothing!"

"Aye, ye dae, Cait!" said Janet.

"I only owe my boys a decent life. Did you know what Hamish did to my husband? Your brother? Did you? Well, listen to this, Janet. He took him out to sea and drowned him, all because he was jealous of him. He told me himself. Jealous! He tried to do the same with Cameron!"

Cait looked to Janet for some surprise reaction or yielding to this revelation. Instead, there was a deep silence from her.

"You – you knew," ceded Cait, resolved as she pieced the events all together – Janet's close bond with Hamish, never growing hungry, not keeping up with the chores with Cait - and it all started to make sense. "And you kept this from me. How could you?"

Alfred stepped in and stood behind Cait in a show of support. "Put the knife down and hand the boys over, Janet, before you regret it."

A moan was heard in the dark night and suddenly, Hamish appeared behind them at the front of his house. He held onto his arm and his shirt was covered in blood as he strained to make his way in. Pushing Morven aside, he staggered inside the cottage.

"Ah will put an end tae ye, ye whore!" he slavered.

Alfred took hold of Hamish. In the commotion, the boys dashed free from Janet's guard and into their mother's arms. Alfred beseeched her to make a run for it as he held a considerably weakened Hamish back.

Cait and the boys made it past Morven, but Hamish struck Alfred in his face, sending Alfred to the floor. He held his nose, which bled profusely, then rolled over on his side to try to stand up but Hamish kicked him in the gut, over and over, making him cough and gag.

"Ye didnae dae as ah said, 'n' noo ye'r gang tae pay!"

Cait shielded Ewan's and Cameron from seeing the violence.

"Stop this! Hamish!" she yelled.

"Gae after her!" Hamish demanded of Janet.

Morven blocked Janet from getting to Cait. With his battered face, Alfred looked at Cait. Full of blood and coughing up phlegm, he muttered to her. "Take the boys; go to my ship."

"I don't know where it is, Alfred! How will I find it?"

"In the cove," he answered.

Hamish held onto his injured arm and kicked Alfred in the stomach once again. Alfred moaned.

"But there are many, Alfred. Which one?"

Alfred thought momentarily, as he didn't want the others to run ahead and harm the ship.

"Terra Incognita," he said.

Cait took the boys outside.

"Ah ken where th' ship is Mummy," said Cameron. As they stood outside the cottage in the cold night, Cait looked up into the crisp night sky full of stars and nodded. "Yes. Yes, alright! Come boys!" She took Ewan and Cameron by their hands and ran, pulling them along.

Hamish stopped beating Alfred, hurled Morven aside and summoned Janet.

"Git them!"

Janet, with the knife gripped firmly in her hand, ran past a fallen Morven and tore after Cait and the boys. She had a steady pace towards them, albeit a slow one, but her determination to keep the boys on Iona kept her going.

Alfred scrambled away from Hamish and stood to his feet, hunched over holding his stomach. He got his bearings together quickly and hobbled towards Janet. He caught up with her before the top of the hill.

Although he was sheepish when it came to asserting himself with women, his fight to keep Cait safe made him forget the fact that Janet was a woman and he wrenched her to the ground by the skirt of her dress. She fell with a thud. Alfred pinned her arm to the ground and ripped the knife out of her hand.

"You coward of a woman!" he scolded her, tucking the knife into his trousers. "You betrayed Cait and put the boy's lives at risk!"

Janet looked to him with revulsion and spat with terrific and precise aim into his eyes.

"You don't deserve them," he said. He got up and ran off, limping towards Cait as Janet grumbled out of breath, "NA!"

.oOo.

With blood still streaming from his shoulder and his movement limited with agony in every step, Hamish pressed on feverishly to catch up. He faltered past Janet.

She reached out to him. "Hamish. Gie me a hand up."

Hamish was too determined on going after the others to bother with her. "Ye stay here."

"Gimme me a hand up!" Janet charged.

But he left Janet sitting there as he pressed onward.

She screamed out to him, "Git them; donnae let them leave!"

.oOo.

With everyone behind them and out of sight, Cait thought they would be safe for a few minutes and slowed her stride. In a final attempt to say goodbye, she looked in the direction of the burial ground and to William's grave. There she stood, knowing it would be her last farewell to him. She had grieved enough for the man who was no longer there and a new chapter awaited her. One where she would be free to live instead of slowly dying, one in which to love and to be loved, a life free of bribes or emotions based on trickery or duplicity. A story of her own where there was no room for deceit in words and conduct, nor would they be the basis of the world around her as it had been on the Isle of Iona. Had she lived a day of truth at all, she wondered.

She dreamed and prayed, relying on and trusting in her faith in God, and it was all finally happening, she thought. In the greater scheme, He had been busy making it all happen for her; arranging all the details like the Master working over her life making the pieces fit, putting things and people here and there. She concluded, all that had happened was meant to happen.

If only her children would never again go hungry or play without irreparable holes in their shoes. If only she could get them off the island, they would learn skills in writing and mathematics like other children and be given opportunities and develop insight into the world so that they could do great and wonderful things in the name of progress and prosperity. Perhaps they would do well enough simply to make some sort of meaningful contribution to the betterment of the human condition.

She had more than enough confidence in them and in their abilities to learn beyond the rudimentary ideals she could give them. Whatever was to come of Ewan and Cameron would be a vast improvement on their current affairs. The only truth she had known had been William's devotion to her, and yet even that was stolen from her at the hands of his murderous brother. It was all in the past now, if she could just get her boys to Alfred's ship.

In the quietude of the night, as she gazed over at William's grave and at his small, simple cross, the dreamy images of a future momentarily passed through her mind. Then suddenly, a gunshot echoed out into the dark blue morning, rippling through the cold air. The bullet struck the ground next to the boys, lifting a chunk of dirt and propelling its dust into the space around them. They shuttered. Numb with fear, Cait pulled her boys to the ground and huddled with them under her arms, shaking in terror.

From much further back, Morven shouted the unmistaken, however obvious warning. "He has a pistol!"

Hamish was making speed and catching up to Alfred. "Am gang tae shoot ye deid!" Hamish yelled to him as he fiddled with the cylinder that seemed to be stuck.

Alfred's only concern was the safety of Cait and the boys.

He shouted out to them. "Keep running! Don't stop!" Cait looked up into the early morning sky and searched the stars. Ahead, she saw Polaris glittering in the sky as if a loyal comrade. Directly below it, situated peacefully in a small cove of white sand shimmering in the light of the moon and surrounded by clusters of sharp, black rock, emerged two masts of the ship, Consolation, whose tips delicately touched the stars.

She could taste the restitution, the indemnification of hardship to something more deserving. "Look, there it is! Come now, boys!" She reached to take Cameron's hand. Ewan turned around to see if Alfred was coming.

"Whit aboot Mr Henderson?" he asked, concerned for his own welfare, but equally worried for the man who would tomorrow teach him how to catch a fish properly.

Cait looked back but she couldn't see Alfred in the dark. "He will come. He has to; I trust him."

"So dae ah. He'll nego - negotshate something," added Cameron.

Cait looked at him, not completely certain of what he meant by that, but it mattered not. Because feeling confident, Cameron took Ewan's and his mother's hands and the three of them ran on towards the awaiting ship.

The Consolation was now in close range. Hamish knew that running with his bleeding shoulder was painful and weakening him, but he was determined to finish them all off. He came to a halt thirty metres away from Alfred to reload. With blurred vision, he aimed the gun at Alfred and set the hammer.

Alfred heard the unmistakable sound of the pistol's click and stopped suddenly in his tracks.

"Tis over, three-legged coward," Hamish blurted. Alfred, unsure of Hamish's skill with the pistol, was certain that the wrecker now had the upper hand, despite being off balance with inebriation and suffering in pain. The fact was that anything was possible given that Hamish was out of his mind with two powerful and yet debilitating emotions – infatuation and revenge, he was an unstable man in every aspect.

Hamish lifted the gun and pointed it at Alfred whilst they both watched Cait and the boys run down the sands, so close to reaching safety.

"Oan yer knees," he commanded.

Alfred dropped to the ground.

"One move fae ye 'n' ah will murder ye first. Now," he said as he straightened his arms out and looked down the barrel. As carefully as he could do in his drunken state, he shifted his aim almost precisely on Cait. "Watch as ah blow apart oor bonnie lassie," he smirked.

"No!" called Alfred, desperately.

Hamish pulled the trigger. Alfred couldn't bear to look, so he squinted his eyes tight. There was a click, but nothing happened, no sound of a fired bullet.

Alfred shouted to Cait, but she was now out of the range of his voice and entering the shallows of the beach. "Run, Cait! Keep going!"

Not understanding why the pistol didn't fire, Hamish rolled the cylinder around to ensure it was moving. It moved well, so he thought he would shoot it again. However, his feet got tangled in the tall grasses which blew all around him in the wind. He tripped himself up, lost his balance and fell backwards onto his backside, dropping the Lefaucheux next to him.

Hamish mumbled something profane in Gaelic as he felt around the grass. Alfred looked back to see what the commotion was.

"Turn yersel' roond!" he shouted as he picked up the pistol.

Alfred watched on as Hamish fumbled about trying to stand up in the clumps of grass. He also knew Cait was too far ahead for Hamish to shoot her.

Still on the ground, Hamish held the pistol out in front of him with both arms locked straight. Realising he could not see Cait very well as she was fading out of sight, he drew it in close to his face so that he could focus the aim better. He was on his last bullet and his final chance to keep Cait from leaving. Hamish held the weapon with his right hand on the trigger and his left hand held the tip of the barrel with the grip pressed into his nose and chin to steady it. Doing this, he regained a better than the previously sketchy focus down the long barrel, and was satisfied it would do, as the pistol was now perfectly aimed at Cait. He moved the barrel along with her movements and followed her with his eyes then pulled the trigger.

Alfred shuddered at the immense sound of it and crouched down into the ground. He looked over towards Cait who was wading through the water with the two boys in tow.

.oOo.

Cait and the boys turned back to look into the vacant field, which was becoming visible at that morning hour. She took an uneasy breath as she searched the distance at the softly rolling ground but could see neither Alfred nor Hamish.

"Alfred!" she screamed.

If Alfred was dead, they might still be able to escape Hamish's wrath if his injured shoulder was bad enough. But Cait knew that his madness would simply mask the pain. She pushed the boys through the water to the boat to safety.

.oOo.

From out of the dark curtain of grasses and thorny gorse came the loud, moanful cry of the boorish Hamish.

The final bullet from the damaged pistol never left its barrel; the gun had backfired.

With nowhere for the bullet to go, it exploded through the cylinder and the hot metal struck Hamish in the face, plunging pieces of it into his left cheek, through his jaw and shredding his ear. The flesh of his head, hands and up his arms were blasted open and dotted with shrapnel. It was impossible to make out if there was any face left at all, as he was completely unrecognisable in the carnage. He screamed again in unendurable agony but the blood masked his cry as it poured into his throat, causing him to gurgle.

Alfred ran off ahead towards his ship.

As if he was attempting to make his final steps towards Cait, Hamish took several long, uncalculated strides, stumbled onto the beach and fell into the soft white sand, staining it with a spray of red. He gurgled again, unable to see through the mutilation; after he rolled in his torment everything which was wet with blood became plastered with sand.

.oOo.

Andrew jumped off the deck and into the water. He took Ewan and lifted him up to Duncan, who leaned over the edge of the Consolation's gunwale. Then Duncan pulled up Cameron. Andrew stood in the water and reached out to Cait, but she just stood there, alone, her arms at her side, unwilling to receive the help, not just yet.

"Come along, Ma'am," then added more gently, "Cait."

She looked at him, curiously. "You know my name."

"Aye, we both do," he replied.

"As does most of Greenock by now," smiled Duncan.

Forgetting the cold and the men who were there to take her to safety and warmth, Cait lingered thigh deep in the chilly sea as her dress floated in the currents and the wind blew all around her. Her hair danced in the morning rushes of air and whipped about in cadence to the white horses of the sea.

She looked eagerly around in the distance for Alfred and waited, whilst at the same time she feared spotting Hamish coming instead.

The moon shone palely in one space of the sky and the sun slowly lifted the morning veil open to the east. Cait could see someone coming. He walked, stumbling towards her with a limp she recognised. She smiled eagerly and breathed a heavy sigh of relief.

Alfred concentrated his focus on her, not wanting her to leave his sight. And her yearnful look to him kept him coming steadfastly while his feet splashed into the shoal of the beach. They came towards each other, and the brisk cold was unfelt in contrast to their warm, longing hearts. Within that short distance they could feel each other's hearts beating in a frenzy, desperately seeking to unite.

They met, stopping just short of reach. He stepped into her space, took her face in his hands and met his lips with hers, kissing her boldly and unapologetically. She leaned her body forward into him, pressing her chest into his as she welcomed this slow seal of affection. With his arms he pulled her close and pressed his body firmly against hers.

Cait pulled away from his kiss to see if what was happening was true and they looked into each other's eyes. They turned to the men who were watching and awaiting to help them board. The boys giggled at the couple embraced in the water as the men began to understand Alfred's vehement need to return to the Isle of Iona.

Duncan pulled up the anchor and both men pushed the boat out of the cove. Inside the cabin, Alfred and Cait gathered the boys to their side and held them close together.

As they sailed away from Iona, the shape of the island eventually disappeared behind them. The morning had broken fully and clouds began to gather and blow in from the west. Alfred was called up on deck by Andrew. He took Cait up with him and together they watched as Dubh Artach lighthouse came into view, emerging due south. Duncan kept the Consolation at a good, safe distance as they passed the skerry and the tall stone tower appeared to be complete. Cameron and Ewan looked out of the cabin to view it as they passed. Their eyes opened in wonderment.

Ewan shot out of the cabin. "Whit is that Mr Henderson?"

"It's the new lighthouse. It's Dubh Artach. Do you see the top of it?"

"Yes?"

"Inside that is a lens which will shine a light and it will burn so brightly that anyone passing within twenty miles will see it flashing and be warned of the dangerous rocks below."

Cameron appeared by his feet and took Alfred's hand.

"Whit mak's th' light?" Ewan asked.

Alfred explained as the boys listened to him with not only interest, but sheer reverence as he told even more about the Scotland's lighthouse legacy.

"All round Scotland and inside each lighthouse live three men. Each man has the duty to keep the lamp inside burning all night and all day. They are called lighthouse keepers, or wickies."

"Why wickies?" asked Ewan.

"The wickie is the man who trims the blackened wick in the lamp to keep the fire going," added Alfred.

"The sailors will see it and can steer away from the black rocks and be safe for the rest of their voyage. Together, the lighthouse keepers will save hundreds, perhaps thousands of lives over the years."

"Tis a grand idea, th' lighthoose," added Ewan.

"'Tis, my boy. Whether it was through storms, sunshine or high waters, the men who built it continued working there for five years until it was finished."

"Whit a story," said Ewan.

"Aye, a real story. And, built by friends of mine."

"Pray fur th sailors," Cait said, softly.

"Aye and do you?" smiled Alfred.

"I always have." She smiled back. "That's why you came back."

"So, I have you to thank?" asked Alfred, cheekily, as if his desire for her was not enough in itself to bring him to her.

"Aye, and I suppose your determined heart had something to do with it as well."

He held her close to him, as her words made him feel valued. As he looked out at the magnificent spectacle standing above the skerry, something was missing. Its light had not yet been lit. He also knew that any anticipation of it would be premature as it was still very early in the morning of the 1st of November. And thought about the craftsmen celebrating it once alight, after the long, arduous labour they encountered in constructing it.

"Out of a great trial comes a great result," he said.

He also wondered about young Louis Stevenson and if his undisciplined, somewhat defiant imagination would get the better of him or if his law studies at Edinburgh University would have tamed his mental acquisitiveness. Perhaps his imagination was best left savage, and why not? Why should a man grow out of his youth to become analytical, arrogant and less playful as Alfred had? Wasn't Lois correct in her observation of him as they walked together to the church, he thought. *"You didn't grow up, you grew old"*, she told him. How perceptive she was.

He was filled with gratitude of Duncan and Andrew's loyalty to him over the years, for waiting for him in the cove, for pardoning his lack of sailing assistance to them and how they always offered to help him with his bad leg. He was grateful for the way Cameron and Ewan reached into his heart with their adventure spirits, yet so much innocence. He thought it would be lovely if they were to keep just a little of it.

On that day, he forgave his father. The way he had behaved was only a product of the man's education and upbringing. He even felt grateful for his father's discipline, his method of punishment by way of polishing brass, sewing the fragmented sails and splicing the ropes. As he had seen by looking after Cameron those many months, he was brought to understand the importance of balance of discipline and nurturing a child. Although he was now more content with teaching the lessons of life whilst living the adventure of it. That style suited him better, he thought.

And then, there was Cait. This was right, this was viable, and she would be good for him. There was so much more to learn about each other. He would look after her and be the man he never had the chance to be with Fiona. A youthful marriage to Fiona was filled with angst, transpired by pleasing his parents, particularly obeying what his father had expected of him. Then, in a matter of a few years, he lost them all and had had no one to please or appease but grief itself. His purpose became the embodiment of despondency as he was urged to sail and die by the sea, resigned to bitter loneliness.

Alfred was baffled by his own shift of emotions, as if he had awakened a new man that same morning, with what God, the Giver of all things, had gifted to him in just one day. That change happened only from the accumulation of events over the years, taking a lifetime to fully come to fruition. Though it felt he had been walking in darkness, the light had always shone on his path and now he was able to see his true purpose.

The verse from the Bible ran through his mind: *Thy Word is a lamp unto my feet and the light unto my path.* In contrast to existing as his own dim, nearly lifeless lantern, he finally saw God as the origin of all things whole and good, the flame within his lantern, his very own lamplighter.

CHAPTER 12

Wilt thou go with me sweet maid
Say maiden wilt thou go with me
Through the valley depths of shade
Of night and dark obscurity
Where the path hath lost its way
Where the sun forgets the day
Where there's nor life nor light to see
Sweet maiden wilt thou go with me

Where stones will turn to flooding streams,
Where plains will rise like ocean waves,
Where life will fade like visioned dreams
And mountains darken into caves.
Say maiden wilt thou go with me
Through this sad non-identity
Where parents live and are forgot
And sisters live and know us not

Say maiden wilt thou go with me
In this strange death of life to be
To live in death and be the same
Without this life, or home, or name
At once to be, and not to be
That was, and is not – yet to see
Things pass like shadows and the sky
Above, below, around us lie

The land of shadows wilt thou trace
And look – nor know each other's face
The present mixed with reasons gone
And past, and present all as one
Say maiden can thy life be led
To join the living to the dead
Then trace thy footsteps on with me
We're wed to one eternity

John Clare
An Invite To Eternity

A sudden flapping of the mainsail threw Alfred's attention back to the present. As the weather turned increasingly wild, the tranquillity in his face changed with the deepening of the colours of the sky. It altered from one which was relaxed and content to concerned and his creases began to show with the changing, shadowing light above, deepening. Alfred knew Tosh would soon be setting sail. If the current conditions did not improve, he would have to return home in time to stop him.

In Greenock, Aemelius was nearing departure for her voyage. John Gallagher had assumed Alfred's usual duty of checking in the passengers, the last of whom had just boarded. He gathered up the papers and left the table and chair behind at the dock.

The small vessel, Consolation, approached Greenock. Although the dark clouds stirred and hovered in the sky, the masts of Aemelius could just be seen further down the Clyde. It gave Alfred tremendous relief to know it had not yet departed.

After the Consolation was tied to her mooring, Alfred sent Duncan to run down to Aemelius to tell them to await departure till the next day instead and give them the report of bad weather and the possibility of not having light from the Dubh Artach lighthouse. Alfred led Cait and the two boys to Tosh's house, as this was closer to the port than his own and he was certain that Marion would look after them.

Marion answered the door with Lois curiously peering behind her, to the four of them standing there tired, looking ragged from the previous night's affairs and out of breath from their fast-paced walk through Greenock's town centre.

"Marion," greeted Alfred rather anxiously. "Marion, Lois, this is Cait, Ewan, and you already know Cameron. I don't have the time to explain, but ..."

Marion interrupted. "No need to. Come in, come in all of you."

He shifted Cait and the boys inside the house, where Lois took them down to the end of the hall before she stopped to listen to Alfred and her mother discuss the voyage.

"I can't," he added. "I must stop Tosh."

"Why?" asked Marion.

"The lighthouse wasn't alight when we passed it."

"But that must have been hours ago. It's probably alight now."

Alfred looked her square in the eyes. "I just have a feeling, and I need to follow it."

Marion drew in her breath. "Then you had better go, Alfred. Let this not be the day I have been long dreading."

Cait came through to see what was happening and Lois

looked through the curtains at the fading first of November light. “I’m sure he would have set sail by now,” Lois said, as she stood under the sitting room door frame.

Marion grabbed his arm and pulled him to the front door. Cait took his other hand and followed him outside for a momentary embrace.

“Hurry, Alfred, go stop him; and all of those travellers!” Marion said, her voice breaking.

Alfred ran off, letting Cait’s hand slip out of his after a final squeeze.

As the sky became dusk, Alfred rushed back to the docks. He could just about see Aemelius's masts and smoke trail as she sailed into the open sea. Alfred ran over to the Consolation. He called out to Andrew and Duncan, who were tidying up the decks of the ship, imploring them to get ready to set sail.

“Andrew, Duncan, why didn’t you stop Tosh?” he implored.

Andrew stepped forward. “Duncan and I both tried to, but he wouldnae listen.”

Alfred was desperate. “Come! We must chase them! They’re headed into bad weather with no promise of the beacon!”

The three men hastened to untie the ship and hoisted up the sails in an attempt to catch Aemelius as she was shrinking out of sight beyond the point of Gourock.

.oOo.

At Dubh Artach, the sea was rough, and the winds gathered intensity. Kumbi and two of the other craftsmen scurried to get inside the lighthouse to light the paraffin. The breaking waves made the short walking passage from the barracks to the tower completely impassable, even with a rope to hold for guidance. The wet rock was slippery and the waves battered against the men as if they were bowling pins.

Alan shouted. "Retreat men! To the barracks. Retreat!" he yelled.

They returned to their metal cylinder, climbed the legs of the structure and into the hatch, locking themselves in.

"I pray we won't be trapped in here for five days again, like the other gale," said one of the men. At this, commotion ensued between them.

Alan lectured them. "Listen, men!"

They looked to him for instruction.

He continued, "I am afraid we will have to wait to light it tomorrow, that is, if the weather makes it possible to do so. For now, we will have to wait out another storm."

Kumbi made his way forward through the crowd of men.

"Mr Brebner, sir, I feel that I must remind you that it was scheduled and announced that on this day the lamp would lit."

"I am aware of that, Kumbi."

"But Mr Brebner, sir, young Mr Stevenson was to inform Mr Henderson of this, and I am sure he would have done so. And, as keen as Mr Henderson was about sailing his passenger ship, I fear, sir, they will be passing the coast this day. I'm certain of this, Mr Brebner. Today."

Once again, the commotion between the men started up. Alan was struck by this complication.

"We cannot reach the light, Kumbi. I won't risk my men."

The wind screamed as it swept between the passage of the barracks and the lighthouse. A fearful silence fell upon all the lighthouse workers. Kumbi took a step closer to Alan.

"Risking one old slave man is better than risking two hundred passengers."

Alan's heart sank at Kumbi's words and swallowed hard.

"Understand me, Kumbi: you have never been a slave here among my men. You are equal to them, and your talent is revered in the highest of opinions. What you and your family have given in the name of loyalty to the Stevenson family and the families before is worth more than the lives of two hundred passengers. I cannot allow you to go."

"Sir, perhaps we should not measure my worth against their great number. It is you and the Stevensons – three generations of them - who have taught me loyalty and a commitment to finish the task. And, what good is a lighthouse without a light? It has no purpose! No one here knows the lens better than I. So, today, sir, I will finish my job."

Alan took Kumbi by the shoulders and squeezed him, feeling the most admiration and respect. "I fear I cannot stop you. You are the bravest of all men, but no."

With Alan's back turned, Kumbi opened the hatch and disappeared. He climbed down the legs onto the turbulent track, holding on with both hands to the connecting rope. He didn't look back to see the men calling him back but focused straight ahead to the new lighthouse.

.oOo.

At sea, the Consolation was slipping further behind Aemelius. Alfred was immensely distressed and tried unceasingly to signal them with his lanterns, one in each hand. Though, as quickly as they were held up, the wind blew the flames out. They failed him and their ship remained unseen.

.oOo.

On the skerry, with every step, Kumbi fought to reach the ladder on which he would have to climb to get to the lighthouse door. Between wave surges, he moved quickly. When the waves crashed at his body, he wrapped himself around the railing rope, locking his arms and legs firmly together to hold his place. However, the waves turned unpredictable. There was no set time or distance between them. In fact, the waves were sloshing through in powerful hits and coming at him from all directions.

Kumbi finally reached the base of the lighthouse tower. He grabbed hold of the fixed ladder and used the same method of moving quickly when he could and locked his arms and legs around the steel rungs when the waves were about to hit.

After climbing thirty-one feet above the rock, he finally made it up to the door of the lighthouse. The sea level rose dramatically, covering the black rock underneath him. As he stood on the ladder many metres up the tower, the waves below him licked at his feet.

At the same moment that Kumbi pulled on the handle of the door to open it, a wave rushed over him. The door swung out whilst Kumbi held onto it and slammed his back against the stone tower. Gasping for breath, he held on with his legs quivering about in the air.

That wave receded and before another could smack him, Kumbi used his legs to push himself away from the stone wall and swing back to the door opening. He pulled his way inside, securing the door shut behind him. Fearfully out of breath, he was able to jostle upward within the tower and rush to the paraffin source. He took hold of the handgrip and pumped it steadily to increase the pressure of the air. He then opened the valve which released the mix. He ran up the straight stairs all the way up the lens at the top and checked the fuel tray, searching frantically, feeling for the matches in his pocket. He pulled out the box and, undoubtedly, they were soaked through.

.oOo.

On board the Aemelius, Tosh had a growing concern. On the open Scottish coast, the sea was in a full gale and he realised that his ship and everyone aboard were in danger. He had increasing difficulty controlling the direction of the ship and was being blown off course. He could not see the reef he was quickly approaching.

.oOo.

Dripping wet from the sea and the thrashing rain, Kumbi looked all around the circular room for matches, but the room was bare of them. He ran down one level to the bunk chambers. After a flurry of opening drawers and cubby spaces which had been filled with neatly folded blankets, he finally found a dry match box inside the window ledge.

He ran upstairs to the lens, trying to ignore the distressing wail of the wind encircling outside the glass lantern room and the noticeable movement in which the structure was built to give way to. He took out a match struck it. It sizzled for a moment until a flame arose. He reached in and lit the fuel tray lamp, then pushed it back in. He then turned a dial to release the vapour and lit another match. It gave another sizzle, then died. Another match was taken from the box. It, too, made the crackling sound, but the cold damp stopped it from lighting.

Kumbi began to panic because the match box had also become damp from his clothing dripping onto his cold hands and an ever so slight chill seemed to pass invisibly through the airtight lantern room. Hovering over his space to make a protective corner against the lantern, he rubbed his hands together to warm them and struck another match. The flame took hold to the wood stick.

Taking a deep breath, he prayed as he steadied one hand with the other in the tremoring tower. When the lit match touched the vapour, it ignited. From within the lens, a colossal beam burst into Kumbi's face, giving a tremendous and sudden illumination on his half of the room, then the other half. Then his side again. He grinned and laughed as the lens rotated around and the beam continued to explode in its movements. His smile gleamed with the timing of the radiance. He fell backwards in complete relief.

.oOo.

As the weather was too turbulent for their small ship, Andrew ordered her to be turned around. However reluctant, Duncan obeyed. He let loose the sails and shouted as if it were any ordinary day, any familiar order, "Ready to come about!"

"Coming about!" Andrew mirrored the mood, yet still he rubbed away those tears which refused to be swept away by the wind. He quickly spun the wheel, and between waves he turned Consolation back in the direction of home.

As she came about between the dips of the waves, Alfred still kept his hopeful eyes and expectations open on the little he could see of the Aemelius. She, too, was pulled up and down within the troughs and crests of the sea and the two ships were out of sync. In fact, the whole black ocean was wildly out of tune with itself in a deranged and chaotic rhythm.

Alfred glanced ahead with the attentive captain, then he turned to take one last look for Aemelius on the horizon, now behind them. His heart stood still. A moment before, the masts and dark chimney smoke of Aemelius could be seen, and now they could not. Alfred looked around, frantically waiting to see the ship rise up with the crests, but it did not. His eyes filled with despair.

"No!" he cried aloud. "NO!"

.oOo.

Inside the quiet Edinburgh family home of the Stevensons, sitting at his bedroom desk by an oil lamp, Louis was studying books on law. He leaned back comfortably into his chair; legs stretched out. An instant glow entered through the window of his room with the nightly switching on of the streetlamp outside. Now distracted from his work, Louis's eyes shifted to the sand glass which sat upon his desk. He put down his book and closed it, took the sand glass and turned it over. He stared closely at the creamy grains pouring through the neck and down into the bottom, watching it both empty and fill at the same time. He then pushed his books aside, took a clean sheet of paper and a pen to dip into the ink. Gently, he tapped the pen against the inkwell until the drop of ink fell. At the top of the paper, he began to write.

I will begin the story of my adventures with a certain morning in the month of June, the year of grace 1751, when I took the key for the last time out of the door of my father's house. The sun began to shine upon the summit of the hills as I went down the road; and by the time I had come as far as the manse, the blackbirds were whistling in the garden lilacs, and the mist that hung around the valley in the time of the dawn was beginning to arise and die away.

There was a gentle tapping on his door, to which he was selectively deaf when engrossed in writing, then the squeak from the turn of the doorknob.

"Mr Stevenson?" asked the soft voice as his old nanny, Cummy, called in on him.

"Oh! Cummy, do come in," said Louis.

"Ah did knock," she smiled. "But I ken yer busy 'n' no deaf."

"Aye, well, you know well enough me by now. I'm only glad to see it was you and that I did not annoy my father again with his surprise visits."

She carried a jug of water to his bed table. "He knows ye by noo."

As she was leaving, she stopped at his side curiously and asked, "What are ye writing aboot th' noo?"

"A summer adventure. Might I read it to you?"

"Aye, Mr Stevenson, later this evening. Dinner is aboot tae be served. Yer parents have asked tha ye come doon."

"Yes, tell them I am on my way; I'm just - into my book." He winked, holding up a book on Scottish law.

Cummy smiled at him before leaving the room.

He slid his paper away into a drawer and set his pen down on its stand, as he was not to be caught out writing poetry and stories during his time reserved for studies.

.oOo.

In the newness of spring, the MacIntosh house was the place for the wedding celebration of Alfred and Cait. Marion, along with John Gallagher's wife Anne, were both still dressed in mourning black which contrasted sharply against Cait's white dress. Lois, heavily expecting her first child, shared a blether with the other women while Douglas, Duncan and Andrew took to their own company and sipped whisky.

Running around outside were the Gallagher children with Ewan and Cameron, playing soldiers together.

Made in the USA
Monee, IL
19 June 2023

36180218R00154